MW00532383

Reaching Riverdale

Geeta Schrayter

PREMA PRESS

Reaching Riverdale is a work of fiction. Names, characters, places, and incidents are either the product of the author's imagination or are used fictitiously, and any resemblance to actual events, locales, or persons, living or dead, is entirely coincidental.

Published in 2011
This edition published 2020

Copyright © 2020 by Geeta Schrayter

All rights reserved.

Per the U.S. Copyright Act of 1976, no part of this publication may be reproduced, scanned, or distributed in any form or by any means, electronic or mechanical, without written permission.

ISBN: 978-1-7349800-0-4

Published in the United States by Prema Press

Cover design by Danielle Christopher

For my Great Aunt Anne

And all those who believe in me, even when I don't believe in myself.

Reaching Riverdale

1

Time is such a funny thing. The way it can seem both slow and fast had always amazed me. Some days move slowly, like a Southerner on a stroll without reason or destination; yet entire years can race by before you know it, as though someone is turning the pages of a flipbook. In my own life at least, that has certainly held true. I could remember times I thought would never pass, but entire periods of my life have ended just as quickly as they began.

I recalled one day in fifth grade, when I glanced up at the clock on the classroom wall. It was during a particularly boring history lesson, and I couldn't wait for it to be over; I looked at the time and was dismayed to find the day was far from finished. The four hours remaining seemed endless, and each minute felt unnaturally long. As I discovered this, my ten-year-old self then realized those hours were nothing compared to the number of years I had until my high school graduation. I counted them slowly on my fingers: sixth grade, seventh grade, eighth, ninth, all the way up to twelfth—seven years that seemed like an eternity. A milestone I'd never reach.

And yet here I was, at twenty-four, celebrating the completion of graduate school. Looking back, those seven years and the six that followed positively flew by. There were many other days like the one in elementary school but collectively, I felt like they came and went in the blink of an eye. One day I was running around the playground and building projects on poster board, and the next I was crafting a thesis and discovering a keg stand wasn't some gymnastics move. Then, just when I felt I was getting used to all that made up college, I was once again in the house I grew up in, with two degrees in my pocket.

As I sat on the familiar sofa in the living room with a glass of wine in hand, I relaxed as light conversation and laughter flowed through the air. The sounds enveloped me in warmth, like a blanket in the middle of winter. The individual voices were lost within the collective hum they created but as I became used to the noise, I started to recognize those of my family. I could pick out a word here, a tone there, a familiar buzz. I made a game of it, tilting my head to the side and listening for the cues. And, following the sounds, I couldn't help but smile when they led me faithfully to a well-known face.

The joyful noises of a baby were the first to catch my attention. Looking across the room, I found my sister Julianne rocking her son Ryan back and forth in the crook of her arm. On the ground beneath her, her daughter April was sprawled on her stomach reading a book, oblivious to the people around her. It was exactly the sort of thing Jules and I would have done when we were younger—left the real world behind for a literary adventure. Looking at the two of them, it was easy to see the resemblance in the shape of their noses, the stubborn jut of their chins and the thick brown hair they both possessed. That, and their mirror personalities, were clear examples of the phrase "like mother like daughter" ringing true.

A sudden childish shriek crashed against the voices that already filled the air, followed by pounding on stairs. No one else paid attention, but I turned and looked just as Haley and Vanessa, my brother's twin girls, came bolting down the steps. Close behind them raced Jules' other son Tyler. His face was flushed with excitement, and as they sped through the room, I caught a glimpse of what looked suspiciously like a toad clasped between his palms. I couldn't help but laugh at the little devil and the way he was always causing trouble. He especially enjoyed terrorizing the twins, who were a prime example of girls made from "sugar and spice and everything nice." I had a feeling they didn't include toads in that category.

Deep laughter drew my attention next, and I peered through the crowd toward the direction of the den. Through the doorway I caught a glimpse of my brother Nathan laughing along with my father. Straining to listen, I recognized the voice of my brother-in-law Derek as well, the three of them forming their own little gang—that is, if gangs told dad jokes and were endlessly kind.

I smiled as I looked at my dad. I wasn't the type who considered men to be the answer to all women's problems, but I couldn't deny my mom seemed to grow younger as the years passed with my father—not older. She was happy, and it showed. Right now I knew she was standing in the kitchen and socializing, while cooking up some delicious concoction for the crowd. I could picture her: smiling and in her element, with features that seemed to heighten as the years progressed. Many people said we looked alike, but I always thought she surpassed me by far. I was taller than she was, and not as delicate. My hair was a dark chestnut color, while hers was a gold-flecked brown that more closely matched my sister's. Her eyes were all sky while mine were bright green, like Irish moss. I knew a healthy diet and good genes played a part in her good looks, but I also knew they weren't the only things responsible. I had to give credit where credit was due—to my dad—and the boundless happiness he brought her. If only everyone could be so lucky.

I thought back to college, and the day I stood in the Metropolitan Museum of Art staring at a painting...

I tried to make sense of the seemingly random dots of paint that covered the canvas. As part of an assignment for my art elective, and in an attempt by the professor to get us to semi-regularly attend the city's numerous museums, every few weeks he had us pick from an art "grab bag." Whatever piece we chose we had to locate, visit, analyze, and write about. I was usually a fan of the task, but I was less than thrilled with my current selection.

"It's not very good is it?"

I turned around and found a chiseled face with green eyes and black hair looking down at me, amused.

"Excuse me?"

He nodded towards the art I'd been staring at. "You've been looking at that painting with a frown for about 15 minutes. So I figured I'd just take a chance and come out and say what you might be thinking."

"Well... it's not so much that it's ugly per say, it's just that... I think my nephew could have done it. He's a toddler."

He laughed and held out his hand. "Too right you are. I'm Rick. I go to school at NYU."

"I'm Annebelle. I do too."

He nodded, "I thought you might. Do you want to grab a drink?" He hadn't released my hand after our introduction, instead holding it firmly in his grasp.

I pointed at the painting. "Umm... well I have to finish—"

"Staring unhappily at this toddler's craft? Have a drink with me now, Google the painting later. I don't think looking at it longer will magically turn it into a Renoir."

I laughed at that, and noted while he wasn't really my type, he was in no way unattractive. "Well... all right."

"Fantastic!"

He released my hand then, and we headed off to enjoy a drink at the Roof Garden Café with panoramic views of the city all around us. He'd seemed so perfectly charming then...

I shook the thoughts from my mind with a shudder and lifted my glass to my lips, only to realize it was empty. Rising from my place on the sofa, I made my way towards the kitchen for a refill, weaving my way through the clusters of people. Just as I was about to break through the crowd and into the hallway, a warm hand caught mine, forcing me to stop.

"Belle." It was said almost as a whisper, like the word hitched a ride on an exhale of breath, but I'd have known that voice anywhere. I glanced up and found myself looking into the recesses of Riley Parker's honey brown eyes.

Another funny thing about time is the way it can pause. You know the world hasn't literally stopped turning, but there are moments when it certainly feels that way. Looking into Riley's eyes was definitely one of those instances. I knew the guests were still talking and the clock was ticking on the mantle, but gazing into those eyes made everything seem to halt. Instantly, I was transported back in time.

Riley Parker was one of those boys-turned-men all the residents in a small town like mine talked about. He had charm, handsome looks, and "a good head on his shoulders" as I was constantly reminded. I met Riley one autumn afternoon when I was eleven, about a year after they'd moved to town. With a book in hand, I'd walked over to the apple tree that bordered our yards, intent on climbing the tough old boughs for a leisurely read. But when I got there, I was surprised to find Riley already sitting among the branches. Before that moment I had only ever seen him from a distance, playing in his backyard with his family's big yellow lab or some rowdy friends. He was fourteen and much bigger than I was, but that didn't stop me from placing my hands on my hips and exclaiming sternly, "You're in my tree."

He'd retorted with something about joint custody because it bordered our properties, and since he was older, he got first pick when it came to whose turn it was. Some other words passed between us, the particulars of which I can't remember, but never before had I seen Riley in that tree so I knew he couldn't be right. He made me mad. And so, I did what any sensible girl in my position would do; I picked up one of the fallen apples and threw it in his direction, hitting him squarely in the head.

We became friends shortly after that. Our mothers made us apologize to each other, and as punishment, we were sent to gather all the apples off the ground, sort out the good from the bad, and peel the former for pies and streusel. So with apple juice on our hands and the scent of fall in the air, a love-hate relationship was formed. We were always sparring with words, and we rarely agreed. In school, Riley couldn't let anyone know he was friends with me: eighth graders didn't socialize with sixth graders. But we learned to share the apple tree, and up in those branches we talked about everything imaginable. When I was in eighth grade and he was a sophomore, he erased my first kiss fear by giving me one himself. Freshman year rolled around, and it was okay for us to be friends then. In fact, it was okay for us to be more than friends, and I went with him to his junior prom. The following year we were practically inseparable.

Our families, then our family friends, then the rest of the town constantly talked about the day we'd inevitably get married. We were named "best couple" in his senior yearbook, and he gave me his class ring. There were other girls with an interest in Riley, but he ignored their flirtations—and I pretended to ignore the envious glances they passed my way. Riley was undeniably gorgeous and a catch even in high school but to me, above all else, he would always be the boy I bruised with an apple.

My best friend Meredith, whose romantic heart skipped a beat whenever I told her about the things Riley did for me, was always saying our relationship was just like Anne Shirley and Gilbert Blythe's. According to her, our marriage was a done deal. I'd just laugh.

When Riley received his acceptance letter from the University of California, Los Angeles, I was the first person he told after his parents. I was lying on his bed, thumbing through a magazine while he played a video game when he broke the news. I sprung up and shrieked in excitement as I congratulated him. I was genuinely thrilled about his future and all of the things he would get to see and experience on the West Coast, but he didn't seem nearly as happy as I was. When I asked about it, he proceeded to say he didn't want to go because of me. I looked at him incredulously.

"What on earth are you talking about?"

"How are we supposed to be together if I'm all the way across the country?"

The idea of Riley Parker—smart, handsome, Riley Parker—giving up the chance to go to UCLA because of me seemed abominable. "You're going to California," I said in the same tone I'd used when I found him in the apple tree that very first day.

He put down his controller and looked at me. "I'm not fourteen anymore, Belle. You can't tell me I'm going to go to college the same way you told me to get out of a tree."

"UCLA is an amazing school. You have to go."

"The only way I'll go is if you come with me."

"I'm still in high school, Riley..."

"Afterwards..." He got up from his chair and stepped over to me. *"Yeah."* He took my hand and his expression changed, and I could

practically see the gears turning in his head as he formulated a plan. "Yeah, that's it. Once you graduate you can come over and meet me. You can apply to a nearby school, or the same one. You're smart enough to get in. Then it will only be two years that we're apart, and once we're both done we can come back here and get married just like everyone expects us to."

My future flashed before my eyes. Everything everyone had ever said about the two of us getting married came rushing back to me, and suddenly it didn't seem like something to laugh about. I had to hit the brakes. How could Riley be so certain we were meant to be together? I loved him—true—but we were young, and it was a big world. I couldn't bear it if he never explored that world because we were together. Neither could I bear it if I stayed with him—went with him—and watched as he discovered there were plenty of other girls outside Riverdale. What if he saw those girls and realized I wasn't that great after all? What if he began to regret us? Likewise, what if I never went to New York City like I'd always planned and spent my entire life wondering "what if?" A million possibilities started swirling around in my head, and I felt my heart speed up anxiously.

I pulled my hand from his and held both up in front of me like I was trying to stop the future I'd just seen. "Whoa, Riley, what are you talking about? That's not how it goes. You're going to college in California. I'm going to graduate and go to college in the city. We've always talked about the things we wanted to do, and that's what we've always wanted to do."

He reached for my left hand and started toying with the class ring that adorned my finger. "I know, but those were just dreams. You and me—that's what's real."

I looked down at the ring and started to get dizzy. How on earth had this happened? I took a step back.

"Riley... you're going to California, not me."

He let out a sarcastic laugh. "Belle, what are you gonna do? Throw an apple at me again?"

I paused and gazed into his eyes. "I don't think that would work this time." Then I slipped the class ring off my finger, placed it on the desk and walked out of his room.

After the initial shock he must have felt at my actions, he tried to talk to me about things. He called me, waited at my locker, wrote letters, sat by the tree. I knew he was hurt; I could see it in his eyes, but I couldn't— I wouldn't—budge. At first, I remained firm because I wanted him to go to Los Angeles so earnestly. He had so much potential; there was no way I was going to let him throw away the opportunities I knew he'd have in

LA. Eventually he conceded, saying he'd go but that we could stay together because he'd come home every break. But I shook my head. Now that wasn't enough.

I remained firm because, in all honestly, I was afraid. I didn't want a broken heart. I couldn't bear it if we stayed together then he called one day to tell me he'd met someone. Or, if that didn't happen, I didn't want to wonder years down the road if he regretted the fact that we'd practically been together since childhood. After all, didn't guys relish moving from one girl to the next in college? Breaking things off meant he could do just that.

When I told him this, he raked a hand roughly through his hair, called me insane and told me I was the one he wanted. But in a way, how certain he was of us—of me—made me stand firmer in my decision. How could someone be so sure of love when they hadn't experienced the world and all it had to offer?

Looking back on it all, I could see now my actions were about me, too; how could *I* be so sure of love if I never experienced the world and all it had to offer? How could I be sure I'd be happy if I left Riverdale only to follow Riley to California then return to town to spend the rest of my days? The same place, the same people, the same old thing... forever? These were questions I didn't know the answers to, but I had to at least attempt to figure them out; breaking up with Riley felt like the only way to get that inquisition underway.

News traveled fast, and everyone in town was completely stunned by my actions. My family asked me about it constantly. Meredith repeatedly said I was crazy. But time kept moving. Riley skipped his senior prom since I wouldn't go with him and shortly after, he graduated. Soon he left town, packing his bags and heading to campus for an honors program months before the semester got underway. Two years later I packed as well and found myself a few hours south studying business at New York University.

I'd be lying if I said it was easy. Riley had been an integral part of my life for such a long time. After my family and Meredith, he was always the first person I wanted to call when something exciting happened. But I was nothing if not stubborn and so, after my finger hovered over the dial button one too many times, I deleted his number from my phone, then willed myself to forget the digits I'd used so often over the years. I threw myself into my studies and made sure "free time" was a rare commodity. Being busy meant I wouldn't think about him. But at times my phone would ring, and although the number wasn't saved, I knew it instantly despite my best efforts to forget. I always wanted to pick up, but forced myself not to.

And then, of course, life happened. The calls came less and less. I was certain there were probably troves of gorgeous California girls— tall, tan, and blonde—fawning over him at UCLA, and I could only assume he'd found one who caught his eye. A dull ache settled in my heart at the thought of it, but I told myself to be happy. After all, this was exactly the sort of thing I'd been trying to let happen by breaking up with him. I was sure, I'd tell myself over and over, that it would only be a matter of time before I found someone else too. And eventually, I did, succumbing to the advances of the smooth-talking Rick Durand from the art museum.

I hadn't seen Riley in years. And now, here he was standing next to me, still every bit as handsome—but different as well. He looked more mature, more self-assured. A smile spread across my face and I tossed my arms around him. I felt his hesitation, but then his arms grasped me and held on tight in return. My smile deepened, and, to my slight surprise, my heart suddenly felt light as air.

"Riley Parker, it is *so* good to see you," I muttered and meant it. I was engrossed in the moment, but not so much so that I didn't notice the intrigued glances circulating the living room at the sight of us. I pulled back and gripped his well-toned arm through the sleeve of his shirt. My eyes locked with his once more. "How are you?"

"How could I be anything but great, with you standing in front of me?" A screen-worthy smile spread across his face. My excitement bubbled. How could seeing someone again feel this good? I dropped my arm, placed my hand on my hip and gave him a good once-over.

"Well, when did you get here? What are you doing now? How's life, love, work?"

"Take it easy, Miss Roth." He laughed. "I'm not about to disappear. Life is good. I'm working at dad's law firm now. Well, more than just working—we're partners."

"Wait, you're partners with your dad? That happened fast!"

"Well it wasn't exactly fast—I mean, you could say it's been on the discussion table since I was born, but it happened once I got back from Cali."

"Which was what, last week?"

"A year ago, actually."

I started to laugh at his exaggeration then noticed he didn't look like he was joking. "You've been back in Riverdale for a year?"

"Yeah. A friend of mine has a practice in Los Angeles so I worked with him for a while after I passed the Bar Exam, then came home."

I couldn't help but note the way he referred to Riverdale as home, even after being gone for so long.

"Well we can just take that theory about everyone knowing everybody else's business in a small town and toss it out the window. How the hell did I not know this?"

"Trust me, that phrase still holds true. But you weren't here when I got back, and you didn't exactly visit much while you were in college."

I opened my mouth to offer up a retort but shut it as I realized the truth to his words. "Yeah, well, New York City is a busy place."

That definitely wasn't a lie. I was in Manhattan for six years, and there was still plenty I'd left undiscovered. But I knew by the way Riley looked at me he was aware there was more behind my lack of visits than a want for time. My thoughts began to travel down a dangerous path, and I felt the walls that had momentarily disappeared in Riley's presence build back up around me. Clearly eight years wasn't long enough to rid him of his uncanny ability to see right through me. I knew he was about to call my half-truth, so I broke our gaze and glanced down at the empty wine glass in my hand.

"Well, speaking of New York, how'd things go?"

I let out a silent breath of relief as he let my white lie slide, and I knew it was best to move on before he called me out on something else; I'd forgotten how effortlessly he read me. "It's easier than a kindergarten book," he used to fondly say.

"Unbelievably remarkable... but we would be here all afternoon if I started talking about it." I shifted from one foot to the other, suddenly uncomfortable under his watchful gaze. "Especially since it would only be polite for me to ask you to tell me more about California afterwards, and that would take forever too. My wine glass is empty." I lifted it, proving that was the case. "And as the recent graduate I have some obligatory mingling to do. So, we'll have to take a rain check."

He raised an eyebrow at me and smiled. "But I'm a guest, so doesn't this count as obligatory mingling?"

I shook my head and returned his smile with one of my own. "You're not a guest, you're the neighbor. It's not like our town is huge... I'll be seeing you." I spoke the last part over my shoulder as I slid past him and into the hallway before he had a chance to respond.

2

I entered the kitchen just as my mom reached in the oven to pull out a tray of white chocolate macadamia nut cookies—my favorite. She glanced up at me, a smile lingering on her face from whatever she'd been talking about with the other two women in the room.

"Hi Sweetie," she said as she set the baking sheet on the counter.

"Why, here she is!" Eyes the same sky blue as my mom's twinkled at me as my Aunt Arlene spoke from her seat at the table.

"We were just talking about you, you know…" My eyes moved to the right where Doris, the town's gossipmonger, sat trying to bait me with her words. Doris Clark had been a part of Riverdale for ages. I had no idea how old she was, I just knew she'd been here since before my mom was born. I used to walk her dog when I was younger, and sometimes I'd help with her gardens. She lived in an old house in the middle of town next to the green, and it was the perfect location for someone who liked to know what was going on at all times and considered it her professional duty to keep the gossip wheel turning.

"At my graduation party? Really? Who would have thought!" I tried to look intrigued as I walked over to the counter. My mom discreetly elbowed me from behind and Arlene shook her head ever so slightly. But I knew my sarcasm wouldn't be noticed, and even if I didn't offer up the slightest bit of interest Doris would still tell me whatever it was she had on her mind.

She nodded in response. "Indeed we were. Did you happen to notice Mr. Parker is here?"

Oh God, I thought to myself. I should have known leaving the living room wouldn't be the last of Riley. I reached for the wine bottle and started to fill my glass.

"I was just speaking with him a moment ago actu—"

"Of course you were. Then you probably know he's done a fine job for himself what with partnering up with his father and all. He's a wonderful presence to have around town, that's for sure. Nearly every time he passes by my house he stops for a chat. He's grown into quite the gentleman."

"I gathered as much."

"...Although he's always been that way. Whoever settles down with Riley will be extremely lucky. Any woman who'd turn him down is a fool and a half."

I gave her a tight smile in response and grabbed one of the fresh cookies off the plate my mom had just set out. I took a bite to avoid responding and she took my silence as cue to continue.

"Yes, quite the fool. I know he'll settle down before long with someone marvelous though. And speaking of settling down, how about you, dear? Whatever happened to that flame of yours from New York? Oh what was his name..." She pressed her lips together and furrowed her brow.

I tossed a glare at my mom and Arlene, wondering which one had spread stories of my college life about town. I couldn't escape. One would think being hours away, living a life completely separate from Riverdale would mean I'd be able to keep some of my private life private. But no, nothing was safe from this place. I was suddenly extra glad I wouldn't be here for long; I loved my family to no end, but I'd probably go insane if I stayed longer than the two weeks I was planning on. And if the theme of the current conversation continued, even that was going to push it.

"Richard! That's it. How are things with you and Richard?"

"We—"

"You should have brought him home with you. I'm sure your family would love to meet him."

"Well—"

"Of course, he must be busy getting things ready for your return. I don't see why you can't come and live in Riverdale though. We could use a new business or two, that's for sure."

"I don't—"

"We have our main businesses of course, and they've been here for ages, so that's all fine in general, but some of the owners are getting on in years, you know. A few young hands could do marvels, I'm sure. Maybe you can talk him into coming here instead."

"He—"

"Besides, I think the city would be terrible for your health after a while. The air quality there is positively dreadful. I'm sure the sights are nice enough and there are some quaint restaurants like that one in Central Park. I think it's called Tavern on the—"

"Rick and I broke up."

Three pairs of eyes turned quickly in my direction. Doris paused midsentence. I hadn't planned on breaking the news so suddenly, and definitely not with Doris around, but for such a small old lady she sure had a lot of wind in her. I knew I wouldn't be able to get a word in edgewise without it being a tidbit worth spreading around; Doris was only quiet long enough to learn more gossip so she could keep on talking.

"Oh my. Well then." I could tell she was trying to act like this new information wasn't making her squirm in her seat. If she could she'd probably leave this instant to go tell someone. I could already hear the conversations.

"That Annebelle Roth let another one go. She can't hold onto a man for the life of her. Doris just heard it from her yesterday at the graduation party."

"Well, what happened?"

"Not too sure of the particulars, but apparently he was asking too much of her."

"So she kicked him to the curb?"

"He probably just asked her to stop shopping on Fifth Avenue so excessively or something."

"I swear there's just no help for that girl."

They wouldn't know the real story though, and I wasn't about to tell them. My thoughts journeyed back to senior year.

"Annebelle!"

It sounded like a growl or rough sandpaper—a far cry from the silken sound of my name when it came from Riley's lips. I cringed at it, slowly looking up from my place in the living room of our apartment. That is, it was Rick's apartment—but he'd insisted I move in, assuring me I'd be able to focus much more on my studies without the chaos of the college dorms.

"Why can't you keep it clean in here!?"

I peered behind him into the bedroom. Everything was neat and in its place—except for an unmade bed.

"Sorry—I woke up late for class this morning." My voice cracked nervously as I replied.

"You got back over an hour ago, didn't you?"

I stood up and started toward the room. "Sorry... I just... forgot. It's just a bed." I knew I wouldn't be able to give him a satisfactory reply, no matter how I tried.

"You're always forgetting!" His voice escalated and as it rose, so did his hand. "Just a bed?! You know I can't focus on my work when things aren't in order!"

I flinched at his raised hand, which he held in the air only a moment longer, before dropping it and pulling me roughly against him. "Don't flinch, baby. Sorry. I didn't mean to yell." He breathed the words, heavy against my neck, squeezing me tightly. "You know I'm just stressed. Make the bed and don't forget again, okay?" He released me as I nodded, and I began to walk past him.

A second later he stopped me with a firm grip on my arm. "Oh, and baby? Don't ever flinch like that when we're in public..."

Doris cleared her throat as a topic transition, and the memory vanished

"Well, in that case, we can probably expect you to be around town longer, no? I'm sure it's for the best anyway—you can move on home. You'd be plenty useful around town, that's for sure. In fact, you could help out at the community center on Thursdays, for starters."

"I'm not staying in Riverdale."

"Well, why wouldn't you? I could easily find you employment. If you don't want to stay at home, I'm sure there's somewhere else for you to live nearby, like the apartments on Valley Road. Just think how wonderful it would be for your entire family to reside in Riverdale. After all, Nathan and Julianne have both settled here. I think it makes sense you would as well."

"No, it makes sense that I wouldn't." The way she was planning everything out aggravated me. There was no way I was going to let my future be decided so easily, in a manner so... expected. It was like a repeat of the scenario with Riley. "I'm only here for a couple of weeks. The company I interned with last year has a position waiting for me with their Atlanta branch so I'm moving there the Tuesday after next. It's a great opportunity." I looked at my mom who was now leaning against the counter watching me thoughtfully. Aunt Arlene's chin rested on her hand as she listened. "You didn't actually expect me to stay in town, did you?"

"Well, what's so wrong with it here?" Arlene chimed in. "Has college made you too good for us?"

"No. It's just... this place is so..." I hesitated. "It's just not the place for me. There are opportunities for me elsewhere. There's a lot more to this world than Riverdale."

Silence followed. Doris started patting her head of short white hair as if fixing it—which was ridiculous since I doubted her perm would move in a tornado. My aunt copied my earlier tactic and picked up an appetizer from the plate in front of her and started nibbling. I looked towards my mom for help.

"Oh come now Doris, it shouldn't come as a surprise that they'd offer her a job. She's too wonderful for anyone to pass up."

I gave my mom a feeble smile, but I could tell she wasn't thrilled with the announcement, either.

"Auntie Belle, Auntie Belle!" The backdoor flew open and Tyler came scrambling in, unknowingly saving the day. His hands still covered what I assumed was the toad. "Guess what I've got!"

"What, a leprechaun?"

He let out a fit of laughter. "No, they only come out in March!"

I placed my wine glass on the counter, knelt down and looked at his hand pensively. "Oh, that's right. Okay then, Tinker Bell?"

He scrunched up his nose at me. "Why would I try and catch Tinker Bell?" He let out a sigh. "I'll just tell you—it's a toad!"

"A toad!" I grasped him by the shoulders and turned him back around towards the door before glancing at my mom. "Well we better head outside so you can show me. If you let him loose in Nana's kitchen she's going to have a fit."

"A big fit?"

"Huge. She'll probably stop baking for a month!"

"Oh no!" He let me steer him outside, obviously appalled at the thought of no more cookies. He stopped on the back step to show me his treasure, and as I peeked in the space he made between his hands, a pair of small beady eyes looked up at me. I stuck a finger in and touched its rough leathery skin.

"Well, look at that. How did you manage to catch him?"

"He was hopping by the swings. I snuck up from behind, and real hurried, I jumped down and put my hands on top."

"He must not have known you were there. You're real good at finding animals, huh?"

"I guess so."

"I know so. You're like Steve Irwin."

The kid was obsessed with animals and the late Crocodile Hunter, and he looked up at me proudly at my assertion. "I am, huh?"

"You bet. Are you gonna let him go back to his family now, like Steve would?"

He thought about it for a second, and then shook his head matter-of-factly. "'Course I am."

I followed as he headed over toward the swings my dad had set up between two tall sycamore trees. Haley and Vanessa sat on them, trying to swing as hard as they could. They saw Tyler walking towards them and let out a shriek.

"Aunt Belle! Don't let him come near us!" Vanessa pleaded.

Haley looked on fretfully. "He's got a dirty toad in his hands!"

I smiled, amused. "Don't worry, he won't bring it near you—he's about to let it go."

"Promise?" They said in unison.

"Of course I do. So does Tyler, right, Ty?"

"I do?"

I gave him a look and he mumbled in agreement. "Yeah, sure."

We walked behind the girls to the grove of old oaks that lined the back of the property. Tyler looked at the toad wistfully. "Don't you think sometimes Steve would keep the animals he found?"

"No, I think he let them all go." I squeezed one of Tyler's shoulders.

"But I bet he gave them names before that so he'd remember them. You could do that if you want."

"You think?"

I nodded.

"Okay. This is... Brad."

"Why Brad?"

"Because it's close to 'grad' and I found him at your graduation party!"

I laughed at his answer. We were clearly part of the same family. When I was younger, I'd always name my pets after something relating to the day I got them; when a bunny was given to me on my birthday I named her "Candles." The fish from the river that runs through town was dubbed "Dale," and the kitten we found one Memorial Day was aptly named "Patriot."

"I think that's a great name."

"Me too. All right Brad, time to go home." Resigned now, Tyler kneeled down and let Brad hop out of his palm.

"Auntie come push Haley and me!" I glanced over my shoulder at the girls.

"Sure thing. Ty, you want to help?"

"Uh... no thanks. I'm gonna go inside and find Uncle Nathan. He said he'd play catch with me."

"Okay, but don't forget to wash your hands." He tossed a wave my way in reply as he started to scurry off toward the house.

I headed over to the girls and began pushing each one alternately. Their laughter started to bubble over as they climbed higher and higher, stretching out their toes in a hopeless attempt to touch the clouds adorning the sky. The setting sun had started to change their color from a brilliant white to a mixture of pink and purple hues; the pale blue backdrop was beginning to darken as the light faded, and a slight breeze sent the fluffy white seeds from the cottonwood trees dancing through the air.

I tossed a wave at Nathan as he emerged from the house with Tyler a few minutes later. I inhaled the scent of spring flowers, listened faintly to the song of nearby birds and laughed along with the girls while simultaneously watching Nathan and Ty begin a haphazard game of catch. I reveled in the moment. Despite the conversation in the kitchen, which had only escalated like it did because I'd been upset with Doris' pushiness, it *was* nice to be surrounded by family—people I knew without a doubt loved me with no strings attached.

"Auntie, you're slowing down!" My attention snapped back to my nieces. I quickly apologized to Vanessa and made sure to use extra force when she swung back into reach. Not long after, the back door opened once again, and Jules stepped out with Ryan. She headed toward the swings, calling over to Tyler as she walked. "Ty, honey, we're going to leave in a few minutes."

He uttered an incoherent reply, or maybe it was a disappointed grunt, and kept on playing.

"Hey Jules."

"Aunt Jules, look at us fly!" The girls sang out.

Jules stopped next to one of the trees, still holding Ryan in the crook of her arm. He reached up with one of his tiny hands and tried to grasp one of the downy seeds as it floated past.

"It's good to have you home again, Annebelle. Believe it or not, we miss you when you're away."

I felt a tingling of guilt, but quickly shoved it aside. "Well, yeah, it's good to visit. I missed all of you, too."

Her smile faded slightly. "Won't you at least think about staying in town?"

"Really? News still travels fast, I see. Everyone stays here, Jules."

"So that's a bad thing?"

"*You* used to want to leave at one point."

"Well, that was then. I was young."

"Oh please, you're still young. Having kids doesn't instantly make you twenty years older than you are."

"No, but it certainly helps you put your priorities in order. ...I just think you're trying extra hard to stay away from this place for some reason."

I could feel my aggravation rising. I was already tired of the prying, and having people question my decisions. I wasn't a child anymore.

"Look, I have not. The job in Atlanta is really good. My path just doesn't end in Riverdale."

"Yeah, because you won't let it! You've been fighting this place ever since high school."

"Well excuse me for believing there are other towns worth living in besides Riverdale."

Ryan began to cry and the two girls, who had been acting oblivious to our squabbling, now saw it fit to talk.

"Dad, Auntie Belle and Aunt Jules aren't getting along very well." Haley hollered over to Nathan.

"Yeah, and umm, Auntie Belle you're slowing down again..." Vanessa called down from her swing.

I stepped over to Jules and held out my arms for Ryan.

"Your turn to push," I ordered. She handed off the baby in a huff and took my place behind the girls. I looked down at Ryan, his big baby eyes returned the gaze, and his crying began to hush.

"Are you two arguing already?" Nathan strolled over with Tyler beside him.

"Only because Annebelle hates her family," Jules decidedly stated.

Tyler glanced up at me with concern. "You don't hate us, do you?

The two girls looked down as they swung back and forth, awaiting an answer.

"Thanks a lot, Jules. Of course not. I love you all to the moon and back!"

"The sun too?" Haley asked.

"Yup, and all the stars as well."

"We could go to the sun and back right now if Aunt Jules would only push a little harder."

Nathan stepped beside the swing and hooked an arm around Vanessa as she swung by, pulling her off the seat as she shrieked in surprise.

"How about instead of making comments like that you say, 'Thank you for pushing me, Aunt Jules.' We're about to leave, so you'll have to try for the sun another time. Go inside and find mom, green bean."

"Bleh. I hate green beans." She squirmed out of his grasp and thanked Jules before sprinting into the house, her dark ponytail twirling fiercely as she ran. Clearly she forgot *I* was the one who pushed her first—what gratitude!

Nathan walked in front of Haley's swing and held out his arms

"Come on brussels sprout."

She made a face at the term of endearment. "Ew, Daddy those are gross." In the next instant she flung herself out of the swing and into his arms.

"They are not. They're delicious—especially with your Nana's cream sauce."

"No, they're gross." He squeezed her tightly as she continued to protest before setting her on the ground and addressing Jules and me.

"Are you two okay to leave alone? I don't want to have to break up any fights."

"We'll head in, too. Derek was just about ready to head out," said Jules. She looked at me and opened her mouth as though she had more to say, then thankfully decided against it.

We headed back toward the house side by side with baby Ryan in my arms, Tyler on Jules' back, and Haley holding hands with Nathan. Once indoors, they went to gather up the rest of their families to make their rather short trips home, and as they said their goodnights other guests began leaving as well. I smiled as a few more people departed. Hugs and kisses were passed along, more "congratulations" and "welcome home" well-wishes were expressed, and I thanked each individual for coming.

An hour or so later I sat quietly on the front steps, once again taking in the moment. The sound of crickets started from the woods—a peaceful sound. I looked up at the few stars twinkling in the sky, the air much cooler now. These were sights and sounds I hadn't seen in years. The city sky was lit up with bright lights instead of stars, and the sounds stemmed from sirens and taxicabs, not crickets and birds. But just like riding a bike after going sometime without, it all comes back—it all feels familiar.

Everyone was now gone. I knew this because I was positive I'd seen every resident of Riverdale walk out our door. Well, almost every resident; somehow a certain guest with a particular pair of honey brown eyes slipped out without me knowing. At the thought of him, my mind once again spiraled back in time.

Suddenly it was summer. I turned to my left and looked into those eyes, laughing as we sped along the highway, the warm wind from the open windows brushing against my cheeks and blowing my hair wildly. Riley reached for my hand, brought it to his lips, then held it in his grasp. The car was filled with the scent of suntan lotion and the sound of The Beach Boys—fitting since the beach was our destination.

In the next instant it was fall. We were lying on the ground in the park gazing at the sky. It was brilliantly blue, filled with clouds drifting lazily about and brightly colored leaves cascading down around us like autumn's version of snow. Our hands, fingers intertwined, rested between us. The remnants of an afternoon picnic were scattered about. Riley sat up and reached for the plate holding his third piece of apple pie—I'd made him his first of the season. He took a bite, grinned widely, then leaned down to kiss me in gratitude. His kiss made me feel like I was melting faster than the ice cream on his pie; it tasted like cinnamon, apples—and Riley.

I snapped back to the present, surprised where my thoughts had led me. I stood up and shook my head. The leisurely moment now broken, I walked into the house. Being back in town was already churning up memories I'd successfully kept at bay for years, and pondering them now, when so much time had passed and so much had changed, couldn't possibly be a good idea.

"What can I do to help?" I asked as I came upon my mom in the living room, cleaning up remnants of the party. My dad sat on the couch I had occupied earlier with a newspaper in hand. Aside from the occasional rustle as he changed sections, the ticking clock, and my mom's movements, it was silent—a stark contrast to both the city and the sounds that had filled the house only hours before.

She looked towards me as she gathered plates off one of the tables. "You can head on up to bed, that's what you can do. You look exhausted."

I sank down into an armchair. "No, it's all right, I'm not tired. I can help you clean up."

"Don't be silly, Belle. It's not much, and besides, I've got your dad here to help. Isn't that right, Matt?"

"Mmhmm," he responded as he flipped the paper over. I smirked at his faux-uninterested reply. He was making it seem like he couldn't be bothered, but once I left I knew he'd put down the paper and help. That had always been his way; he tried to act tough in front of other people, even his kids, but mom and him were a team, and he couldn't stand a mess any more than she could.

I thought back to when I played soccer in middle school. My dad was one of the coaches, and his tough character was famous on the field. He was convinced every one of us had the skills to become professionals and treated us as such. He always pushed our limits, his gruff voice filling the air while we played, ordering us to work harder, go faster, play better...

The opposing teams probably thought we had a drill instructor for a coach, but if one of us ever got hurt, it was easy to see he was truly a softy. A downed player meant he'd be out on the field in half a second. The day Meredith broke her wrist from a fall, I swear he was by her side before she'd even realized what happened. The memory of his concern made me smile.

"Hey coach?" He glanced up at the mention of his old title. No matter how long he'd been retired from coaching, I knew he'd always answer to that name. "I love you," I stated.

He placed the newspaper down and looked at me curiously a moment, then nodded and smiled in return. "I love you too, Junior."

"Go on ahead. This won't take long," my mom urged. "We'll talk more tomorrow." I nodded and stifled a yawn, suddenly glad she didn't want my help. I stood and started toward the stairs.

"Annebelle?"

"Hmm?" I paused and looked back at her loving face.

"Congratulations. We're so very proud of you. And it's good to have you home."

Home—technically, this wasn't my home anymore. I mean, I hadn't lived here in six years, and now I was only stopping by for a couple of weeks. That wasn't nearly long enough for me to stake claim to this house as being home anymore, was it? I thought this but smiled at her.

"It's good to *be* home. Good night Mom. Night Dad." I walked up the stairs and into my room, where slumber impatiently waited.

3

I woke to the smell of coffee—a scent that was all too familiar considering I could probably be diagnosed as a caffeine addict. Starbucks was my asylum quite often during college. Before I'd moved in with Rick, my roommate and I would take turns heading to one of the many that lined the city streets, returning with coffees to help us get through our work. Sometimes I'd venture down on my own to sit and study—or sit and pretend to work as I watched different people coming and going. On other occasions it was a meeting place for Rick and me to catch up. We'd sip a latte and talk before heading to work or class, and during those moments I'd think about how perfect we must look to passersby, sitting there talking about our day over coffee…

But I didn't want to go there. I stretched, turned on my side, and let my eyes gaze across the bedroom—seemingly untouched by time. Everything looked just like it did the day I left for school; my old teddy bear was still sitting on the chair in the corner looking solemn and neglected. Decorative perfume bottles still graced the dresser top. A stack of books was piled on the bedside table, and a dried rose from high school—a gift from Riley—still hung in front of the window. Of course, I knew it had been entered occasionally—my mom would have come up to dust. But for the most part it was like traveling back six years, or realizing you'd changed while everything else stayed the same.

"Where is she?" A familiar voice came rushing up from downstairs. I broke out in a grin and tossed back the embroidered quilt my grandmother had made when I was a baby.

"She's still sleeping?! She's always been such a sloth!"

My bare feet hit the cool wood floor just as footsteps began thundering up the stairs. I grabbed one of the pillows and held it ready. As the door flew open I tossed it, hitting Meredith Kinney in the face.

"Annebelle Roth, you brat!" She threw the pillow back at me, and then followed the flying cushion, tossing herself on the bed and tackling me with a giant hug. "My God have I missed you!"

"You've sure got a funny way of showing it. If you don't get off me I'm going to suffocate, and then you'll be sorry!" I laughed as she pushed herself up and sat on the bed, looking at me. "And I resent that sloth comment by the way—I am not!"

She stood and tugged on the bottom of her shirt. "Oh, you heard that?"

"This house is far from soundproof."

"Well you know I was kidding. But this is no time for sleeping in. It's after nine. Your mom has breakfast downstairs, it's a beautiful day, and we have to go walk around town together so I can show you off to everyone. I bet we could find ourselves a delicious lunch at Amy's, too."

"You're ridiculous." I stood up and ran a hand through my mess of hair. It was so good to have Meredith standing in front of me. Her bright hazel eyes twinkled at me from a lightly freckled face framed with wispy dark red hair. Her outfit of faded jeans and a white T-shirt fit her personality and her job as the town veterinarian. Meredith had *always* cared for animals, big and small, so no one was surprised when she became a vet. As children we'd hold funeral services for any unfortunate rodents the neighborhood cats got a hold of. She mended birds with broken wings, raised a baby rabbit on her own when she was only seven, and had the uncanny ability to soothe just about any agitated animal. We used to make believe we could talk to them, but sometimes I didn't think it'd been all pretend with Mere. She had a gift, that much was certain. And although time had changed her from a girl to a woman, and she mended larger animals now, too, I knew she was still the same friendly, intelligent, fun-loving Meredith Kinney I'd known since preschool.

"I guess I could handle spending some time with you, but I'm not going to Amy's. I'm not in the mood for lunch with a side of town chatter. You know just as well as I do that going to that diner means running into half of Riverdale."

"That's entirely the point! I'm not going to have you hide in your room the whole time you're here."

"I just got back! I wasn't going to hide."

"Sure you weren't. You were probably going to get a few books, cozy up, and read until it was time to bail out of here as fast as you could."

I kept quiet, thinking about my plan to go to the library for some books later. "You think you're so smart. Fine, I'll go, but know I'm not excited about it. And now I have to take a shower... You could have called, ya know."

She smiled smugly at me. "Why would I call when I can just waltz on over? I haven't been able to do that for years!" Her smile faded then and her expression turned serious. "I'm really sorry I couldn't make it to the party yesterday. The mare at Spring Meadow Farm had a really tough pregnancy and the labor wasn't much better. I was over there until well after midnight... but everything turned out all right in the end and now there's the cutest little foal to show for it!"

I stepped over to one of my suitcases and started rummaging around for some clothes. "It was pretty selfish of her to go into labor when she did. I expected everything to just halt for my graduation party. Horse pregnancies included."

"Still as sarcastic as ever I see. "

"It suits me. Don't worry about it though, you're here now and that's what matters." I paused to look at her once again. "And I've missed you, too, Merekins."

"I haven't been called that since high school!"

"Well, it's about time then. Okay, I'll jump in the shower real quick, and then we can go do whatever silliness you had in mind."

"Good. But hurry it up. Your showers can take forever."

"Hey, I already said 'quick.'" I walked to the bathroom and left her to head downstairs and visit with my mom. Then, one "fast" shower later I slipped into some clothes and followed suit, heading towards the scent of espresso beans. I found the coffee, Meredith, and my mom in the kitchen as expected.

Mere was devouring a piece of what turned out to be a warm blueberry scone, compliments of my Mom. I poured a mug of the hot, energy-infused liquid and sat with them, eagerly reaching for one of the scones. I spread lemon curd across the lightly golden top and took one bite, then another, savoring the taste.

I was convinced the ability to create delicious food was genetic, like eye color or intelligence. And whatever gene it was that allowed a person to whip up a batch of buttery scones from ingredients that tasted no good on their own—like flour, salt and baking soda—seemed to run in my family.

I was pretty good at cooking, but I absolutely *loved* baking. I could remember standing on my tiptoes as a child, watching my mom roll out the dough for a pie, or making a mess of things as I tried to make my own creation from tiny bowls of ingredients my grandmother would set before me. Although my first attempts led to inedible creations, I caught on before long and had been baking ever since. I even found ways to put that interest to use while I was at college, whipping up treats and giving them to my friends. I'd change the recipes so they contained ingredients college students would be drawn to (see: alcohol) and crafted desserts with a twist, like pies with Kahlua flavored pudding or brownies with Baileys Irish Cream. They became a kind of phenomenon, and soon, instead of giving them to friends for free, I had people paying me to make them for parties or gifts. It was a fun way for me to make some extra cash while it lasted (that is, before Rick put a stop to it).

But no matter how many times my service was requested or the number of people who told me what a great baker I was, I always knew I wasn't nearly as good as my grandmother had been or my mom still was, and to me that was the way it was supposed to be; they might teach you what they know, but the original is always best. I could bake all I wanted but I'd still come home, take a bite of my mom's heavenly creations and consider them the most scrumptious things in the world.

After I devoured two scones and downed a cup of coffee (it took some effort to resist a third scone and a second cup), Meredith and I headed to town. I decided to stick with my previous plan and head to the library for some books, and Meredith told me she needed to pick up a few groceries and some paint from the hardware store. I knew these trivial errands were a ploy to get me in as many stores and in plain sight of as many residents as possible so Meredith could "show me off" as she'd said earlier. And while I would have definitely preferred going to the library straight away and then heading home to hide, I decided to humor my best friend.

All three of her intended destinations would achieve the goal of putting me on display simply due to the layout of town. For the most part, Riverdale was spread out parallel to the Diamond River—close enough to be scenic, but far enough away to be safe from floods. Main Street, where the majority of Riverdale's stores sat, ran along the south edge. Quality Home & Hardware, which was our first stop, was sandwiched between the bank and gas station on one side, and Amy's Diner and the General Store on the other. It was perfectly positioned so anyone eating at Amy's or pumping gas could easily see who was going in and coming out. Consequentially, what should be a simple trip becomes a town event. Whether it's for paint or a plunger, it's likely more than one person will catch a glimpse of whatever you're buying and make assumptions about what you're doing—if, that is, they don't already know by some other means.

Across from this stretch of stores was the green—an expanse of lush grass shaded by ancient trees with a few well-placed benches. On the edge of the green sat Doris' white farmhouse with its wrap-around porch and various chairs placed at different angles for her viewing pleasure. In the past, she'd often catch me on my way to visit Riley at his dad's practice which neighbored her yard, or stopping in at my favorite place across the street, The Apple Blossom Bakery (an establishment with yet another phenomenal baker, Mr. Carter).

East of town headed into farmland and eventually the highway, while the opposite direction led by the library and the post office before winding into the forest past numerous properties, like my parents' place. South of the green was the town hall, the old church, fire and police stations, Riverdale's schools and more houses beyond. The town was bigger north to south than east to west, with the majority south of the river; crossing the bridge to the north side led to Meredith's vet and a few more farms like Spring Meadow, its fields full of grazing animals and newly planted crops.

Most of "downtown" could be navigated on foot, which I often did as a child. I'd walk to the gas station for a soda, sprawl out on the green with a newly borrowed book, or stop in at the bakery for a piece of pie. Even though Meredith often accompanied me on these strolls, today she insisted we drive. And so, we drove the short distance from my home to Quality's and pulled off the road to the parking spaces out front, the gravel crunching beneath the tires.

Seconds after stepping foot inside the door, the tiny bell tinkling above us, I heard the first call of acknowledgement.

"Why if it isn't Miss Annebelle finally come back to see me." I flashed a smile to my left where I knew I'd find the owner, Mr. Palmer, just as I always had. And there he was, leaning against the well-weathered wood countertop. His hair was grayer than before I left, but he looked generally the same in an old plaid shirt, chewing on what I assumed was tobacco. The faded red register sat to his right, along with a row of big glass pickle jars filled with nickel candy.

Every time I came into Quality's as a child I'd buy two peppermint patties and a piece of butterscotch from those jars and in a silly way, it made me quite happy to see they still sat where I saw them last.

"Mr. Palmer. I see you haven't changed much at all since I've been gone. You're still stuck behind that counter and still chewing on that tobacco that's bound to be the death of you."

"Now Annebelle, don't go making assumptions that aren't founded. You know as much as I do that I love being right here in this store. And this isn't tobacco. It's gum."

To prove his point, he put his lips together and blew, revealing, to my surprise, a pink bubble.

I let out a laugh. "So it is! God bless whatever woman finally convinced you to kick the habit."

The bubble snapped, and Mr. Palmer looked at me questioningly.

"What makes you think I gave it up for a woman? It's bad for me, that's all."

"I've been coming here and bothering you for most of my life, and there wasn't a single thing I, or anyone else, could say or do to get you to stop chewing. Trust me, it's for a woman."

He changed positions, crossing his arms in front of him, looking at me intently and making another bubble. The pink substance looked silly against his rough features. "Meredith Kinney, why'd you bring this sass bucket into my store?"

"Um… because you asked me to?"

I turned to look at her. "Oh, really? I thought you said we were coming in here for paint?"

She tossed a sheepish look back at me. "We were, I mean, we are. Well… that is, I don't have the paint sample with me. I left it back—"

"Meredith, don't you dare try to make up some story! You know as well as I do we're not painting any bathroom."

Mr. Palmer let out an amused laugh, stepped over to the pickle jars and started unscrewing the container with the peppermints. "Come on now, I don't want the two of you squabbling in here. It's bad for business. Have a candy."

"Annebelle Roth, is that you I hear?"

"Of course it is. Who else would cause a scene in a hardware store?"

I turned toward the new voices and waved a hand at Janis and John Carpenter as they approached. Not surprisingly, I went to high school with them. I always knew they'd marry each other.

"Yep, just me, causing trouble like always."

"I can't tell you how many times I came into this place to find you gallivanting around." John said. "It was like you worked here—or lived here!"

"Well, I always did have a fondness for the smell of woodchips and fresh paint."

Janis tucked her arm into John's. "I see school in the big city didn't rid you of your sarcasm."

I smiled sweetly at her. "Oh no, definitely not. In fact, I took a class all about honing my sarcasm skills. They're all for that kind of thing in Manhattan."

"Really? I didn't know they had that type of course. I would have preferred to use my time better I should think, on philosophy or something like that."

John let out a chuckle. "She was kidding love, there's no such class. She was being, of all things, *sarcastic*."

Janis' cheeks reddened slightly. "Oh, well obviously. Well, we've got to get on home. We're painting our bathroom."

"You are?!" I grinned at Meredith. "Mere, they're painting their bathroom!"

"Shut up, Belle."

"Did we miss something?" John asked.

Mr. Palmer shook his head and reached into the basket Janis placed on the counter, pulling out a container of paint. "Only the usual Meredith-Annebelle antics. Riverdale has been extremely quiet without them."

"Miss Annebelle! I haven't seen you since you were a beanpole of a thing!"

I turned around as Sam Taylor, one of the local farmers, came walking over. I took a breath and smiled yet again. Then I punched Meredith squarely in the arm to let her know just what I thought about being shown off around town.

4

An hour and five more residents later, Meredith and I left Quality's. Of course, not before Mr. Palmer gave me a butterscotch to go with my peppermint and made me promise I wasn't mad at him for having Mere bring me down. I told him I wasn't, and the truth was I didn't think I could ever be mad at Mr. Palmer. John Carpenter wasn't exaggerating when he said I was there a lot growing up. I found something comforting in the scents of the hardware store and Mr. Palmer's company, so even though I rarely needed anything, I'd often stop in for a visit. And no matter how many questions I asked, how many times I badgered him to let me mess around with things, or how often I ran around exploring the aisles, he never seriously got mad at me... Except for the time I dropped a hammer on my foot while pretending to fix a shelf, but even then it was only because he was worried.

"So who's the lady he gave up tobacco for?"

Meredith looked at me skeptically. "Aren't you going to yell at me for bringing you here?"

"Of course not. I'm not dumb, Merekins. I knew what any trip to town would mean—I did grow up here after all—and I doubt your mom would let you paint the bathroom anyway. You can't even stay in the lines in a coloring book."

"Good point." She smirked and unlocked the car door on the passenger side then walked around the front. "I need some gas. And then... Amy's after?" Meredith gave me a straight puppy dog look upon saying the last part.

I let out a sigh and shook my head. "Ugh. Alright, alright, fine. Amy's after."

She let out a little squeal of excitement as she slid into the car. "And it's Ms. Ferris."

"Ms. Ferris! The librarian?!" I said as I followed her inside. "I love her! But how on earth did that happen? I don't think I can picture Mr.

Palmer venturing in for a book or Ms. Ferris needing a hammer and nails at Quality's."

She started the engine and backed out. "They started spending time together after the picnic two summers ago."

"Go figure. Well, I like the idea of them together."

As we turned into the gas station and pulled next to a pump, Meredith tensed up and started looking nervously around. At the same time, I happened to glance at the dash and realized her gas tank was half full.

"Mere, you still have half a tank!"

"What? Oh… yeah. I don't like letting it get any lower. It drops pretty fast once it's beyond that."

I laughed. "There's no difference between the first and second half, Meredith. What are you keeping from me??"

She looked at me as she shut off the engine. "Nothing! I just think that…" Her stare moved from my face to somewhere behind me. "Uh, well… I wanted to…"

"What are you looking at?"

I turned my head in the direction she was gazing and tried to figure out what caught her attention. The small store that sold nothing but soda, tobacco, bait, beer, and oil didn't seem interesting enough, neither did the garage next to it with an old car lifted in the single bay. There wasn't some random animal running around by the dumpster and… I looked back over to the edge of the garage and noticed someone leaning against the side. He had one foot resting on the brick wall and a hand holding a lit cigarette to his lips. He turned toward the car, and as he did so I heard Meredith inhale a sharp breath and start to open the door. I turned back toward her and grabbed a fistful of shirt.

"You hold on just one second missy! Who's *that*?"

"Who's who?" She tried to pull herself away and step out of the car, but I held fast.

"Don't play dumb with me, you know who I mean, and I'm not about to let you out of this car until you spill it." She tried to shrug me off again and when it didn't work, she tossed a glare at me. "Meredith Kinney, I swear, you act like we haven't known each other since the days we ate Play-Doh. You have half a tank left. I know you. You're the kind of girl to run out of gas on the road somewhere because you keep putting off filling up. Remember the time we went driving through the woods in Somerville with the Lacey girls AND GOT STUCK because you ran out of gas? And don't think I don't know when something or someone's got you distracted—that guy has you distracted. So who is he??"

29

I could tell she knew exactly what I meant. She stopped pulling and settled back in her seat, crossing her arms in front of her. "That's Jeremy."

I waited. "And?"

"And, well, I like him!"

The idea of kind, loving Meredith having a crush on a cigarette smoking, jean-clad, oil-covered mechanic was not what I expected. It wasn't the type of guy I always pictured her liking—and remembered her liking. She used to go for the shy, sweet ones and I didn't think this guy was likely to be shy *or* sweet. Even so... I considered it a best friend's duty to help in the romance department.

"That much is apparent, Merekins. You're practically sweating. So what have you done about it besides stalk him at work?"

"I'm not stalking! I'm a paying patron!"

I raised an eyebrow.

"Oh, fine. Whatever. Sure. I make trips to the gas station more often than I probably need to. Big deal. It's not like I drive by his house at night or anything... well, I mean, unless I have to make any house calls in that area... or something."

"Seriously?! Have you ever tried... oh, I don't know... talking to him?!"

She looked at me sheepishly.

"Well, today's the day. You get out of this car right now and—"

Her eyes widened and her hand flew down to my leg and squeezed tightly. "He's walking over here. Belle, what are we gonna do!?"

I pried her hand from my leg to prevent bruising, just as there was a knock on the car window. "Relax, would you!" I pushed the button on the door and as the window retracted, I looked up at the man we were just discussing. His bright blue eyes softened his rough, suntanned skin, and a face covered in pale blond stubble. He took his cigarette from his mouth, his fingernails black around the edges from a constant companionship with car grime and oil. He tossed the butt on the ground, stepped on it, and gazed back. There was something familiar about this guy.

I gave him a smile and broke the silence. "Hi! Can I help you?"

"This pump's not full service anymore."

This guy thought I didn't know my own town! His response made me bristle. "We're well aware. We were having a conversation, and unless there's some hidden line of cars waiting behind us to use it, that shouldn't be a problem. Thanks anyway."

Instead of sauntering off at my brusque tone the way he had sauntered over, which was what I thought would happen, he broke into a grin.

"Don't get saucy with me Annebelle, I was just kidding." I paused and looked at him again, wondering how on earth he knew my name. He noted my hesitation. "You don't know who I am, do you?"

I wasn't about to lie to the guy. There was something familiar about him, but I couldn't quite place it. I shook my head. "Sorry..."

Meredith spoke up from beside me. "You don't remember him?!"

He smiled at Meredith. "It's not the first time." He extended an arm through the window for a greeting. "We'll do this all official then. Annebelle, I'm Jeremy Larson. Welcome back to Riverdale."

I grasped his hand, removed my sunglasses, and looked at him with wide eyes and an open mouth. Jeremy Larson? Well there goes my theory about this guy being the opposite of shy and sweet. Jeremy Larson was the *epitome* of shy and sweet in high school. He was also about a hundred pounds heavier and dressed in wrinkled khakis and screen-printed T-shirts all the time. He'd rarely ever approach us, but Meredith and I always made it a point to talk to him. He was such a nice guy. At the time, there was never anything romantic in it on either side, at least not that I could see, but now... now I could see something, and I liked it, just as I liked the idea of Mr. Palmer and Ms. Ferris. Who knew small-town Riverdale—where everyone knew everybody else—could produce such cute couples? Then again, it did produce Riley and me, but that was beside the point. Far be it from me to try and prevent Meredith from spending time with Jeremy. That is, if I could get her to *start* spending time with him in the first place. He just still better be as sweet as he was back then, otherwise I'd have to take a step in between them like good friends do. ...And the cigarettes would definitely have to go.

"Oh my god. It is, isn't it!" I exclaimed. "It's good to see you! You look great."

I heard Meredith get out of the car and start working on the gas, so I got out as well, leaning against the car and giving him a none-too-subtle appraisal.

"You too, and thanks." He took a step back and hooked a thumb on one of his belt loops.

"So... what have you been up to?" I asked. I couldn't believe this was the same Jeremy Larson. This town was so strange—such a mixture of things that stayed the same and things that change—I barely knew what to think anymore.

"Working a lot, saving up," he replied. "I've got plans to buy some land on the north side of town before long, right near Spring Meadow actually..."

"Shit!" I heard from behind me and spun around towards Meredith. Cuss words weren't something you often heard out of her mouth, but I had a feeling her mishap had to do with his reference to Spring Meadow: it'd always been a dream of hers to own property on that side of town.

"You okay?" I asked.

"Yeah." She mumbled back. "I didn't stick the nozzle in the whole way... I spilled all over the place."

Jeremy let out a well-meaning laugh and walked over to her. "Here, I guess I can make this full service just this once." He took the pump from her hand, and I smiled inwardly as I watched her look at him in awe.

"Good thing you put out that cigarette, Larson, otherwise we might have had a fire on our hands" I taunted. "Mere, I'm gonna take a walk over to Doris' place real quick. I think I see her on the porch."

Meredith looked at me with a silent plea not to go, but clearly my best friend needed a little prodding. If Meredith wouldn't get the guts to ask him out, I could only hope Jeremy would do it instead. I smiled at the two of them and started to head up the road as Jeremy called after me, "When isn't she on her porch?"

"That's a very good point, but five bucks says she's got drinks with her. I could use a nice glass of iced tea."

"I guess you haven't forgotten anything about the ways of Doris."

"Nope!"

I'd get hell from Meredith later for leaving her, but it'd be worth it. That girl was just as friendly as I was, *except* when it came to men. She could like someone for years and never do a thing about it, which was inconvenient because she's had her wedding planned out since the day she got Barbie hitched with Ken. We didn't play with them too often, but when we did, pulling them out of the trunk that sat beneath her bed, that was usually the storyline.

My doll, on the other hand, usually came for the nuptials as the maid of honor. After a few glasses of champagne from a tiny pink goblet, she'd end up with one of the groomsmen. They'd date for a while, maybe even going so far as to get engaged. But before she made her way to the altar, she'd break things off and opt for adventure instead. So as Meredith bought the Barbie mansion and decorated the nursery, I'd go zooming around in the pink convertible, exploring different parts of the bedroom-turned-world.

Thinking about the lives we imagined for ourselves as kids made me smile, especially considering they'd be pretty close to reality if only Meredith could find her groom. Jeremy, I decided right then, had potential.

Bringing my thoughts back to my current mission I crossed the street, nodding to the cars that passed. I walked along the edge of the green, tossing a wave at a few of the people relaxing among the trees. As I approached Doris' porch she looked up from the book she had in hand as though she wasn't already well aware I was heading over. I wasn't kidding when I'd said I saw her; she was sitting in one of the chairs angled in our direction, pretending to read. I doubt she actually looked at the pages. More than likely she was peeking at the gas station, waiting to see if I'd stop over. If I didn't, she'd later comment about "hearing" how I'd been in town and grumble something about avoiding her.

I took note of her appearance as I walked up the steps. Someone who didn't know her would think she looked sweet and slightly feeble. Time had given her more wrinkles while stealing some of the weight she lacked to begin with. She had always been a small woman—it was her bark that made her seem twice the size. She had a permed head of snowy white hair, bright eyes, and lips that were always covered in bright red lipstick. Her attire was always meticulous; from her sweater tops and blouses down to her slacks and shoes, she was a fashionable little thing, and I always found myself wondering what she was like as a young woman. Quite the ticket, I'd bet.

"My, my, my, this is a sight I haven't seen in a while. You haven't come walking up my porch steps for ages."

She placed her book on the tiny table beside her chair, which also held a pitcher of iced tea, just as I expected. I was slightly surprised however, to see there wasn't a plate of doughnuts or cookies from the bakery next to it. Doris had always kept a beverage and a pile of something sweet on hand for anyone who stopped by. It was part old-timey manners and part bait; the kids in town knew she'd have a treat for them if they went over but once there, they rarely left without helping her out with some sort of task… which, I supposed, was just how it ought to be.

"It's about time you made your way over. My garden's a mess."

I scanned the perfectly lined rows of tulips in bloom. "I'm not here to garden. Besides, they look just fine."

"One of the young Harper girls started coming over once you skipped off. She doesn't do quite as well as you did, that's for sure. The other day she pulled up a bulb instead of a weed."

"I'm sure she's doing great…"

"If you just came on home more often that wouldn't have happened. Care for some iced tea?" She started pouring a glass before I had a chance to answer.

"Are you going to give me a hard time? Because if you are, I can just go get some tea from the store…"

She flashed a look at me as she thrust the glass in my direction.

"There's no iced tea like mine. I'm not giving anyone a hard time. I just want my flowers to bloom. What brings you into town today? Did you go on over and visit Mr. Palmer? He's been praising you to the moon since hearing you were back."

"Yeah, I was over th—"

"But of course you did. You always were fond of him. I never could quite figure where the connection came, but then again, you were a friendly little thing and it's not like Tom had a family of his own to occupy his time. I wondered for the longest time why he never married. There was a time he used to sit on my porch and sip cold tea like we're having right now. He offered to take me out a time or two as well, but he's much too young for me and after my Harry passed on, well that was it for me. Did you ever meet Harry?"

I took a step back and rested against the porch beam in the corner, sipping my drink and listening. There was really no sense in trying to edge a word in at the moment. It didn't matter that I seriously doubted Mr. Palmer had any romantic interest in her, or that I'd heard about her Harry more times than I could count. Once Doris got to telling a story, she meant to finish it.

"I'm sure you did, but you would have been quite little. He was a good man, my Harry." She paused for a moment, staring down the street, as if she were looking for him to come walking up. "Anyway, like I was saying, Tom's a nice one, but I had my time with love already. Now, did you hear about him and Virginia? That's something I was glad to catch wind of. I don't think anyone would ever suspect the two of them going on together, that's for sure. But I think it's a good thing. She'll get him out of that store, and he'll get her nose out of those books."

I nodded in agreement even though I was sure she wasn't paying me much attention. I looked up the road toward the farmland where she'd been gazing moments prior. I stared at the street angling off into the distance before it disappeared behind a group of trees. Tiny spots, which I assumed were cows, dotted some of the lush, green fields. I drew my eyes back up the street and came to focus on the building next to Doris' house. The freshly painted sign out front read "Parker & Parker, Attorneys at Law."

So there it was, proof Riley had really gone and done all he claimed to have done—proof that he really had grown up from the boy I used to sit with under the apple tree. I smiled a little wistfully at the thought, glad that my actions—harsh as they may have been—sent him off to California, but sad that so much time had flown by without so much as a word between us. But it was my own fault; I had wanted it that way. Well, at least at first. And then, of course, Rick happened...

"Annebelle... you're not listening to a word I'm saying!" I guess she was paying attention, after all.

"Sure I was, Mrs. Clark."

She looked at me sharply. "Don't insult my intelligence. You were not. And it's Doris to you, dear."

"Okay, okay, sorry. It's been a long day already, and I was distracted by the Parker's office. I was looking at the sign."

"I told you he's done well for himself. Did you know he finished school a year early, too? He could have easily stayed working out west. He had a good thing set up with his friend over there. But instead he decided to come back here, and we're very glad he did so. He knows a good thing when he's got it."

The underlying meaning behind everything she said about Riley was so blatantly obvious. Doris Clark had never, ever, let go of the whole situation regarding the two of us. Before I left for college, she'd update me on his status whenever I saw her around town. She'd praise his accomplishments and make sure I knew just how great he was turning out to be, what a catch he was, and how all the women in California were practically fighting over him. News of all Riley was doing was spread around town like wildfire, and Doris was always sure to give me the latest edition—although I had an inkling she embellished some aspects and added a few additions of her own.

Apparently I *didn't* know a good thing when I had it. I figured by the time I got back from school she'd have learned to let the past be the past, but it looked like that wasn't going to happen anytime soon.

"Anyway, as I was saying, Arlene is coming over this evening. We're going to the church to play cards. It's such a nice way to pass the time. I see many of my friends there, those that are still around that is. Your aunt is such a blessing. She's just wonderful, always stopping over for this and that. I'd be quite desolate without her, that's for sure. I didn't see her nearly as much while your cousins were growing up, but now that they're off on their own she's been around much more. It's mostly due to boredom I think, but let me tell you..."

My stomach let out an angry grumble, the coffee and scones from breakfast long gone. I looked again toward the table that usually held a plate of treats.

"Doris?" I interjected, and for once—surprisingly—she actually paused. "How come you don't have any cookies out? Or cake—anything? I'm not trying to be rude but you always used to."

She pressed her lips together as she always did when someone mentioned anything unpleasant. "Word lemons," she called it.

"For all you know I could have stopped doing that the day you left. That would mean there hasn't been a plate of anything out here for a long time."

"That's doubtful."

"Time didn't stop while you were away, you know. Things happen, people get older. Like Mr. Carter, for example."

She gestured across the street and I looked, for the first time, toward The Apple Blossom Bakery. The windows were dark and dusty, and the sign on the door read "closed." The whole building could use a good painting, and the once carefully tended gardens were in need of some TLC. I was appalled at myself for not noticing earlier, considering it had truly been my favorite stop in town growing up, outside the hardware store.

"What happened to Mr. Carter?" My stomach dropped as I thought about the possibilities. Mr. Carter had started up the bakery ages ago with his wife, Clarissa. Although she passed away when I was very young, he always spoke fondly of her, saying she was the sugar in his life. He used to say without her around to make the baked goods sweet, they weren't half as tasty. Even so, everyone in town knew he was the best baker around. But he was a grumpy one, too. Most people went in, got what they wanted and headed out. But me, I'd skip on down and stick around whether he liked it or not. It'd been a love affair between Apple Blossoms and me ever since the day I had my first sticky bun as a toddler. I never let his attitude get to me. Instead I'd make jokes about it, even giving him the nickname "Mr. Sourdough" when I was older. He'd scoff at my comments and tell me to scat, but other folks could see he had a soft spot for me.

"Oh, he's still there."

I let out a sigh of relief.

"But he doesn't do much with the bakery anymore. It's too much work. Sometimes he opens it up for a day or two, but it's mostly closed now. I'm afraid he's turned into a bit of a hermit. And you know how he is—stubborn as a mule. He was doing fine with the bakery on his own for quite some time, but he can't do it all anymore and won't let just anyone help him out."

I definitely knew that to be the case. More than one high school kid stopped in over the years to see about a summer job, and he'd turn them away faster than you could say "hot cross bun." After they left, he'd slide a plate of something warm and delicious in front of me and say, "You don't work in a bakery for spending money. You work in a bakery because you want to. You have two people make the exact same recipe— one who wants to make it and one who *has* to make it—and you see which one tastes better. There's an ingredient you can't buy in stores that goes in on its own when you *want* to bake somethin' delicious—it's called passion. Got that?"

I'd nod in agreement, licking white frosting off my fingers. Now, the bakery looked so sad and neglected. I couldn't stand to see it like that, so I turned back towards Doris only to find her eyeing me with intent.

"You know…" She tapped a finger on her chin.

"What?"

"I bet Benjamin would let *you* work for him."

I started to shake my head profusely. "No way."

"He always did soften up like the butter he baked with once you stopped on in. You should help out with the place, bring it back to life."

"I'm not about to—"

"That *is* what you went to school for, isn't it? Business? And don't try to say you don't know a thing about baking, because I know you do—probably just as much as he does, if not more. Your mother and grandmother knew their way around an oven and I know they taught you. I heard about your little baking business at college, too."

"Doris, I'm not about to do that. I can't fix a place up in a week's time."

"Don't be silly, of course you can't. You'd have to stay longer. An inconvenience for you I know—you're so anxious to leave us all behind—but Apple Blossoms is practically a Riverdale landmark. Think of what you'd be doing for the town!"

I balanced my glass on the railing and started down the stairs, shaking my head as I went. "You just knock that idea right out of your head, Mrs. Clark. It's not gonna happen. I've got a ticket to Atlanta for two weeks from now, and I plan on using it."

She stood up from her chair for the first time during my visit and walked to the edge of the porch, placing her hands on her hips and looking like some kind of den mother. "I told you to call me Doris!"

"Thank you for the tea *Doris*, but I better be off. Have a nice time at cards this evening. Say 'hi' to my aunt for me."

"Annebelle Roth, you think about what I just said. I know you're not half so uncaring as you pretend to be."

Uncaring? I didn't know I was pretending to be uncaring at all! That woman, I swear! I started to walk back towards the gas station leaving Doris, Riley's practice, and the bakery behind—but not before glancing once again at its darkened windows. Doris may have suggested a crazy idea, but I really did need to stop over to see Mr. Carter. I'd love to see if I could still make him crack a smile.

Back at the gas station, I was glad to see Meredith still talking with Jeremy.

"It's about time you came back," she exclaimed as she caught sight of me, tucking a stray piece of hair behind her ear. "I thought she convinced you to start right in on the gardens."

"Believe me, she tried. How come you didn't tell me Mr. Carter practically shut down the bakery?"

Meredith's face dropped. "I didn't want to upset you. I know how much you love that place. If he'd just let someone in to help with everything…"

"He's had plenty of people interested in helping," Jeremy chimed in. "And plenty of offers to buy it, too."

I shook my head knowingly. "He would never let just anybody help out—he's not like that. And there's no way he'd sell. At least, I don't think there is. I bet he'd rather close it up for good than sell it to some jerk who'd go and change everything he and Clarissa built together."

Meredith nodded in agreement. "If only there was someone he'd trust enough to help turn the place around." She held her gaze with mine a second longer than necessary, and I couldn't help but feel she was thinking the exact thing Doris had just voiced.

I tried to shrug my shoulders in a manner that suggested it wasn't too big of a deal. "Time changes everything I suppose. So what about Amy's? Are we still heading over for a bite? I'm starving, and if we wait any longer I'm gonna bail and head home for a sandwich."

"No, no, we're going." She looked at Jeremy, hesitated for a moment, then nervously shifted her weight from one foot to the other and glanced my way.

I took that as a cue to offer an invite. "All right then, Jeremy, you gonna come along?"

"As much as I'd enjoy accompanying you ladies, I'm not done here until five."

"Well, considering it's Amy's we're going to, there's no telling how long we'll get caught up. Maybe we'll still be there when dinnertime rolls around."

He let out a laugh as he started to back away toward the garage. "I'll be sure to take a look after I'm through."

"You do that. Good seeing you, Jeremy."

"You, too, Annebelle." He nodded his head in our direction. "Meredith."

I was pretty sure he winked at her as he spoke her name. I held back a smile as he turned away.

"Come on Merekins, let's go get some food."

"I thought you weren't at all excited about eating there today?"

Once again we headed over to the car so we could move it to an actual parking space. "I'm not but I'm hungry, and I told you I'd go, so I will. By the way, this whole driving around town thing has been really annoying. It would have been so much easier to walk."

Her eyes twinkled at me. "Yeah, but I needed gas remember?"

I let out a snort of amusement. "Yeah, you needed gas all right. Liar. Next time, let's just go in for a soda and some bait or something."

"Oh because we fish now..."

"Hey, whatever gets you and Mr. I-Turned-Out-To-Be-Gorgeous over there together works for me."

5

Walking into Amy's Diner, as with most of the places in Riverdale, was like opening a box of memories. As I stepped through the door with Meredith, I took in my surroundings. The walls were still pale green and covered with framed photographs of Amy's family and parts of town from throughout the years. Sunlight still poured in from the front windows and delicious smells tickled my nose. The same tables were scattered across the cream tiled floor, and two of the walls were still lined with the same vinyl upholstered booths, a couple of which were currently occupied by a group of high school kids; their happy chatter mixed with the sounds coming from the kitchen and the voice of Elvis crooning in the background.

As we entered, all eyes turned in our direction as the kids searched for familiar faces. I smiled slightly at them, thinking of all the times I'd come here with my own friends. It was always the same routine—a bunch of us would pile into a car or walk over after school. Although Amy's had all kinds of food, we'd usually settle for the traditional fare of burgers, golden fries, sizzling mozzarella sticks, frothy shakes and a bunch of laughs—and if we were feeling really daring, a heaping sundae for dessert.

The kids turned their attention back to their meals as they realized we weren't anyone worth stopping over. I shot a wistful look at Meredith.

"That was us back in the day, huh?"

"It sure was. This has definitely always been the after-school hangout. We had some good times in this place."

"Yeah we did. Remember when Lucy Stevens tossed her shake at Bobby?" We started to walk toward the stools in front of the counter as she laughed.

"How could I forget! That was the last of *their* relationship."

"And a waste of a damn good shake."

As we took a seat, my eyes once again roamed around the diner. A part of me was glad not too much had changed. The meals I had enjoyed here, surrounded by either family or friends, were countless. There were memories in almost every nook and cranny: the booth in the corner Riley and I always claimed, the soda fountain that had been there for eternity, the jukebox my sister and I would fight over, an old picture of my friends and me at a summer picnic. It was like a 3-D history book.

I shook my thoughts away. What was I thinking? I didn't even like history, and Riverdale wasn't supposed to have any kind of nostalgic hold on me. It was only supposed to be a place I'm passing through...

"...beat the rush."

I realized Meredith was talking to me, and my focus returned to the present. "Sorry, what was that?"

"Daydreaming about Riley?" She teased. "I *said* it looks like we beat the lunch rush."

The first part of her comment caught me off guard, but I chose to ignore it and nodded my head in agreement. "Thank God. I'd still much rather eat my lunch in quiet."

"You're not going to take a swipe at me for that comment?"

I let out a breath. "You and just about everyone else I've spoken with so far has tried to get some kind of rise out of me by mentioning Riley, but it's not gonna happen. We've been over for years. There's nothing between us anymore. And as my best friend I'd expect you of all people to just *let it go*."

My statement succeeded in making her look a bit sheepish. "Oh jeez, you're totally right. I'm sorry Belle. No wonder you want to leave this place, what with everyone badgering you about your choices and trying to tell you what to do. It's just that I always thought maybe you and him..."

She trailed off as our waitress walked over in the same pale-yellow dress and white apron that had always been the uniform at Amy's. It completed the scene, making the diner look like it was straight out of a '50s film.

"Welcome to Amy's, my name's Laura," the girl said, pen and notebook in hand. "Can I start you off with some drinks?"

"Diet coke with lemon for me, please," Meredith offered up.

"I'll have a shake—half chocolate, half strawberry. Thanks."

Meredith laughed. "I guess *you're* not on a diet, although you sure look like it."

"If I do, it's only from years of walking around Manhattan. Life's too short to give up milkshakes, Mere. And it's definitely too short to play shy around a good-looking guy like Jeremy." I winked at her for emphasis, and she laughed in return.

"He is good looking, isn't he? He's really sweet too... but I always get so flustered around him." The dreamy look that had momentarily appeared in her eyes vanished. "I end up looking like an idiot."

"Oh please, you do not. He probably thinks it's cute."

She mumbled some incoherent retort that was drowned out by the sudden sound of our names.

"Meredith! Annebelle! Ah! I can't believe you're here!" A woman came rushing out of the kitchen and over to where we sat, wiping her hands on a towel. Instantly, I knew it was Amy's daughter Sarah. She looked a lot like her mother, with cheeks that appeared permanently flushed from being in a kitchen all day, and a figure that looked like she'd certainly had her share of good food. She was boisterous, talkative, and fiercely loyal to Riverdale and its traditions. She was several years older than Meredith and I—closer to my brother's age—but we'd still seen each other around town often enough to be friendly.

"It's so good to see the both of you sitting here!"

"It's good to see you, too, Sarah." I smiled genuinely at her as she approached.

"It's been a while."

"I told you I'd get her out and about as soon as she got back." Meredith grinned from beside me. I should have been annoyed at her for making all these promises to people about bringing me around, but I couldn't seem to regret seeing some of them—like Sarah—even if it was a bit overwhelming.

"Yeah you did. What can I get for the two of you? This meal's on the house."

"Oh! Do you run the place now?" I asked.

Sarah let out a laugh. "Oh no, I could never handle it all with the kids back home causing a ruckus. Usually my parents and I do it together, but I sent them on a much-needed vacation, so I've had to take the reins while they're away. I've got good help though. Natalie, my eldest, helps out a bit. So do a few of her friends, like Laura over there. And Nicole Trenton's son Tim works in the kitchen. My husband is usually here too but being a Saturday, he's at home with the rest of the kids." She frowned for a second as she looked at the lack of food in front of us. "Listen to me chatter on while you're sitting here hungry. Let me know what you want and I'll get it to you straight away."

Meredith and I asked for a chicken Caesar salad and a BLT, respectively, and Sarah bustled in back to let Tim know. Moments later she returned with a plate of mozzarella sticks that she slid in front of us as she continued talking

"I thought you could use those while you wait.

Meredith groaned. "There goes my diet."

"You don't need to diet," Sarah stated matter-of-factly before turning her gaze back to me. "It's a good thing I've got so many people from town to help out around here, and it *is* really good to have you back, Belle. Too many people skip out of this place these days, and that means we get all these newcomers trying to push their way in." She shook her head disapprovingly.

I had to bite my tongue to refrain from commenting. I could see why people would leave, being one of them myself, but I couldn't exactly see why people would move here. It's not like this town was thriving with reasons to call it home.

"Just the other day this wispy little thing of a girl came in to ask for a job. I said no, of course. I'd never seen her before in my life! I'd rather set up a playroom in the back for the kids and run this place by myself than hire someone I'd never even met before. I doubt she'd last five minutes if I let her anyway. She looked scared as a rabbit and talked like she was from Texas or something. But that's beside the point. We start welcoming just anyone into our town and before you know it we won't even know our own neighbors!"

As she said all this I thought about the city, where you could walk past thousands of people each day and not know a single one. It was definitely a far cry from Riverdale, where you worried about the day you wouldn't know one of your neighbors. In Manhattan you could go about your daily business without worrying about other people butting in or trying to tell you what you should or shouldn't do. Everyone was so busy they only had time to think about their own lives, their own business. In the city you could have a life of complete anonymity if that was what you wanted. It was practically the opposite in Riverdale.

But then, if I let myself admit it, there *was* something uncanny about the whole situation—walking down streets filled with people and simply being "one of the crowd" as opposed to Annebelle Roth. I guess there were some days I wanted to go for a walk and see familiar faces like I had earlier this morning, but I always forced those feelings quickly aside. Who would want to live a life without mystery or adventure? Not me, that's for sure—which was another good reason why I couldn't stay here. All the mysteries had been figured out, all the adventures had been taken, and it had all been done decades before I came around.

Sarah left again and returned with our food, which I hungrily started in on. Between bites of salad Meredith conversed with her about

different things: things happening in town, the vet, and Sarah's family—
which Sarah lightheartedly compared to a barnyard. I would have been
content simply listening to them as I enjoyed my sandwich, having had
more than my share of talking for the day, but of course I couldn't get
off so easy. I heard the door open behind us, and Sarah rolled her eyes
before waving at the newcomer and retreating back to the kitchen, clearly
avoiding a conversation with whoever had just come in.

I turned around, and my eyes came upon Alexis Peterson. She looked
exactly as she had in high school. Her blonde hair was pulled back into
a ponytail; her slim figure was covered in low-rise jeans, a pink tank top,
and a white jacket. Her lips formed a perfectly glossed O of feigned
surprise as she saw me, and I tossed her half a wave.

I'd never been friends with Alexis Peterson. It wasn't that she was a
terrible person or anything, it had more to do with Riley (why does
everything have to do with him?). Sure, she'd never been my first pick
when it came to potential friends, but there wouldn't have been a chance
even if I *wanted* to be a part of the same squad, because along with being
captain of the cheerleading team Alexis was captain of team jealousy, of
which Riley was the obsession.

Alexis could have gotten any member of the football, soccer, or
basketball team that she wanted. Only, instead, she insisted on trying for
Riley, and he was the one guy who didn't jump at the opportunity. And
that was because of me. I guess she always figured there was no way
Riley would say no to her, especially considering I was two years
younger and not as good looking according to the standards set by
Cheerleaders of America. So when "no" is precisely what he said—again
and again—that was too much for a girl like Alexis to handle, and her
dislike of me was cemented.

But that dislike was always hidden behind fake friendliness—at least
when Riley was around. Being mean to me would have made him upset
with her, and even though he wouldn't accept her advances, she took
what she could get and Riley, ever the nice guy, was always civil toward
her.

Considering years had passed since I'd last seen her, and Riley was
nowhere to be found, I couldn't hide my surprise as she started in our
direction and her ultra-giddy voice pierced the air.

"Meredith!" She exclaimed excitedly. "What a surprise! Why didn't
you tell me Annebelle was going to be here? I'm sure you must have
known when I saw you for your hair appointment last week. You two
don't keep a thing from each other." She let out a bubbly laugh.

I cringed at the way she always said my name, pronouncing it like it
was spelled "Annie bell" instead of the "Ann-eh-bell" my mom intended

when naming me to honor my great grandmother. No matter how many times I told her otherwise she kept at it, and I'd swear it was just to annoy me.

It was also doubtful she didn't know I was coming home—she did live in town after all. What was she trying to do? Her behavior was suspicious.

"I figured you'd hear it sooner or later." Meredith gave Alexis a charming smile, but I knew it was the type that was completely forced and sprung up when she was annoyed.

Alexis stepped closer to us and called over to Laura for an ice water. "Hmmm. It's funny really, this little reunion." There was a glint in her eyes, and I had a feeling it wasn't for a good reason.

"Why's that?" I inquired, only half caring.

"Well, taking the past into account, you'd think it would be *you*, Ann*i*ebelle, not me, who was about to have lunch with Riley."

I took a sip of my shake before answering—it suddenly seemed harder to swallow. "Lex, Riley's allowed to eat with whoever he wants to, and so are you."

I could tell that wasn't the reaction she was looking for, and I mentally took back my previous thought about her not being a terrible person: once a bitch always a bitch. I yawned slightly and glanced at Meredith. "You just about ready?"

"Yup!" She responded as she took the last bite of her salad.

"It was fun seeing the two of you. I'm sure we'll run into each other again soon." Alexis smiled way too brightly as she headed toward the booth in the corner—the same one Riley and I used to dominate.

"God, I hope not," Meredith muttered beneath her breath.

"Oh no, not that one hon. Sorry, it's reserved."

Meredith and I looked over to see Sarah direct Alexis to a different booth, and we couldn't help but smile knowingly.

"Reserved?" Alexis argued. "Since when does this place take reservations?"

"Oh, it's just something new we're trying out." Sarah placed Alexis' drink on a different table before letting her know Laura would be right with her. She walked back in our direction with a smug look on her face. "You two gonna stay for some dessert?"

"Um, no, I think we've had enough for today," I stated, hoping she'd catch my drift—it wasn't the food but the new company.

"Got it. You better come back soon, okay?"

I smiled at her, honestly glad to see her again. "Sure thing, Sarah."

"Thanks for lunch," Meredith added as we stood to leave.

We turned around just as the door opened once again and in walked Riley. He stopped as he caught sight of us, then smiled and took a step in our direction, clearly intending to strike up a conversation. But he was quickly intercepted by Alexis' voice once again calling out.

"Riiiiley, there you are!"

She was on him before he had a chance to respond, linking her arm through his and leading him to their table. He looked over his shoulder at us, but I pretended not to notice, and Meredith and I stepped out of the diner.

"That was fairly awkward," Mere said as we walked over to the car.

"Something like that," I said absentmindedly.

"Alexis can be such a brat."

"I was leaning more toward 'bitch' actually."

"Yeah, well... at least she's good with hair." Leave it to Mere to try and lighten up the situation. "She's got a salon in Harwinton with some other girl. It's pretty nice actually."

I gave her a look. "Would you knock it off already? Salon or not, I still say she's a B. And I'd rather drive back to the city than get my hair done by her."

"Okay, okay, so maybe she is. Happy now?"

"I'd be happier if you said it."

"Said it?"

"Yeah, that she's a bitch."

"How would that make you happier?" she inquired as we got in the car.

I shrugged. "It just would."

Meredith glanced over at me. "Well, that's mature."

I crossed my arms in front of my chest and glared at her.

"Okay, fine. Alexis is a bitch."

"I feel better already!" I put my head against her shoulder for an exaggerated moment of sentiment. "Not that I really care or anything" I added as I straightened up. "I mean, she can do whatever she wants. So can Riley."

"Right, but..."

I held up a hand. "But nothing. Not another word. Let's just forget it, Merekins. Ancient history."

"Okay..." There was silence for a moment, then Meredith started up again. "Well, do you still want to go to the library? I dragged you through enough for one day."

I thought about how nice it would be to curl up in my room with a good book, the spring breeze rustling my curtains and happy birds chirping in the trees outside. If only some books would magically appear in my room—I didn't feel like perusing the library and bumping into more people just now and so, I shook my head.

"I'll stop in tomorrow. Just take me home. I think I'm getting a headache."

"Of course! But don't think you'll get rid of me for long. I'll be back."

I laughed. "I hope so. I don't know what I'd do without you!"

"You'd be perfectly fine. You were for the past six years anyway."

I glanced at her, catching a look of hurt on her face that disappeared a moment later. I silently berated myself. It was becoming clear I'd hurt more than one person's feelings by pursuing a life outside Riverdale and staying away so long. It may not have been all my doing, but that didn't change that facts.

I watched Meredith back out of the driveway before I turned toward the house—the home I had grown up in. Like many of the houses in Riverdale, it was an old colonial. Its white exterior was accented by dark green shutters and well-tended gardens, thanks to my parents' green thumbs.

I walked up to the yellow daffodils that lined the front pathway and knelt down to smell one of the blooms. The feeling of ease I felt whenever I was here started to envelope me again, and the encounters of the day began to drift away as I walked around the side of the house, enjoying the way the spring sunshine fell warmly across my face. One of the windows was halfway open, and the peaceful strains of classical music flitted through the air alongside the notes of cheery birds and the quiet drone of worker bees.

My eyes came to rest on the apple tree in front of me, which still stood proudly along the edge of our yard. Its thick trunk rose into the air and its branches, covered in pale green leaves that weren't quite full yet, stretched to the sky, beckoning the sun to shine on them. Purple and white crocuses were scattered along the base, and a chipmunk rustled around among them in search of a nibble. Looking at the tree, beautiful in all its springtime glory, it was nearly impossible not to think about the different things that had transpired there—all of the beginnings.

Almost involuntarily, my gaze moved to the left and found Riley's home. It looked as though it had recently been painted, but it was still familiar with its pale blue siding, cream trim and screened porch off the back. The yard was still neat and orderly with closely trimmed greenery for decoration, and the old shed that used to house all of Riley's toys sitting in the back corner.

I looked up at the window I knew had been his. Long gone were the days when the two of us could be found hanging out up there. He had a place of his own—where *did* he live now?—and, at present, he was enjoying lunch with Alexis Peterson. I rounded the corner to the back and tried to push the image from my mind.

"Annebelle, hi sweetie!" I found my mom sitting in a lawn chair with a book on her lap. A warm smile came across my face at seeing her, and I crossed over to sit in one of the chairs beside her.

"Hi, Ma."

"Did you have fun?"

"I guess so. It was strange seeing a lot of the people I grew up with. Honestly, it was a little overwhelming."

"Well, everyone's excited to see you."

I kicked off my sneakers. "I think they're all placing too much significance in my being here. It's not that big of a deal."

My mom placed a marker in the crease of the pages she was reading and closed the book. "It's a big deal to the people who love you."

I pulled my socks off and nestled my toes into the grass.

"Haley and Vanessa will be over later," she continued after a sigh. "They're going to spend the night. Nathan says they've done nothing but gush about you since the party."

"Good. I love spending time with them."

"They haven't had much of a chance to get to know you over the years. They were infants when you left for school."

"Well, I'm here now, and soon they'll be old enough to just hop on a plane and come visit me."

"They would have loved to have seen you more, especially during the holidays. Everyone would have."

"Mom, we've been over this. You know how busy I was. You know I needed to stay on campus to work and take extra courses when I could."

I started ripping up pieces of grass with my toes, thinking again of Rick and how he'd beg me not to go every time I'd plan to visit Riverdale for a holiday. Sometimes I'd stay back because he'd ask so sweetly, telling me he couldn't bear to spend it without me. Then, other times, I'd stay because he frightened me.

"You know I don't see my family, baby."

He never did tell me why.

"And you're just going to leave me here by myself?" That sandpaper growl would start to take over. *"What kind of a girlfriend are you?"*

Never mind the fact that I'd always tell him to come with me. He always had a reason why he couldn't, and a reason why I should stay with him instead.

"I know." The sound of my mom's voice broke the thought, and it was a welcome interruption. "And that's why I just dealt with it, despite how much I missed you. I thought once you graduated you'd be back, and then I'd get to have my holidays with you. But now, now I still won't see you." She hesitated for a moment. "Why Georgia?"

I knew this was coming. "I told you, it's a great job. I'm lucky they asked me to join them after the internship, Mom, especially with the economy the way it is. Who knows how long it'd take me to find another job?"

"Don't be silly, Belle. I know you could find a position anywhere."

"I thought you, of all people, would be supportive of my decisions."

"Of course I'm supportive. I just don't understand them."

I stood up and gathered my socks and sneakers. "You don't have to understand them." I chose not to add that I wasn't entirely sure of them myself.

"Well, I wish I did," she said, standing as well. "I just don't want you making decisions for the wrong sorts of reasons.

"Such as?"

She looked at me knowingly. "Fear. Or...or running from something."

I shook my head incredulously. "I hardly think moving over a thousand miles away is something that could be done out of fear." I started toward the back door. "I'm gonna head upstairs and take a nap. I have a headache coming on."

I opened the door and stepped into the house, and when the screen door slammed shut after me, I was acutely aware it felt symbolically like my past coming to hit me from behind.

"Shh! You're going to wake her up."

"That's the point, silly—grandma said we could."

I felt the mattress move as extra weight was added. I took my arm from across my face and halfway opened an eye. Vanessa sat cross-legged on the bed, grinning at me. Haley stood against the side, her hands folded, waiting for my reaction to their intrusion.

"Hey," I offered sleepily

"Auntie Belle, I told Vanessa not to get on the bed, but she doesn't listen to me," Haley said in defense. Although they were both daddy's little princesses, Haley was the shyer of the two as well as peacekeeper; she didn't like anyone to ever be hurt or upset.

Vanessa swung one leg down over the edge. "Grandma said we could."

"Oh she did, did she?" I sat up, rubbing my eyes and yawning. "Good thing! I'd hate it if I slept through a visit from the two of you."

At my response, Haley broke into a grin like her sister. "You'd see us at breakfast. We're having a sleepover!"

I acted as though I didn't already know, a surprised expression on my face.

"You are! That's awesome! In that case, what do you want to do?"

"First we're gonna eat dinner," started Vanessa.

"And dessert!" Haley chimed in.

"Yeah, and we're gonna watch a movie!"

"But right now..." Haley hesitated and looked at her sister.

"...we were wondering if we could play with your dolls." Vanessa finished.

"My dolls? Well, I don't have too many. Aunt Jules had more than I did. But!" I slid my legs to the floor.

"I think they're all in that closet over there." I stood up and walked over to the door. Opening it, I reached in and took out a box from the back. "You've played with them before, haven't you?" I asked, opening the top. The girls scrambled over beside me.

"Sometimes," Vanessa said, reaching in and taking out one of Julianne's Barbies.

"But now that you're back grandma said we shouldn't until we asked you." Haley went for my old American Girl doll as she spoke.

I smiled as I watched. "Well, from now on you can play with them whenever you'd like."

"Really?" they said in unison, looking at me excitedly.

"Mmhmm. I don't think they like being boxed up too much."

"Can you play too?" Haley asked.

"Umm..." I glanced at my desk where there sat a stack of papers from my soon-to-be employer in Atlanta that I'd barely looked over. "Actually, I have some things I need to do, but I'll be right here in the room."

I took a seat and started looking through the pile. There was so much to fill out—so much business jargon to read to get things ready for my official hire, on top of a potential acquisition I'd been tasked with analyzing to showcase my abilities. I let out a quiet sigh, listening to the girls prattle on behind me and thinking about how much I'd rather be playing. I shuffled some of the forms, aggravated at my inability to focus. This was a great opportunity. Sure, working for a mergers and acquisitions firm wasn't really my first choice, but I didn't see any other option at the moment; it was stable, and it would get me out of Riverdale, where I refused to be stuck. That's what I wanted, right?

I knew at some point I wanted to be a part of something more positive—something that focused on solutions for business owners that *didn't* end in a sale or merger (of course, I left that out of my interview), but I'd get paid well at A.J. Pratts, the sister company to where I interned. And, who knew, after a while maybe I'd get the kind of opportunity I was hoping for, or at least make the connections to help me along the way.

"Auntie?"

I looked to my right to find the girls standing next to the desk. "What's wrong?" I asked. "Are you bored already?"

Vanessa shook her head adamantly. "No, we just wanted to ask you something."

"Go ahead!"

They paused, then Haley was the first to speak. "How come you have to go all the way to Georgia? Mom says that's like... reallllyyy far."

"And we miss you when you're gone." Vanessa pitched in.

"We don't ever get to see you!"

"Yeah, and we like when we can. Why can't you find a job up here?"

"I bet you could," Haley prompted. "You're so nice!"

I let out a laugh and pulled both of them in for a hug. "You're both really sweet, and I miss you too when I'm not around... But I have to try some new things."

I knew talking on and on about the benefits of the position wouldn't help any, so I settled for a different route. "I've never seen Georgia. I heard it's nice."

The girls looked at me with their big eyes, and Vanessa bit her lower lip thoughtfully. "Well, what if Georgia came up here?"

I started to laugh again then stopped at her serious expression. "That's not possible. You can't move an entire state, sweetie."

"But we get peaches from Georgia, don't we?"

Haley's eyes brightened. "Yeah, Vanessa, we do!"

"So, then, Georgia *does* come up here!"

"That's not..." I contemplated trying to explain things further then decided to simply go with it. I reached over and tucked a piece of hair behind Vanessa's ear. "Ok, sure, sometimes I guess pieces of Georgia come up here, in a way... but I'd need more than peaches to keep me from going. That's not a very big piece of Georgia is it?"

They shook their heads in response.

"We'll find a bigger piece of Georgia. We just *have* to! Right Haley?"

"Yeah!"

I swallowed hard and hoped our conversation wouldn't end up backfiring and upsetting them. I supposed there was no harm in letting them try at the impossible. Still, I decided it was best to steer the conversation elsewhere.

"All right, how about I play for a bit, then we can head down for dinner? I bet it'll be ready soon."

The girls squealed in excitement as I got up to choose one of the dolls.

———————

The slumber party was a success. As I drove through a steady drizzle toward the general store the next day, I couldn't help but smile thinking about it. I'd donned a pair of cotton pajamas to match the girls and dragged an old sleeping bag down from the attic. We set up base in the living room talking, playing games, and braiding each other's hair before nestling down in our cocoons and starting a movie—the girls slipped into dreamland long before the credits.

The next morning, not even waking up to a cloudy sky and raindrop-covered windows was enough to dampen their spirits. We enjoyed a breakfast filled with enough laughter to brighten the gloomiest of days, and when Nathan arrived, the girls didn't hesitate to attach themselves to my legs in protest of leaving. The only thing that got them to finally detach was letting them know we'd all be together again for Sunday dinner that very evening. Knowing they enjoyed spending time with me so much was truly bittersweet. It made me feel silly for thinking presents in the mail made up for my being away, and regretful again at what my impending departure would mean.

The general store was mostly deserted, the rain clearly keeping many would-be shoppers at home, and I maneuvered through the aisles without interruption. I found the items my mom needed for dinner in record time, and as I walked toward the checkout, I aimlessly scanned the signs stating which items were held in each row. When I came across the bread aisle an idea suddenly struck me, and I took a quick detour to pick up a particular loaf of bread before heading out.

The dark clouds that loomed overhead warned of an impending storm, but after putting most of the groceries in the car, I walked up the road with my small parcel from the bread aisle and set my sights on The Apple Blossom Bakery. As I neared, I took in the peeling paint, the overgrown gardens, and the windows dark with dust. It was a far cry from the bakery I remembered. I lifted a fist and rapped on the old wooden door as the rain began to increase. I waited... nothing.

"Mr. Carter?" I knocked again as the droplets started to soak my shirt. "Mr. Carter!" I said, louder this time.

He had to be home, and there was no way I was leaving without stepping foot inside the bakery—not when I was getting soaked waiting for him. In the next instant, the drizzle transformed into a downpour and lightning flashed above me, followed almost immediately by a clap of thunder that had me jumping. I let out a surprised shriek and my knock turned into a pound. A light flickered on in the back of the bakery, and a minute—that felt much longer—later, the door creaked open. Mr. Carter's scowling face appeared just as lighting brightened the sky once again.

"What kind of crazy, lunatic little—"

Another clap of thunder filled the air.

"Mr. Carter, yell at me in a minute. I'm about to get struck by lightning, you old grouch!"

I pushed past him, catching an eyebrow raise in surprise as he realized who I was. I headed over to the counter and took a seat on one of the stools, letting out a breath of relief and ignoring the dust and the slight smell of must that filled the air. I heard him close the door behind me and then his footsteps, softer and slower than I remembered, headed in my direction. He had always walked with a heavy determination, like he was dead set on making the best baked goods around. But now, his pace was that of someone defeated; almost like someone who had given up the fervor of living. I didn't like the change one bit.

He walked around the counter and came to face me.

"What'd ya think you're doing?" he began sternly, "Rushing onto my property and into my house before I even say 'come in'? Which, might I add, I wasn't gonna say to begin with seeing as you ain't welcome." I rested my chin on a hand and smiled warmly, waiting for him to finish. "This what all that fancy schooling taught you? Barge into people's homes like they're your own? Hmph." He paced from one end of the counter to the other. "I'd get my money back if I was you. You leave for the big city a lady an' come back acting like Eliza Doolittle before that professor gets a hold of her." He paused and crossed his hands in front of his chest. "Well? Whaddya have to say for yourself?"

I cleared my throat and, still smiling, gave him my best *My Fair Lady* impression. "The rayn in Spayn—I mean Rivadayle—falls mainly on the playn."

He stood for a moment in the same position, looking me over with an expression that said he was less than amused. I stared back as intently as he did, taking in his white hair and a face furrowed with frown lines mixed with age lines (that had increased significantly since I left), and lines at the corners of his eyes and mouth. And the latter, I knew, were proof that he used to laugh.

When I was a kid I used to dream up stories about Mr. Carter from the days when he laughed, wondering endlessly about what it was that snatched it all away. My mother always said even when his wife was alive his laugh never quite reached those lines at the corners of his eyes, which always made me believe there had to be something else...

"What do you want?" I jumped slightly at the sudden bark of his voice.

"To see you!" I exclaimed, feigning astonishment at the fact he even asked.

"You saw me." He started to walk back around to the front of the counter. "Now leave."

I hopped off the stool. "No way! I'm not going anywhere, Mr. Carter."

"That's what they all say." He mumbled so low I almost didn't hear.

"Excuse me?"

"Didn't say a damn thing." He walked over to one of the dust-covered windows and crossed his arms again, gazing out at the rain.

"Mr. Carter, stop being such a grump and pretending you're not as happy to see me as I am you. Although, from the looks of this place..." My gaze roamed over the bakery and the darkened doorway leading into the kitchen. "...I'd say you haven't baked anything sweet in a long while, so I'll just attribute your attitude to a lack of sugar."

He turned toward me at that last part. "What would you know about when I last put something in the oven?" He snapped. "It's not like you've been around to see one way or the other."

"Okay, fine" I replied slowly. "I guess I wouldn't, being away at school and all... but if you don't get rid of that attitude, I'm gonna take after Hansel and Gretel and put *you* in the oven."

I tried to keep calm, even though it frustrated me he was just like everyone else in this damn town, giving me a hard time about living life elsewhere. Keeping away as much as I had may not have entirely been my doing, but no one had reason to think that. If I wasn't willing to talk about it—which I wasn't—I'd have to deal with the attacks. I just wished they didn't happen to begin with. I turned back toward the counter, and, taking the bread I'd bought out of the bag, placed it on the wood surface.

"No sense in caring for someone if they just up and leave you one day." He continued from behind me, but his tone started to mellow until it almost seemed like he was mumbling to himself. "You can spend years with someone—your whole life with someone—then they just decide you're not good enough no more, so they up and leave you behind... no sense."

"What was that?"

"Gah!" He started back toward the center of the room. "Makes no difference, dammit. What's that?" He nodded in the direction of the bread.

"It's for you. It's a loaf of bread!"

"Don't get smart with me, I know what it is, missy. But what do you think you're doing bringing a loaf of bread into a bakery and givin' it to a baker?"

"Like I said before..." I pointed toward the breadless shelves and the empty display case beneath the counter. "Doesn't look like there's much baking going on here. And besides, it's a special type of bread."

"Special type of bread, eh? There ain't no bread in this town or any other that's better than what's made right here in this bakery." He stepped beside me and turned the loaf to glance at its label. I inhaled the familiar scent of pipe tobacco that surrounded him and noticed the smells it used to mingle with—flour, butter, and sweat—had faded.

"Sourdough? Ain't nothing special about that. Just basic old sourdough," he grumbled.

I looked at his profile as he stood next to me, and I was pretty positive I saw the muscles in his jaw tighten and his lips twinge at the corners as though he was stifling a smile. There was no way he'd forgot about the nickname I'd given him. A wave of affection washed over me, and in a sudden move of impulse, I leaned over and kissed him on the cheek.

"It sure is good to see you again, Mr. Sourdough. I'll come back soon, and I'd like a plate of something sweet when I do."

And with that, I hopped off the stool and left him standing by the counter with his loaf of bread.

6

The rain was still falling steadily, and I ran through the cool drops to the car. I fell into the driver's seat and let out a little laugh as I turned the ignition; I sure had missed that grouchy old man. I pulled onto the road and headed east so I could head around the green toward the library — the storm made a stop for books absolutely necessary. There was nothing quite like a blanket, a cup of tea, and a good read on a day like today.

I thought of Mr. Carter as I drove. He seemed like he needed someone to cheer him up a bit — someone to get the determination back in his step — and I decided I'd try to see him every day while I was in town. If only he'd hire help. That place had always been his pride and joy.

I pulled into the spot closest to the library entrance and looked lovingly at the building. The walls had been decorated by nature in places, with areas of moss and vines of ivy growing along the brick. Tulips lined the front, and above them, tall windows trimmed in white provided a glimpse of the treasures kept inside. In my opinion, the thunderstorm served as the perfect backdrop — it gave the library a mysterious air, tucked as it was along the edge of the forest.

As I walked up the steps to the old double doors painted hunter green, I felt myself drifting back to childhood. How many times had I gotten lost in my own little world here, or those gifted to me by the books I chose to read? The doors opened with a creak and I entered to find the place darkened. The only light came from the windows, and the day was too gray to provide anything more than a dull illumination. A quick flip of the light switch next to the door told me the power was out — no doubt caused by the thunderstorm. But I wouldn't be deterred. Exploring a library in semi-darkness? It seemed very *Jane Eyre*. I glanced at the mahogany counter that served as the checkout and noticed it was unoccupied.

"Ms. Ferris?" I called out, my voice echoing down the hall. I walked over and picked up a piece of paper that was lying in the center of the counter.

Miss Belle – I went to church. Don't forget to sign out your books, same as always.

Welcome back!

Ms. Ferris

I shook my head in wonder as I headed toward the stairs. She left the library *unlocked* with a note reminding me to sign out my books. If that didn't sum up Riverdale, I didn't know what would. I guess I should have known she'd be expecting me. I hadn't thought about it today, but Sunday had always been my library day over the years. Some people started their week with prayer, I started mine with a fresh pile of books. Ms. Ferris knew this because she was always here, which—come to think of it—made me wonder why she was at church. I started up the spiral staircase and stopped suddenly as I remembered Mr. Palmer. Of course! Mr. Palmer *always* went to church. So if they were a pair, she must be going right along with him. I found myself laughing again as I continued on. The idea of the two of them was as sweet as ever.

I started down the center aisle and felt myself relax as the smell of books—one of my favorite scents in the world—came to greet me. I knew the library like the back of my hand and wandered past rows housing romance, fantasy, and poetry before pausing at the classics and contemplating a visit with Mr. Darcy or Heathcliff. But then, a combination of the storm outside and the darkened library had me heading to the collection of mystery books instead. I started picking various novels off the shelves and reading the jackets by the light of my cell phone. Town secrets, strange disappearances, and unsettled spirits— it was all very intriguing. I was in the middle of reading a synopsis about one such spirit haunting an Irish village, when a sudden sob had me dropping the book in surprise. It sounded faint and far off. I stood completely still, my heart speeding at the noise. I'd thought I was the only one in here...

A moment later, the howl of the wind and a rumble of thunder convinced me I'd imagined the noise, and I bent down to retrieve the novel. Perhaps it was best if I stick with the classics after all. I returned the book to its shelf and started back toward Mr. Darcy when I heard the sound again—it was definitely a choked sob. A million ideas started rushing through my mind as my heart began to pound. I heard it once more, and this time I could tell it was coming from the small sitting area in the back corner of the library. I grabbed the heaviest book I saw nearby and started cautiously toward the noise.

"Okay," I reasoned with myself. "It's not a ghost. A ghost wouldn't suddenly decide to haunt this place while I was away, and I think something tragic would have had to have happened... I'm pretty sure nothing tragic has *ever* happened in Riverdale."

I approached the last row before the room opened up into the small area filled with overstuffed chairs. "It's not a man," I continued to reason. The sob was definitely that of a girl, so chances were I could overpower whoever it was if they proved hostile. Although, considering they were *crying*, I doubted that would be necessary.

I tiptoed into the aisle and peeked through a gap between the books. My thoughts stopped as I noticed a gray mound quivering slightly in one of the chairs. Muffled sniffles rose from within what appeared to be the folds of a giant sweatshirt with the tips of two sneakers poking out from underneath. I watched for a moment, trying to decide my next move, when the cell phone in my hand began to vibrate and suddenly, the sound of my ringtone pierced the air.

"Shit!" I exclaimed as I scrambled for the silent button. I pressed it, but it was too late. I watched as the hooded head snapped up and the figure jumped from the chair, revealing a full-length person with legs covered in pink sweats. I hurried around the front of the aisle, trying not to look like some crazy stalker popping out from behind a stack of books. "Sorry! Sorry, I didn't mean to startle you!"

The person—a girl, as I had assumed—took a step back. "No, no, *I'm sorry*. I shouldn't be in here, I know. It's just..." She broke off as another sob escaped. She was clearly in distress.

"Whoa, whoa, it's fine." I walked over and guided her back into the chair. "It's okay, don't worry about it. There's no reason you can't be in here. It's open. Are you all right?"

"I'm, I'm..." She was stammering ridiculously, trying to get her words out between sniffles and sobs. "No," she finally managed before covering her face with her hands for another round of tears.

I took a seat in the chair next to her. "Okay... it's okay..." I patted her lightly on the shoulder, not really sure what else to do. "Why don't you tell me what's wrong?"

"I don't even know you," was the muffled response.

"Fair enough. I'm Annebelle. You?"

She lifted her head to look at me warily through brown, watery eyes on a tear-streaked face. "Clara."

"Okay, Clara, so tell me, why are you crying all alone in the library?" The word "alone" sent her over the edge again, and I fished around in my purse for a tissue. "Here, use this."

She looked up again, took the tissue and wiped at her nose. "You're right. I *am* alone," she wailed, as if this fact were new to her.

"Well, why? Where's your family?"

Her lips quivered like she was going to break again. "I'm not from here. What do you care?"

Her response was tinged with bitterness, and without her voice muffled by the sweatshirt, I detected an accent. Aha! This must be the girl Sarah had mentioned yesterday. The "tiny wisp of a thing from Texas" looking for a job. I'd never seen someone so upset about not getting to work at a diner before.

"Ohhh. Did Sarah set you off? Listen, it's nothing personal. The people in this town are actually really nice—probably the nicest you've ever met. We just don't take lightly to strangers. Stick around awhile and they'll warm up. And look, you don't have to cry. If you want it that bad, I can take you over with me right now and we can talk with Sarah together. If you get one person in this town to trust you, the rest will soon follow."

Clara looked at me, confused. "What? Who's Sarah?"

"Over at the diner... you *are* the girl who went in looking for a job aren't you?"

She pushed back the hood on her sweatshirt revealing a mass of black hair.

"How'd you know about that?"

"First thing you'll find out about Riverdale: everyone pretty much knows everything about each other."

"Oh. That's how it was back home... I mean, back where I was before."

"Hmm." I thought for a moment about what to say, worried about mentioning something that would send her into hysterics again.

"But I wasn't crying because I didn't get the job at the diner. Well, not just because of that."

"Oh. Well then, what is it?"

She started fiddling with the frayed ends of her sweatshirt strings. She looked like a scared kid, which she probably was. She didn't look any older than me, and in fact, she was likely a couple years younger.

"I'm just... I don't have any money. I don't have a place to stay, and I'm... and I'm... I'm..." She broke off again and let out a sob.

"Aw, it's all right."

She lifted a hand to wipe at some more tears, and I noticed an engagement ring on her finger. "What about your fiancé?"

She let out a heart-wrenching sob, which, had I still been in another part of the library, would have definitely made me think there was a ghost. "He's... he's dead," she managed between sobs.

"Oh, my God," I exclaimed. I moved over and knelt beside the chair, unable to keep from hugging the girl at such an announcement. "I am so sorry. I'm *so* sorry, Clara. I didn't mean to..." I held on for a moment and was surprised when she wrapped an arm around me and held me in place when I began to move away.

What could have easily been fifteen minutes later, her sobs had turned to sniffles and she pulled away. "That's why I'm here."

I offered her another tissue. "What do you mean?"

"I couldn't stay where I was living anymore and... I mean, his family... they didn't like me. They never liked me. When they told me... that he... he'd died overseas, they said they expected that now I'd have to find a way to make a living on my own. They told me I couldn't... not to expect anything from them, since we were only engaged."

"Clara, that's terrible. But how did you end up here? Don't you have any other family?"

She paused for a moment, nervously picking at her fingernails. "It was just my ma and me... but mostly just me. She wasn't around much and took off as soon as I was eighteen."

"Isn't it the child who's supposed to leave once they're eighteen?"

She shrugged. "She wasn't one for settling down, so after my fiancé... well, after I didn't have him anymore, I had no one. I didn't know where to go, so I left. I took all the savings I had, which wasn't very much, and started on a train. I just kept going 'til I couldn't go anymore and now here I am. I can't go any further, only now I don't have money or a place to stay or... anything."

She looked about ready to cry again so I replied hurriedly, "We'll figure something out,"

"We?" she asked in surprise.

"Yes, I'm not just gonna leave you here in the library like this. I can help you find a job and a place to stay. I mean, if you want. You can come home with me for the night, too. You can't sleep in the..." I stopped as a realization suddenly came to me. "Wait, when did you say you got here?"

"I didn't. I got here on Wednesday."

"Have you... have you been sleeping in the library since then?"

She looked away, clearly embarrassed, as she nodded in affirmation.

"Okay then, well that won't do at all. Let me just call my mom to let her know there'll be one more for dinner. She's likely worried about me being out in the storm anyway." I also made a mental note to tell Ms. Ferris she needed to do more thorough checks of the library before closing—I think Mr. Palmer had made her a little too love-scattered.

"Are you serious? Annebelle, I mean, are you sure it's all right?" Clara sniffled.

"Call me Belle. And of course it is. What kind of a person would I be if I just left you here while I went off with my copy of..." I looked down at the book I had grabbed as a weapon. "*The Whispers at Willowbrook Hollow*"? I tossed the book aside and punched in my mom's number.

As I soothed her nerves by explaining I'd been at the library the whole time and promising to come back soon with the groceries, I watched Clara as she grabbed her backpack from behind the chair. All her possessions were in one meager backpack. I just couldn't believe she'd been staying in the library since Wednesday. If Sarah ever found out the girl she turned away was homeless, she'd be mortified with herself. And what a sad, sad story she came with—a military fiancé who died overseas whose parents didn't like her, and apparently no family of her own. It certainly made me feel thankful for my own relatives.

After getting off the phone and assuring Clara once again it was all right for her to join us for dinner and spend the night, we got into the car and headed for my house. There were plenty of questions I had yet to ask her, but she didn't quite seem in the mood for talking—she was still crying, silently now, the tears streaming down her face as steady as the falling rain. I let the short drive pass in silence, and as we pulled into the driveway minutes later, my mom appeared at the door. I stepped out of the car and Clara slowly followed, looking slightly surprised to see the house already.

"You can get just about anywhere in Riverdale by foot," I explained, taking a guess at what she'd been thinking as I grabbed grocery bags from the backseat. "Except for some of the farms further off."

She nodded slightly, walking beside me and watching my mom as she opened the screen door for us.

"Annebelle Roth, if you had been any later Sunday dinner would have turned into Monday breakfast!"

The grin that followed let Clara know her stern tone was all in jest. Her smile alone was enough to make anyone feel welcome, and I knew instantly that bringing Clara here was the right thing to do.

"Sorry, mom, I couldn't resist stopping in at the library—can you believe Ms. Ferris just left it unlocked like that and went to church?! And then, well, I came across Clara!" I replied. We headed up the stairs and moved beyond my mom into the entryway. She closed the door behind us, blocking out the rain and ushering us into the bright kitchen.

"Well it's a good thing she interrupted your literary escapade and got you home with my groceries." She took the bags from me and placed them on the counter before she wrapped her arms around me for a hug. "You'd skip breakfast, lunch, dinner, and an entire night's sleep if the book was good enough." She let go and turned her smile on Clara.

"Mom, this is Clara..." I trailed off as I realized I didn't even know her last name.

My mom took in Clara's disheveled appearance and watery eyes and tossed formalities aside for a warm embrace. "Welcome home, Clara." She peered at me with questioning eyes over the girl's shoulder.

I mouthed the word "later," and she nodded slightly before letting go and stepping back. "Well Clara, would you like to sit down and relax while we get dinner ready? Do you want some wine? My other daughter should be here shortly, and my son and his family will be here in an hour or so."

"Actually, mom, how about I bring her upstairs to her room? She'll probably want a shower before dinner. That work for you, Clara?"

She gave me a grateful smile and shook her head. "That'd be great." Her voice was soft and wispy and edged with exhaustion now that the hysterics had subsided.

"What was I thinking?" My mom exclaimed. "Of course she does! Go ahead and do that, then come back down and help me with the potatoes, Belle. There are fresh towels in the bathroom, and I already put some sheets on the bed in the guest room."

I smiled gratefully at her and beckoned Clara to follow me. We walked down the hall and up the stairs, and when I pushed open the door to her room, I thought she was going to start crying again as she glanced around.

"Oh Belle, your house is beautiful! I haven't slept in a room this nice since... well... since ever, really. But it reminds me of..." She broke off and bit her lip.

I pretended not to notice, worried I might cause her to cry again, and looked around the room. The walls were cerulean blue and balanced by dark cherry furniture. A four-poster bed with cream-colored linens was positioned between two windows covered in lace. An antique clock and a vase of fresh flowers adorned a small table beside the bed, and a pale green chair sat across the room next to a dresser topped with a stack of books and an old mirror.

"It's my favorite room apart from my own." I walked over and opened the door to the adjoining bathroom. As promised, there was a pile of fresh towels folded on the counter. "There's shampoo and everything already in the bath, so you should be all set." I turned back to her and caught sight of her backpack again. "Hmm, do you have anything to wear?"

"I have a couple pairs of clothes, but they're all dirty now."

"No problem. Just throw your things in the basket behind the door, and we can put them in the laundry after dinner. You can wear some of mine for now. My room is two doors down on the left, and I'm sure they'll fit you—if anything they'll be a bit big."

I started heading toward the hallway.

"Belle?"

"Hmm?" I turned toward her. She looked so small standing there in her gray sweatshirt and pink sweats, clutching her backpack and staring at me from the center of the room.

"Thank you. For everything. I think you saved my life."

The idea she'd been feeling *that* desolate when I found her made my stomach flip, and I was infinitely glad I decided to get some books when I did—even if I ended up leaving empty-handed.

I smiled warmly at her. "Don't even think about it. I think we're going to end up good friends, Clara." I meant it. There was something very endearing about her, and I intended to help her out in any way that I could. "Dinner's at seven." She nodded in affirmation and I closed the door behind me and headed to the kitchen.

As I passed the living room, I caught sight of April sitting in one of the chairs reading a book. I stopped in for a quick hello, not daring to keep her from reading for any longer than that. Then, following the smells into the kitchen, I found my sister and mom hard at work.

"Hey, Sis."

Jules looked over from her place at the counter where she was mixing up a salad. My mom stood next to her slicing a loaf of bread. "Hi, Belles."

I greeted her with a kiss on the cheek, then walked over to where Ryan sat in his carrier. When he noticed me, he stretched his little arms in my direction and let out a soft coo. I picked him up and snuggled him against me. He let out a happy laugh and started playing with my necklace.

"God, Sis, would you just have a kid or something already?"

I rolled my eyes at my sister and walked over to pick an olive from the salad bowl. She tried to swat my hand away, but I was too quick and popped one into my mouth.

"No thanks. Rent-a-baby is much better. Where's Tyler?"

"He's in the garage with Derek and your father," answered my mom.

"How masculine." I rolled my eyes and tried to reach for another olive, but this time Jules got me with the back of the salad tongs. "Ouch!" Ryan let out an amused gurgle.

"How about you do something useful instead of stealing my olives?"

"All right, what do you want from me?"

Amused, my mom piped up from beside us, "Go mash those potatoes."

"Yes, ma'am." I walked over to the pot she'd beckoned toward and used one hand to mash while keeping hold of Ryan with the other.

"So Belle, tell me, what's with the stranger you brought home for dinner?"

I kept on working but turned my head to look at my mom for a moment. "That was fast."

She shrugged in response and Jules laughed.

"Oh, what, you wanted Mom to keep quiet about the fact that a random girl, who could be a fugitive or a serial killer for all we know, will be joining our family for dinner?"

"She's not a fugitive."

"Then who is she?"

"I found her in the library."

"What do you mean you 'found her in the library'?"

"I mean, I went to the library for some books, and I found her crying in the back."

"Why?"

"Well..." I walked over to the fridge and grabbed the cream. "She doesn't have any money or a family or any place to stay. She tried to get a job at the diner a few days ago, but Sarah turned her away." I poured the cream into the pot, then grabbed some butter from the nearby dish and dropped it in as well. "And to top it all off, her fiancé was in the military, he died overseas, and his parents don't like her so they told her to get lost after his death." I grabbed the salt and added some to the pot followed by some fresh ground pepper, then went on mashing. "She got on a train with nothing but a backpack's worth of belongings and let it take her as far as her money would bring her. And *that* happened to be good ol' Riverdale."

I took a scoop of potatoes and tasted the finished product, then gave a bit to Ryan. "All done." Turning around, I saw Jules and my mom had stopped what they were doing and were watching me. I looked from one to the other. "Awful, huh?"

"Awful?" Jules asked, astounded, a hand clutching her throat. "That's devastating."

"I could tell something had broken the poor girl, but I didn't imagine anything like this," my mom added. "What on Earth can we do for her?"

"Well, we can't bring her fiancé back, which would be the ideal solution, but I already told myself that I would help her. I can at least help her find a place to stay and make sure she has a job before I go, you know?"

We stood silent for a moment, then the stove beeped behind me, and mom took what looked and smelled like a blueberry pie out of the oven. "Well, I guess that's certainly something."

Jules came over and held out her arms for Ryan. Reluctantly, I handed over the warm little bundle. "You're a good person, you know that, Belle?"

"Oh please, it's what any decent person would do."

She placed a kiss on the top of Ryan's head. "Decent people are getting harder to come by these days."

At the sound of crunching gravel, Jules walked over to one of the windows. "Nathan's here."

"Perfect," exclaimed my mom. "All that's left to do set the table. Belle?"

"I'm on it." I headed toward the dining room to take care of the settings. I took dishes from the cabinet and started placing them on the table as I listened to the twins rush in from outdoors.

"It's raining cats!" I heard Haley exclaim.

"And dogs too! We almost *drowned*!" Vanessa added dramatically.

I placed glasses on the table and listened to the happy chatter increase as Kate and Nathan came in. I was laying the last napkin when I heard Haley ask where I was, and a moment later the twins burst into the dining room joined by April.

"Aha!" I exclaimed as they ran in for a hug. "Just in time for the silverware!" They groaned in protest of my greeting, but grabbed the piles of forks, knives, and spoons and went to work. "Goodness, I love you girls!"

"Yeah right, you only love us when you need us!" stated April, and the twins nodded in agreement.

"No way!" I laughed. "I love you all the time! I just love you a tiny bit more when I get you to help."

The sudden addition of male voices told me the boys had come in from the garage, and I left the girls to go say hello. When Tyler saw me he instantly began telling me how he had helped grandpa and his dad work on the car. I expressed my excitement as I gave him a squeeze, then walked around for a hug from everyone else.

"I think seeing you twice in three days should do it for a couple years," joked Nathan.

I punched him in the arm and took the glass of wine Kate poured for me from the bottle they'd brought. We stood laughing and talking in the kitchen as we waited for everything to be ready. The ease and friendliness between us all made me think, yet again, how nice it was to be with them. My family wasn't perfect, but they certainly had their moments. When my mom went to take the chicken from the oven, I headed off to get Clara. The girls had retreated into the living room and as I passed through, I told them to go wash up. I rounded the corner to the stairs and found Clara heading down them in a pair of my leggings and an oversized tunic.

Her damp hair was pulled back into a bun instead of loose and wild, and the hot water had brought some life back to her face. She looked much better than she had when I found her, but the sense of exhaustion and sadness still surrounded her. I held out the glass of wine I had brought from the kitchen.

"Feel better?"

She took it from me and gave me a feeble smile. "Much, thank you."

"Good, we're just about to sit down, so you're right on time. I'll introduce you to everyone once we're settled."

The noise that had been in the kitchen had moved to the dining room, and as we headed in that direction she looked at me uncertainly. "Am I interrupting a party?"

"Nope." I laughed. "Just my family."

Tyler, who had always been the observant one, was in the middle of asking why there was one too many place settings when I walked in with Clara. The voices died down as the kids saw the newcomer, and Clara looked down nervously.

"Everyone," I stated. "This is my friend Clara. She's here for a visit." There was a moment's pause, then a round of greetings rang out from around the table.

Nathan, whose chair was on one side of Clara's, jumped up and pulled it out for her as Kate asked in jest why he didn't do that for her. Everyone laughed in response as we took our seats, and the food began circling around as I started naming my family.

"You met my mom already. That's my dad, Matthew. Then there's my occasionally chivalrous brother Nathan, his wife Kate and their two terribly angelic twin daughters, Haley and Vanessa."

The girls couldn't agree whether "terribly angelic" meant they were good or bad, and Haley said "thanks" while Vanessa exclaimed "am not!" and I laughed and continued on. "Then we have my sister Julianne, her husband Derek and their kids Amazing April, Terrific Tyler and Ridiculously Adorable Ryan."

The children laughed at the names I gave them, and I looked over at Clara with a smile before noting her expression. "Don't worry, you don't have to remember them all right away."

"Sure you do," my dad piped up from the end of the table. "We plan on giving you a quiz before dessert, and if you don't do well, you only get one slice instead of two. Jane made blueberry pie, and trust me, you'll want two." He winked, and I heard her let out a rush of air in relief as she realized he was joking.

"Oh, don't listen to him," Jules said. "He's only trying to suck up to mom so she'll give *him* two slices."

Mom smiled knowingly and handed the bowl of potatoes to Tyler. "Give those to Clara, would you? Have some potatoes, Clara. Belle made them, and they're delicious."

Clara took the offered bowl and smiled. I could sense her uneasiness dissipating as my family's friendliness became evident.

"So, Clara," began Nathan, who hadn't been around to hear me explain her situation. "What is it you do?"

Only *the* most typical icebreaker, I thought, and rolled my eyes.

"Well," she began hesitantly from beside me, concentrating on scooping out some potatoes. "I, um, right now, I'm not... I mean, I'm in transition."

"What is it you're *looking* to do then?" asked Jules, who was putting salad on Tyler's plate with one hand (to his obvious grimace) and feeding Ryan with the other.

Clara seemed more certain of the answer to this question. "I plan on, well, at least, I hope to do something culinary. I like being in the kitchen—making things."

I watched the twins start whispering together and glancing at Clara as Kate raised an eyebrow.

"And you decided Riverdale would be the perfect place for this?" my brother continued.

"Not entirely." She put a forkful of chicken into her mouth and paused, glancing my way.

"All right, what is this, an inquisition? Let the poor girl eat." I said it lightly but shot a quick glare around the table.

"It's okay," she mumbled after swallowing, but my mom took the hint.

"No, no, let her enjoy her dinner."

"We'll continue the inquisition during dessert, eh boys?" prompted Derek, who had previously remained silent. "Nothing like pie and a few questions to make you cry!"

The boys laughed, but Clara's eyes shot up suddenly, a worried expression on her face.

"He's kidding," assured my sister with a quick swat at Derek's shoulder. "Right?"

"Of course!"

"How's the chicken, dear?" My mom inquired.

"It's absolutely delicious, thank you," she replied. There was a general murmur of agreement, and a silence followed as we enjoyed our food. As dishes were passed around for second helpings, my family stuck to conversing about various town topics and things that were occurring in their own lives, leaving Clara to temporarily eat in peace.

"Does anyone need more wine?" Kate asked as she rose from her chair. She received mixed responses, left for the kitchen then returned with the bottle, making her way around the table for refills. She stopped beside Clara's chair and looked at her full glass. "Don't like wine?"

"What?" She looked up surprised, then glanced at her glass. "Oh, no. I do. I'm just a slow drinker."

"Clearly!" Kate smiled as she continued on.

The girls, who had kept silent apart from their whispering, now seemed inclined to speak. I looked at them as I heard Vanessa pressuring Haley to pipe up. "Go on, you said you would!"

"But you're the bravest."

"Yeah, well *it was your idea*, Haley."

"Okay, okay, fine..." She looked toward Clara and cleared her throat. I waited for what I hoped wouldn't be an embarrassing question. "Um, Miss Clara?" She paused as Clara and the rest of the table looked at her. "How come you talk funny?"

My family burst out laughing at her innocent question, and Kate came close to spilling wine across what was left of Nathan's chicken.

Haley's cheeks turned the color of cherries, and her eyes flew to her plate. I took a breath and tried to squelch the laughter, hoping she wouldn't feel bad for asking.

"Haley, sweetie," began her mom. "Clara talks different because she's from a different part of the country."

"It's called an accent," continued Nathan. "If we were to go where she's from, people would think we talked funny too."

"Right," I added. "Clara talks different because she's from... Texas?"

"Actually," Clara said, "I'm from Georgia."

The sudden squeals that filled the room startled the entire table, and this time there was no "almost"—Kate splashed wine across Nathan's plate. Haley and Vanessa were up in an instant holding hands, jumping up and down and shouting "she's staying! she's staying!" Confused glances were tossed around as the twins ran into the living room and continued to shout. As Kate tried to wipe splashes of wine from the tablecloth, she sternly called the girls back in. They obeyed, but their excitement couldn't be contained. It was impossible for their smiles to be any wider. Nathan, who rarely spoke a harsh word to either girl, instead gave them a look that had them back in their seats trying their hardest not to move. We all looked at them for a moment, wondering what had caused such an outburst. They wiggled impatiently in their seats.

"All right ladies, what was that all about?"

It was all the encouragement they needed.

"Dad!"

"She's staying!"

"She told us—"

"She promised!"

"She's not going!" They concluded together.

An idea of what they were talking about suddenly dawned on me, and I cursed under my breath and took a large gulp of wine, wishing I could vanish beneath the table.

"Who's not going? Clara?" wondered my mom.

"No, Auntie Belle!"

"That doesn't make any sense, sweetie." Kate looked at Vanessa curiously.

"Yes, it does!"

"It does," Haley stated in support.

"Okay then, one of you try explaining again—but not so fast, all right?" Nathan encouraged.

My dad and Derek were leaning back in their chairs, amused. Even April and Tyler kept silent watching the twins.

"Actually... I think *I* can explain." All eyes turned in my direction. "When they slept over, we talked about my decision to go to Georgia. I told them I had to go, but—"

"But she said if we could get a big enough piece of Georgia up here than she wouldn't have to!" Vanessa said, still endlessly excited.

"I tried explaining that wasn't possible—"

"But it is!" The excitement in Haley's voice was mounting. "We get peaches from Georgia and now Clara's from Georgia, and she came to us, so Auntie Belle doesn't have to go—"

"Georgia came to Riverdale!"

Clara was looking from face to face, probably wondering what on Earth was going on. I looked from Kate to Nathan apologetically. I may have gotten away with hurting their feelings yesterday, but I had an inkling they were going to hurt even more now. What were the odds of Clara being from Georgia and suddenly ending up in Riverdale right before I was supposed to move there? It was just my luck. I listened as Nathan and Kate started explaining to the girls that I still had to go. I felt awful as I watched the smiles slowly melt from their faces to be replaced by frowns. Tears started welling up in Haley's eyes, and Vanessa looked at her sharply, her frown turning to an angry scowl.

"Don't." She ordered. She took her sister's hand, and the two of them got up again—without any of the previous excitement. Vanessa looked at me, and I could tell she was trying to stay angry so she wouldn't cry as well. "You said!" she shouted suddenly, before stalking out of the room with a tearful Haley trailing behind.

"Vanessa!" Her dad called after her and got up to follow.

"Oh dear" my mom sighed. There was a moment of silence, then, in an attempt to brighten the mood, she did what she does best. "Well...pie anyone?"

The blueberry pie was delicious. Or at least, that's what everyone said; I hadn't actually been able to taste it. The pain I'd caused the twins kept me from enjoying the slice that was placed in front of me—it was the last thing I'd intended to do. I was hoping to pass my entire visit leaving nothing but good memories with my family but of course, I had to go and foul it up by placating their worries with a little promise. Well, it wasn't a little promise anymore.

The girls had refused to come back into the dining room. Instead, they were given their pie in the living room with their dad, who sat on the couch with one on either side, trying to tell them between mouthfuls that they shouldn't be mad. Personally, I thought they had every right to be, even though it felt dreadful knowing they were upset. Kate told me to give them a day and they'd come around, but I wasn't too sure. It made me go back to thinking things were probably best when I just stayed away and sent my love via presents in the mail. At least that way I wouldn't make feeble promises I couldn't keep.

We kept apologizing to Clara about the outburst, but she wouldn't hear it. She was dead set in saying it had been one of the best dinners (food *and* company wise) she had ever experienced. I supposed up until the situation with the girls, it had been pretty great. Of course, to someone like Clara, who was pining for her fiancé and had no real family of her own, the entire thing was probably wonderful and exciting. It certainly showed how much we all loved each other; the girls were so excited when they thought I was staying. *So excited.*

I let out a sigh and turned to my side, gazing out the window into the night. Everyone had left shortly after dessert to get the kids into bed and up in the morning for school. I stayed downstairs to help clean up along with Clara, and then we both retreated for an early night. She really was a sweet girl. There was still an intense feeling of sadness and worry about her, but I didn't think that would soon go away. All I could hope was that I'd be able to help her find a place to work and live before I left. At least now I had something to go on—culinary. Now all I had to do was figure out a place that was looking for help. It wasn't likely to be in Riverdale, but Harwinton might work. She was car-less of course, but there might be a place for rent downtown, close enough so she could walk. I'd run it by her in the morning. I let out a yawn and closed my eyes, trying to focus on helping Clara instead of the heartbroken faces of Haley and Vanessa.

7

The first clear day following a storm always seems brighter. The sky looks bluer, the sun shines stronger, and the air feels fresher. The window I'd cracked open before drifting off to sleep let a light breeze into my room. It ruffled the curtains and brushed across my cheeks, beckoning me to wake. I opened my eyes to find rays of early morning sunshine streaming across my bed. I smiled and stretched my arms above my head. Then, as memories of a dream I'd had came rushing back to me I paused, arms in mid-air.

Well, *that* was interesting. I always tried to pay attention to dreams. Sure, some were downright nonsensical and meant absolutely nothing—for instance I was pretty sure I wasn't going to buy a dozen eggs and find out one belonged to a dinosaur—but there were times my dreams felt eerily lucid. Maybe it was about trying something new—something you always thought you'd be afraid of—but when it happens in the dream you surprise yourself by discovering you're not. I've often found I wake up feeling braver when that happens, perhaps even willing to face the fear in real life. Of course, when what happens in your dream is completely different from the plans you've already made for yourself, it can be hard to decide to go along with it. Interesting as last night's dream was, it fell under the latter category so I decided to put it on the back burner for later contemplation and to see how things played out.

I pushed the covers back and slipped my feet onto the cool wood floor. The clock on the bedside table read 8:37. I stood up and put my bathrobe on before heading into the hallway. The door to Clara's room was still shut, so I tiptoed past and walked lightly down the stairs and into the kitchen. As always, my mom was already there, sitting at the table sipping coffee. Oddly, my dad sat against the wall, the newspaper held up to his face, a mug of coffee steaming on the table in front of him.

"Morning! Dad... don't you have work?"

My mom looked up, and the newspaper moved aside revealing not my dad, but Clara. "Oh! I thought you were still asleep! I thought it was a bit odd for my dad to still be here."

He worked at some top-notch financial institution about an hour away and was usually gone by six every morning. The drive was tough but the pay, he said, made it worth it. At least I could say I didn't have to worry about my mom in that regard—and he'd helped out with my tuition as well. Yep, on top of his personality, I loved the guy for all his hard work, too.

"Clara here is an early riser like me," my mom smiled at her.

"Hey! I'm an early riser too. Well, sometimes..." I poured myself a cup of coffee and joined them at the table.

Clara smiled in response. "I'd love to be a late riser but haven't been able to sleep well in a long time." Her face dropped briefly, and my heart went out to her for putting on such a brave face.

"Well, give it time. Riverdale air is bound to help. There's just something about it, seems to make everyone sleep like a baby."

Clara's eyes flew from my mom to me with a brief look of uncertainty, then she dropped her gaze to her coffee and picked up the mug for a sip. Strange.

"Hey, so what do you say to heading out early? I just have to jump in the shower."

She glanced up again. "That sounds great. Hopefully we can find some place so I don't have to impose on you much longer."

"Oh please," scoffed my mom. "There's no rush, sweetie, you can stay here as long as you need, or as long as you'd like to."

"Well, either way, I have a few places in mind," I added. So we'll see what happens. Did you eat?"

She nodded in response.

"Great, I'll be back in a bit." I got up, took another sip of coffee, then headed back upstairs to get ready.

After another record-setting shower I returned to find my mom had recruited Clara as garden assistant. I looked out the bay window above the sink to find her kneeling in the dirt beside my mom, pulling stray weeds from around the flowers and newly sprouted vegetables. I shook my head and pushed my way out the back door.

"Mom, I leave for twenty minutes and you've already got her digging in the dirt... you're starting to remind me of Doris! Sorry, Clara."

My mom beamed at me mischievously, and Clara sat back on her heels and smiled along with her. "No, no, it's okay. I wanted to. The outdoors is so tranquil. I like it."

"Well, all right then. You can play in the dirt with her all you want once we get back."

"Sounds perfect." She placed one of her hands on the ground for support and pushed herself up. It seemed to take a bit more effort than it should have for such a young person.

"Are you okay?"

"I'm fine, why?"

"It looked like you had a little trouble getting up just then."

"Oh... well... my back's been a little sore. It's probably just a delayed reaction to being on the train for so long."

"Or sleeping on a chair in the library maybe?"

She laughed. "Yeah that too."

"We'll grab you some ibuprofen on the way out."

"Oh! No, no, it's okay, really. I'm fine. It's not that bad." She smiled feebly at me again and brushed the dirt off her hands.

"Suit yourself." I nodded my head toward the direction of the garage and we headed off. "Bye, Mom!"

"Thanks, Mrs. Roth."

"Anytime. Belle, put some gas in the car, would you dear?"

"Sure thing." I turned around to give her a smile and saw her raise an eyebrow at me then look toward Clara as if she were trying to tell me something. I looked at my companion and took in her outfit—a pair of my black leggings, her old sandals, and another tunic top. It wasn't the most fashionable attire, but who was I to judge? I wasn't about to make her change into something else if she was comfortable. I gave my mom a slight shrug before rounding the corner.

We sat in the car and as I pulled out of the driveway, I began telling her about the places I had in mind for finding her a job.

"Okay," I began. "So you said you like to cook. I figure we can try and find you something that falls into that category. I could bring you back over to Amy's and introduce you properly, but it's almost completely run by the family. They only hire some of the local kids to help during the summer, so I mean it could probably work, but it wouldn't be permanent."

Clara nodded beside me as I headed toward the center of town.

"But Amy's isn't the only place that requires cooking, you know? I was thinking an inn or a bed & breakfast might work because they might give you a place to stay, too—if you're any good, that is. I'm assuming you're pretty good?" I glanced at her again as I pulled into the gas station and she nodded.

"Great, well, the Tea Rose Inn or Oak Hill Bed & Breakfast might be perfect. Personally, I'd go for the Inn. It's real sweet. Plus, you might get some perks—the spa there is fantastic."

I conveniently left out the reason I had fond memories of the Inn, which happened to be that Riley had taken me there for a weekend getaway during my sophomore year. I still couldn't believe our parents had been okay with it, but then again, they *had* already assumed we'd marry. It wasn't long afterwards that I broke things off, but I still remembered it as one of my favorite weekends. He'd picked me up on a Friday evening and refused to tell me where we were going, but I knew as soon as we turned onto Pleasant Street. I'd turned to him with a grin.

"We're staying at the Inn!" I'd told him on more than one occasion that I'd always liked the look of it—but why would I ever stay at a place that was only a town away?

"What gives you that idea?" he'd replied teasingly as we rounded the bend and the house came into view.

It was a beautiful Victorian that stood out against the dreary hues of late winter with its mauve walls and white trim. I'd thrown my arms around him and planted a kiss on his cheek as we pulled into the driveway. "Riley, you're wonderful!"

A middle-aged woman greeted us as we reached the door. "Riley, welcome!" she'd acknowledged him, then turned her smile on me. "And you must be Annebelle."

I looked from her to Riley, wondering how they knew each other. Riley answered my silent question. "She is. Mrs. Kensington, this is Annebelle. Annebelle, this is Mrs. Kensington. She and my dad have known each other for quite some time."

As we walked in I looked around to find myself transported back to the Victorian era. Dark wood, floral wall coverings, lace curtains, ferns and an upholstered settee the color of cream greeted me in the entryway. The scent of roses pleased my senses. I loved Riley even more for taking me there after seeing the decor, considering it was a far cry from the sort of place I knew he'd prefer to stay. The term "masculine" certainly didn't apply, and I couldn't help but kiss him again out of gratitude.

"Thank you for coming here with me."

He let out a hearty laugh. "Are you joking? I'm not staying here. I'm just dropping you off." He saluted me then turned around, reaching for the doorknob.

I looked at him open mouthed, my eyes wide. He opened the door, then shut it again and turned back around. "Just kidding."

I pushed him playfully. "Rude!"
"I can't believe you thought I was really leaving..."
"I didn't!"

And so began our weekend. We had a light dinner after I was
thoroughly pampered at the in-house spa, then spent the next two days
having breakfast in bed, playing cards and billiards, watching movies,
going for hikes out back, and simply enjoying each other's company. We
were only forty-five minutes from Riverdale, but it felt like a different
world.

On Sunday evening, Mrs. Kensington informed us it was tradition on
the last night to eat in the formal dining room. So I slipped on a dress
and Riley donned a button down, and we had a five-course meal on bone
china complete with sparkling cider in crystal glasses.

While we were waiting for dessert to be brought out, Riley handed
me a rectangular box wrapped in a satin bow.

I took it from him, and my heart fluttered.

"What's this?"

"A gift, obviously." He smiled and I looked into those honey brown
eyes I loved so much.

"I know that, but why?"

He shrugged. *"Well... my other girlfriend didn't want it, so..."*

I kicked him underneath the table.

"Ouch! I mean, just because you're wonderful." He paused
thoughtfully, then added, *"The apple of my eye, actually."* He chuckled
then, as though he'd just told a joke.

I didn't understand the punch line until a moment later when I untied
the ribbon and opened the box. There I found a silver necklace with a
tiny charm in the shape of an apple. I lifted it off its velvet bed, and the
charm glistened from the light of the chandelier. The fruit sparkled red,
the stem green.

"Riley, it's gorgeous! I love it."

He stood up and took it from me, then fastened it around my neck.
*"Apples are rather symbolic to us, you know. They did bring us together
after all."*

I touched the necklace admiringly. *"Apples didn't bring us together,
your trespassing did."*

He wrapped an arm around my shoulders and rested his chin on my
head. *"I beg to differ. If it weren't for that fantastic aim of yours, I'd
never have wanted to get to know you. You were like Mariano Rivera."*
He pressed a kiss to the top of my head then sat back down.

"Who?"

He looked at me as though I were crazy for not knowing. "Mariano Rivera? Pitcher for the Yankees? Saved like...570 games?"

I glared at him. "What! I only interested you because I reminded you of a baseball player?!"

He grinned mischievously. "Why else would I spend the afternoon peeling apples with an obnoxious eleven-year-old?"

"I was not obnoxious. And if I recall, our mothers made us peel those apples. Although I'm pretty sure I did most of the peeling while you just ate them."

As if on cue, he took an apple from the bowl of fruit on the table. "Either way, it had to do with apples." He took a bite, the crunch emphasizing his statement.

I followed his lead and picked up an apple, bringing it to my lips.

"Actually," he announced a moment later, crossing his arms in front of his chest thoughtfully. "The reason I climbed that tree in the first place was because I wanted to meet you. I'd seen you in it plenty of times before. I thought you were cute."

I paused mid-bite.

"I didn't expect to have fruit thrown at me, though. I thought you'd be a little lady." He said it seriously, but one look at his face told me he was having a hard time not laughing.

I reached my arm back as though I were about to recreate that first meeting and throw the apple across the table at him. "I am a lady!"

"Oh no you don't!" He lunged out of his chair, leaned over the table and pulled my arms to my sides, knocking the apple to the floor. We both started laughing then—silenced only when he kissed me. A moment later Mrs. Kensington entered with our dessert. "I hope you two lovebirds like apple streusel..."

Now my neck was bare. I'd left the necklace hanging on my mirror for some time after we broke up but when I packed for college, I'd slipped it into an envelope with Riley's name on the front and left it in the Parker's mailbox.

I shook the memory away as I got out of the car. I tossed a wave at Jeremy, and as soon as he realized who I was, he got up from his chair in front of the garage and sauntered over.

"Morning, Belle. You're not gonna try and get me to pump your gas again, are you? 'Cause I told you before, this—"

"Is self-service now. Gimme a break! I know." He tossed me a grin, and I gave him one in return. "Anyway, you pumped Meredith's gas not mine. Speaking of whom..." He slipped a hand into his pocket and looked at me expectantly. I stuck the nozzle into the tank and pressed the lever. "Seen her lately?"

His grin transformed into a crooked smile with a dimple piercing one cheek. Oh my God, he had turned completely adorable! "Actually, I have."

He had? Dammit, I hadn't actually expected him to say yes! I silently berated myself for forgetting to call Meredith yesterday, but what with finding Clara, dinner with the family, and the fiasco with the twins, it completely slipped my mind. I knew Meredith would want to tell me everything, but I couldn't help but try to pry some details out of Jeremy.

"Oh really? Do share!"

He smiled. "I took her out to dinner Saturday night."

"And? How was it?" I asked excitedly.

"It was fine."

"Fine! I'm going to need a better adjective than that, Jeremy Larson!"

His dimple deepened. "It was fantastic. That better?"

My heart did a little skip for joy. I was so happy the two of them were together. "Much!" A click from behind me signaled the tank was full, so I replaced the cap, handed Jeremy some money, and reached for the door handle. The sight of Clara's black legging-clad legs in the passenger seat reminded me I wasn't alone.

"Oh! I'm sorry, Jeremy. This is Clara. Clara, this is Jeremy. We went to high school together."

He walked over to the passenger side and stuck his hand through the window for a shake. I got in the car and heard Clara give him a shy hello.

"She's new in town, but I'm sure you'll be seeing her around," I said, leaning toward the window.

"Sounds great. Have a good day, ladies." I heard someone pull in behind us, so I turned on the car, tossed Jeremy a wave and shifted into first. It wasn't until I had turned onto the street and was driving past the station that I realized the car belonged to Riley. He was standing beside it talking to Jeremy, but his gaze followed us as we passed. I looked at him, and our eyes met for a moment before I turned back toward the road. Involuntarily, my heart jumped into my throat at the sight of him. Stupid.

"He looks nice."

"What? Who?" Had she noticed Riley too?

"Jeremy."

Oh. Right. I tried to shake the image from my mind along with the memories that had been cropping up far too often lately.

"He is. He's always been really sweet. I think he's perfect for Meredith—that's my best friend. You'll meet her soon."

We passed the rest of the stores, the green, and Doris' house, then rounded a corner and the river came clearly into view. The sun scattered across the water, making it sparkle as though it were full of diamonds. On the far side, farmland stretched as far as the eye could see. To the right, trees with bright green leaves lined the street, shading various side roads that wound into the forest toward more homes, including Meredith's family's house.

"Wow, this place is beautiful," Clara exclaimed.

I looked around some more, taking in the curves of the road as it followed the flow of the river, and the wild flowers that were blooming on the grass between the two. A new sort of awareness came to me.

"You know, it is pretty beautiful, isn't it?"

She looked at me curiously, at the tone of my agreement. I smiled at her. "It's easy to forget when you've lived here your whole life."

She looked back out the window. "I guess so. But if I lived here, I'd try and never forget."

"You do live here."

"I guess I do now, don't I?" Her tone sounded either contented or resigned—I couldn't tell which.

We drove quietly for a while, basking in the silence and the beauty of the day. Harwinton was fifteen minutes away, and as we neared the town center, Clara broke the silence.

"Riverdale's a lot bigger than I thought it would be."

"Oh, no, this isn't Riverdale," I corrected her.

"What!" Her head snapped in my direction.

"Riverdale's pretty small in the scheme of things. We're in Harwinton now. The Oak Hill Bed & Breakfast is here, and the Tea Rose Inn is over in Madis—"

"No, no, no, no. We can't be here." She was starting to panic beside me.

"What are you talking about?"

"I have to stay in Riverdale. I can't... I won't... I just, I don't want to go anywhere besides Riverdale."

"Whoa, calm down." I was always trying to get this girl to calm down. She was either one extreme or the other—put-together and quiet, or freaking out and emotional. "Harwinton's only fifteen minutes from Riverdale. It's not like you chose Riverdale anyway, you just ended up there."

She took a breath beside me. "I know. It's just that..."

I had pulled the car off to the side of the road and was waiting for an explanation.

"I don't want to go anywhere else now. I like the people in Riverdale. I like what it looks like—and what it feels like. It's just, it feels like home."

I stared at her incredulously. "Okay, first of all, the first person you met wouldn't give you a job. Since then the only other people you've met are me, my crazy family, and a guy I went to high school with. Second of all, it looks like every other small town. And third of all, up until last night you were sleeping in a library, so you tell me how on earth this place feels like home? I'm beginning to think you're crazy, Clara. That, or there's something you're not telling me."

She bit her lower lip and looked nervously at me then out the front window. The sound of the wind rustling the nearby trees was the only noise for a few minutes, and I tried to hide my impatience while I waited for her to speak. Finally, she turned back to face me.

"I'm pregnant."

My mouth dropped open. "Wait, what?"

She let out a nervous laugh. "Yeah. I'm *really* pregnant."

Images flashed through my mind, and things that had seemed random and unexplainable only seconds ago were now connected and *very* explainable. She was over emotional (but I had accepted that one, considering she lost her fiancé and all). She didn't drink her wine at dinner, she chose to wear the biggest clothes I owned, she said she had a sore back "from the train," and she'd refused ibuprofen. And then of course, there was my mom. She must have figured it out and was trying to tell me before we left with that look I'd just shrugged off.

I let out a burst of laughter and covered my mouth with my hand. "You are, aren't you!"

She nodded sheepishly, not quite sure what to make of my laughter.

"Why on earth didn't you tell me?"

"I don't know...I guess I was just used to keeping it to myself. It's not like I had anyone to tell really." I pictured her fiancé's cruel parents and thought about her all alone in Georgia, finding out she was going to have a baby, then being told the one person she'd want to share the news with the most had died. No *wonder* she left. She'd probably been searching for someone—anyone, to care for her.

Instinctively, I wrapped my arms around her.

"Congratulations, Clara. You're gonna be a mommy!" She let out a sob, and I silently swore for making her cry. Crap, she *was* emotional. At least now I had something to blame it on. "Hey, none of that!" I opened the glove compartment and gave her a tissue. As I handed it to her, I saw her expression wasn't exactly one of complete sadness.

"No one's said that to me yet. And I... I was so happy when I found out. I was so excited to tell Jack when he got back, but then..." She paused to blow her nose. "Then his parents told me everything, and suddenly I was alone. Just me an... and the baby."

"Well, you're not alone anymore."

She looked at me with a grateful smile and watery eyes, and I knew I'd do everything I could to make sure that was the truth. "So, your fiancé... his name was Jack?"

Her eyes took on a distant look, the same way Doris's had when she'd talked about "her Harry," and I knew she was thinking of him as she nodded.

"It was. Jackson Everett Cunningham III."

I whistled. "Wow, that's a pretty impressive name."

She nodded again and let out a humorless laugh. "Yeah, it is. His parents placed a lot of importance in names. You know, in what they stood for: family, history... how worthy someone is. If you've got Cunningham at the end of your name, you're practically royalty where I'm from. But my Jack hated all that. He didn't care about names. He always said it was the person who made a name worthwhile, not the other way around." She was brought back to the present and placed a hand across her stomach. "He didn't care that I was only Clara Larkin. He thought I was perfect."

"Clara Larkin." She looked as me as I said her name. I smiled. "You never told me your last name."

"I didn't? I'm sorry. I guess I've turned terrible at socializing."

"Stop apologizing so much. Goodness, it's all right... but is there anything else I should know about you? I mean we never really had a Get to Know Each Other 101 course or anything. So, are you on the run? Or a hit woman perhaps?"

She let out a laugh. "No, I'm not. I'm just Clara Larkin. I'm 22-years-old. I grew up in Savannah, Georgia, and I fell in love when I was sixteen. I lost the man of my dreams, but now that I'm in a new place, I'm gonna try my hardest to keep on living... What about you?"

"Good. Especially since you've got someone else to think about now." I nodded in the direction of her stomach. "And as for me, well, I'm in the middle of trying to figure some things out, so I'll pass for now."

"That's not fair."

I grinned, ignoring her. I started the car again and was about to pull off into the road and head into Harwinton when I remembered the reason we'd stopped in the first place. "Oh! Wait, I'm still a bit confused. Why won't you leave Riverdale? I promise you'll like Harwinton, or even Madison. They're sweet towns. Bigger though, and closer to the highway and all... which will probably be better considering you're having a baby."

As I said that, I realized the fact that she was soon to be a mom was going to make it much tougher for her to work. In fact, how on earth *would* she work? I wasn't sure how far along she was, but obviously she'd need to take maternity leave at some point. And then once the little one was born childcare would need to be sorted out. And if it wasn't Clara who was caring for the baby childcare, I knew, would be expensive. She couldn't work just anywhere now. She'd need a flexible schedule. She'd need to make enough to support the both of them. I began to frown.

She noticed the look and began to apologize again, before I told her to quit it.

"Is it a problem that I want to stay in Riverdale?"

I softened my expression. "No, it's not. In fact, now that I think about it, maybe it'll be better that way. My entire family is there, and I'm there for now, so you'll always have someone who can help out with things. And even the other residents will warm up to you after a while, then you're not likely to be alone ever again! I was just wondering how, and where, we're going to find you work. I mean, especially now."

The smile that had returned to her face disappeared. "Oh. You don't think I could get a job anymore, do you?"

"It's not that. I'm sure you could, but for how long? You should be resting, not working." I tapped my fingers on the steering wheel. "If only there were some place you could do what you like doing but would be able to care for a baby as well. Some place close to wherever you'd be living. I mean, you don't have a car, so you can't exactly get far. It may not be cooking." I looked at her earnestly. "Riverdale doesn't have much, Clara. I mean, the only places that even require cooking of some sort are Amy's and..." I paused as the dream I'd had the night before came rushing back to me.

"Are you okay?"

"Hmm. Yes, I'm fine... you know what? How about this, my mom said you can stay with us as long as you need, so let's not worry about that right now. I haven't seen Meredith in a couple of days, so let's go into Harwinton like I originally planned. Only instead of job hunting, how about we do a little shopping and then meet her for lunch?"

"Er, yeah. I'm okay with that... I mean, I don't want to intrude..."

I held up a hand. "Stop right there. I don't care what the end of that sentence was going to be because you won't be intruding. Besides, now that you don't have to hide this baby of yours, I think you could do for some new clothes. Oh! And maybe some things for the baby, too!"

Her face dropped. "Belle, I don't have any money for that."

"Don't worry about it. I love shopping, I love babies, and did I mention I love shopping? This trip's on me."

She started to protest, but I glared at her. "If it bothers you all that much, you can think of some way to pay me back... in fifty years or so."

She crossed her arms in silent protest, but the smile on her face told me she was excited. Honestly, I couldn't help but be so as well. Of course, the dream was nagging impatiently at me, but I needed to think about it when I was back home—preferably alone and in bed after soaking in a bubble bath for an hour or so.

I glanced in the rearview mirror and noticed a car approach us, slowing down as it neared. I squinted to see it better, and as it started to pull off the road behind us, I recognized it as Riley's.

"What is he, following us or something? That's the last thing I need." I hit the gas and sped onto the road, kicking up dirt and pebbles in my wake.

"What is?"

"What? Oh, did I say that out loud?"

"Er, yep."

"Just some guy I don't want to talk to right now. He was pulling over behind us."

"He was probably just wondering what we were doing. Why are you avoiding him?

"What? What makes you think I'm avoiding him? Maybe I just don't like him."

"Do you?"

"Do I what?"

"Dislike him."

"Oh. Well... no. I don't."

"Well, okay then."

Okay then. She had a point. Why was I making such an effort to avoid him?

8

I stuck my toe in the water to test the temperature. After deciding it was hot enough to soothe without scalding my skin, I slipped into the tub and sank beneath the lavender scented bubbles. I let out a sigh, closed my eyes, and thought about the day.

The shopping trip and lunch had been a lot of fun. Harwinton was certainly no city, but it was bigger than Riverdale and had access to the highway. Because of that, the downtown area was substantially larger and geared more toward passing travelers and tourists looking for a "New England atmosphere" than its residents. Main Street was neat and manicured, with brick sidewalks lining either side, strategically placed trees, and an array of stores. Some of them were quaint, little gift shops and places owned by locals, but others were part of various chains. There was a Starbucks, for example (which I admit to nearly crying at the sight of), the Paul Mitchell salon Alexis co-owned (thank goodness I didn't need a haircut), some restaurants, and a few retail stores like Anthropologie and J.Crew.

After we found a place to park and I rushed over to get a venti caramel macchiato—with an extra shot of espresso—I took Clara on an excursion to find some clothes that actually fit her, and to buy a "few" things for the baby. At first she'd been a bit apprehensive considering I was the one who'd be paying, but after a dozen or so assurances that it was truly fine—and several instances of me shoving exceptionally cute baby outfits in front of her—she couldn't help but become excited. She looked positively serene perusing the racks of baby clothes in one of the simple dresses we'd just purchased. I'd told off one of the young salesgirls who tried to tell me we couldn't actually change in the dressing room (what exactly are they for then!) and forced Clara to slip her small (apart from her stomach) frame into the cream dress with navy flowers I'd tossed over the door. When she stepped out, it was as if someone had flipped a light switch; she was glowing the way an expectant mother should be.

A while later, when we were in the middle of deciding whether a particular outfit was neutral enough for a boy or a girl, my phone started ringing. I took it out and answered it excitedly when I saw it was Meredith. She probably came close to fainting when I told her I was shopping for baby clothes.

"You're *what*?" she'd shouted back at me.

"Shopping for baby clothes." I shook my head at Clara as she held up a onesie the color of pea soup.

"Is there something you want to tell me?"

I smiled mischievously to myself, knowing she assumed I was the one having a baby.

"Oh my God, there's *so* much I want to tell you. Meet me for lunch, will you? I'm in Harwinton, so come to Antonio's. I've been craving the raviolis, and you can get a salad if you're still on that silly diet of yours. Get there at one."

"I'll be there." She hung up before I got in another word.

"Meredith thinks I'm the one who's pregnant," I announced to Clara.

"You didn't tell her otherwise?"

I laughed. "Nope. She didn't tell me she went on a date with Jeremy, so I'm just gonna let her think I didn't tell her I'm having a baby." I winked and took a pack of newborn socks off the shelf, tossing them in our basket.

"You're something else, Annebelle."

"Oh, I know."

I probably would have bought everything Clara needed for the baby on that one trip, but as I started wandering toward the cribs and things, she conveniently reminded me she didn't have a place to put anything yet.

"I guess you're right," I admitted, looking dejected. "We'll come back as soon as you do!" I glanced at my phone to check the time. "It's not quite one, but we can head to Antonio's now anyway. We can have a drink... I mean, *I* can have a drink and you can have a seltzer while we wait."

Once we paid for our things and left the shop, we made our way to the restaurant, but halfway there I realized I didn't have my bag of clothes (there's no way I could spend the day shopping and not come out of it with some things for myself as well!). I told Clara to continue on, and I ran back to the store to find my bag sitting on the ground beside the rack with the awful pea-green outfit. When I walked back outside, I turned up the street to find Riley heading towards me. There was no way for me to duck out of an interaction this time, not without what I was doing becoming blatantly obvious, so I stood where I was and gave him a half smile and a wave as he approached.

"Belle." There it was. I'd never been able to understand how the sound of my name coming from his lips had the ability to go right through me. I probably never would.

"Hey," I responded.

"Are you okay?"

"Yeah, why?" My heart started to flutter at his concern, and I silently berated myself for my conflicting emotions.

"When I was on my way over here I saw you on the side of the road. I was going to pull off to see if you needed any help, but you left."

"Oh that. Well yeah, there was a situation, but everything's fine now. Thanks."

"Okay, great." he paused for a moment, looking at me curiously.

"So, what brings you here?"

"I was just paying Alexis a visit at the..."

The flutter skidded to a stop. I knew he'd paused midsentence because he remembered that the two of us didn't get along. But then again, how could he forget? Why would he even tell me that in the first place? He wasn't dumb. Maybe he had just turned into a jerk... but... no, I couldn't believe that.

"Um, what about you?" He tried to recover.

"Just doing some shopping." I swung the bag in my hands forward slightly, assuming he'd glance at them. Instead, he looked up at the store's sign behind me where it read "The Nursery" in giant pink and yellow letters. I watched his expression change from confused to surprised as he realized what he *thought* was the reason behind my shopping there. Pettily, the fact that he'd been with Alexis made me not at all inclined to tell him otherwise.

"Are you..."

"Well, I've really got to run. I'm with a friend and we're meeting Meredith for lunch." I knew I wouldn't be able to flat out lie to him, so I went for avoidance instead.

He nodded at me, unable to keep from glancing briefly towards my stomach. "Tell her 'hello' for me."

"Sure will. Nice to see you."

"You too."

I started past him, and he once again called my name from behind. "Yes?"

"At your party we said we'd catch up sometime. I know we've both been busy... but I know you're leaving soon, so would you want to..."

"Hey listen, I don't want to keep them waiting." I started walking backwards. "We'll figure something out soon." I tossed him another wave and turned back around. Oh, so he thought I'd want to catch up with him right after he got done spending time with Alexis? What was he playing at? Did he want to have two girls at once? Or did he think we could just be best friends now? I didn't exactly like either of those ideas. Why did emotions have to be so confusing?

I walked into Antonio's to find Clara and Meredith standing next to each other in the lobby. When they noticed me they both waved, and then looked at each other curiously. Clearly they didn't realize they were about to be introduced to each other. I let out a laugh as I walked over.

"Meredith, this is Clara Larkin. Clara, this is my best friend, Meredith Kinney."

"Oh, hey!" Clara exclaimed. "I've heard so much about you."

Meredith gave her a smile and they shook hands, then she turned her attention back to me. "So, Belle, is there something important you'd like to tell me?"

"There sure is. But let's sit down first. I could really use a cocktail."

Meredith stared at me wide-eyed as I headed over to the hostess. "Belle, are you sure you should be..."

"Oh please, Mere, don't get preachy."

Clara followed behind us as we took our seats, an amused expression on her face as she watched the interaction between the two of us. Our waitress came over a moment later, and when I ordered a martini, Meredith tossed me a glare.

"You know, I've been thinking about taking up smoking. I read somewhere some people can lose weight that way."

Meredith nearly choked on the water she was taking a sip of. "Belle, that's the most ridiculous thing I've ever heard and that is *not* okay. You can't drink and smoke when you're having a baby! And *how* could you not tell me!"

There was silence as I let her statement hang dramatically in the air for a moment. Our waitress came back and placed our drinks in front of us, and I took a sip of my martini before responding. "Um, Meredith, I'm not having a baby."

"What?" She looked at me, dumbfounded. "But you said—"

"That I was shopping for baby clothes—for Clara." I nodded in her direction and Meredith looked at Clara, sipping seltzer, one hand reflexively resting on her stomach. She realized her mistake.

"Belle, you jerk!" She landed a punch on my shoulder. "You *knew* I thought it was you who was pregnant!"

I placed my glass on the table to keep it from spilling. "You think I wouldn't tell you? Unlike you, I believe in communicating in this friendship."

"What are you talking about?"

"Psh, 'what are you talking about?' I'm talking about the fact that you didn't tell me you went on a date with Jeremy, that's what!"

She started to respond, then stopped, and snapped her mouth shut. Clara sat in her chair, watching our display of "friendship" with wide-eyes.

"That's right. You don't have anything to say now, *do you?*"

"Sorry."

"What?" That wasn't the argument I'd been expecting.

"I know I should have told you. I swear I was going to, it's just..." She paused, and a dreamy look crossed her face. "Oh Belle, it was so wonderful. He's so sweet! I had such a great time that I... Well, it felt like a dream! I just wanted to keep it to myself for a while. Besides, if you recall, I *did* tell you to call me yesterday."

I tossed my arms around her and squealed. "I know, I know. Sorry about that. I'm not really mad... I'm so excited for you, Merekins! He's a nice guy, and that's just what you need."

I leaned back and looked at her face—she was beaming. I let out another squeal of excitement. "Ahh, I love it! Meredith, you're dating Jeremy. Clara, you're going to have a beautiful baby, and Riley thinks I'm pregnant." I let out a laugh. "This is great!"

"What!" Meredith raised an eyebrow at me.

I took another gulp of my martini. "Yep, I ran into him on my way over. He was fresh from visiting Alexis at the salon, and I was walking out of The Nursery."

"You didn't correct him?"

"Nope! It's not any of his business really. Anyway, I'm hungry. Let's order!" I said as our waitress approached.

Meredith shook her head at me. "Well, calm down with that drink, will you? No need to get wasted at one in the afternoon. You have to drive. And what's the news anyway? I know your pregnancy ruse couldn't have been it."

"No worries, I've got a forced designated driver in Clara." I smiled. "Can I get the raviolis with tomato basil sauce, please?" I told the waitress. "And, no, I wanted you to meet Clara, too." I paused as they both ordered their lunch. "We came to Harwinton originally to see about finding her a place to work and live, but she's gotten fond of Riverdale and wants to stay around there."

Meredith nodded in approval. "Clara, you've got good taste. You know a good town when you see one."

I rolled my eyes at her. "Anyway, I think I've got the perfect place."

"Amy's?"

"Nope, even better. But I have to sort a few things out first. I'll let the both of you know tomorrow what I've decided."

"Decided? Why so mysterious?"

"Just trust me. I need to think it over and settle some things either way. We'll get a coffee tomorrow and I'll let you know then."

"Clara, looks like Belle's keeping secrets from us. Guess we'll just have to team up and start keeping some from her in return."

I laughed. "I'm serious! This will be a huge decision for more than one person, including myself. It literally just came to me on the way over here... well, and partially in a dream last night. So just let me ponder things for a while."

I watched both their expressions. Clara was curious but trusting and nodded in agreement. Meredith looked at me questioningly, and an expression of hope crossed her face, then disappeared a moment later. I wondered if she had any idea...

A knock on the bathroom door brought me back to the present.

"Annebelle, are you all right in there?" My mom's voice slipped in from under the door.

I opened my eyes and saw that most of the bubbles had disappeared. The water had cooled down significantly, so I leaned forward and turned the hot faucet back on. "Yeah, I'm fine. I was just thinking."

"All right. Well, don't stay in too long—you'll shrivel up like a prune!"

I smiled at the way she spoke to me, as if I were still a little girl who needed taking care of. In a way it was nice knowing she was still there, ready and willing to care for me like I was ten again. I guess that feeling never goes away.

I poured more lavender soap beneath the faucet, watched as bubbles started to form across the water, and thought about the dream I'd had the night before. It served as kindling for various ideas and possibilities that didn't fit into my original plan, but life never really follows a set course, does it? I knew it was important to write your plans in pencil—not pen— that way you could erase, edit, and change them as things progressed. Yet despite that knowledge, I tried my hardest to keep my plans steady. I'd go for the pen more often than not and as a result, some plans went as I'd hoped but others didn't, leaving messy scribbles across the paper of life where I'd crossed them off.

The dream hadn't been long—it was a single scene, really. It was me, in a kitchen, baking. Only I wasn't alone. Clara was there and so was Mr. Carter, and although the room looked different in dreamland, I knew exactly where it was. It didn't seem significant at first. There were plenty of occurrences that had happened during the day that could have easily translated into that scene during the night. Conversations, visits— everything leaves some sort of an imprint that can end up in a dream. But when I'd talked with Clara later in the day and discovered she was pregnant, a dream I would have deemed meaningless and eventually forgotten suddenly seemed important. Clara needed a place to work and stay, and I knew of a solution that could work for her while making more than one individual in Riverdale happy. But it would require my help as well, which meant I wouldn't get on that plane next week. So the question now was, would this solution make me happy, too?

I thought about the two paths that loomed in front of me—one led to Georgia, the other led just down the road; one was written in pen, and one hadn't been written at all. Which to choose? I thought about all the paperwork sitting in my room, paperwork I hadn't touched since that night with the twins. The twins. How happy they would be! A slow smile spread across my face. Well, what's one more scribble? I sunk my head beneath the water and let out a rush of air.

9

When my eyes opened the next morning I slipped out of bed and glanced out my window. Bright streams of color peeked between the trees lining the backyard, telling me it couldn't be much past seven. I knew I'd go crazy if I put off what I planned to do—once my mind was set on something I liked to get started right away—so I immediately headed over to grab some clothes. I was about to pull on a pair of jeans, when another look at the pretty spring morning caused me to switch course and reach for running clothes and sneakers instead. I pulled my hair back into a ponytail, wrote a note to Clara and slipped it beneath her door before tiptoeing down the stairs. It wouldn't take long to run there, and the morning exercise would give me energy the whole day through.

After walking to the edge of the driveway, I set off at an easy pace. My muscles were stiff at first, annoyed with me for making them work so early in the morning. It would only be a twenty-minute run, but as I headed up the street my mind, as always, began running its own sort of race. On those occasions I decided to go for a run when I was in New York, I'd usually get lost in my thoughts—which caused me to get lost in real life by missing a turn or going quite a bit further than I intended—but in Riverdale I knew that wouldn't happen. My feet knew the pavement here like the back of my hand; I could run with my eyes shut and still end up where I planned.

I kept my breath steady, inhaling the cool morning air as I rounded the corner to Main Street and began tossing waves to other early risers as I passed. I looked across the street and waved to Jeremy who was in front of the gas station. Amy's was open, and I knew the morning crowd would consist of Riverdale's older residents chatting over coffee and breakfast. In fact, there was a good chance Doris was among them. I ran past without looking in the windows but smiled at the thought of her catching sight of me and leaning over to see where I was headed.

The scenery momentarily blurred as I focused straight ahead and sprinted. When the green came to an end and I found myself approaching Doris's porch, I crossed the street then halted, inhaling deep breaths of air to slow my breathing. My eyes scanned the building in front of me. The once bright white paint had weathered to a grayish tint. The doors, which used to be a vibrant red, had darkened to maroon. The dark green shutters showed extensive peeling. The sign reading "The Apple Blossom Bakery" sat on the wall beside a giant bay window, and was half hidden behind the overgrown apple tree that sat out front, and vines that snaked their way along the building. It looked less ominous than it had on Sunday with all the rain, but the sunlight highlighted the neglect and the building's need for TLC.

I walked up to the door, lifted the knocker and dropped it against the tough old wood, listening as it echoed throughout the empty bakery. After waiting a moment, my impatience and—I'd admit it—excitement, had me walking along the path on the left side of the building that led to the door to the house. I rapped there as well. The bakery was built as an extension on the front of the Carter's home, which was originally an old saltbox. With the addition, the entire structure was shaped like an upside down *L*. My foot tapped impatiently on the ground as I gazed around, noting the gardens that edged the building needed tending as well. Then, as I heard the door creak open and Mr. Carter's grumble, I looked up.

"Can't make a damn decision... have to knock on both doors, do you? Make me walk one way then another. Who's—" He stepped into the open doorway and paused when he saw it was me again.

"Good morning, Mr. Sourdough," I gave him a grin.

"Of course it's you. Hmph. I better invite you in before you rush on by me again."

He moved to the side to allow me in, and I placed a quick kiss on his cheek as I stepped past him into the living room. A quick look around told me his home was cared for much better than the bakery. Then again, I don't know what I was expecting—dusty furniture and sofas covered in sheets? It was actually quite cozy with wood floors covered in places by braided area rugs, a dark blue sofa and a deep red chair with tiny white flowers on the fabric. A table between the sofa and chair held a lamp and a stack of magazines. A television sat across from them, and on the wall behind it were three framed black and white photographs. The room smelled of pipe tobacco.

"Ahem." Mr. Carter cleared his throat beside me and I gave him a smile.

"Hi."

"Mind explaining why you're knocking on my doors at the crack of dawn?"

"Oh come on, you know this isn't the crack of dawn. Once a baker always a baker—I'd bet money you've been up since before five."

His silence told me I was right. He turned on his heels and headed out of the room, and I followed without comment. We walked into the kitchen, a room with pale yellow cabinets, white laminate countertops flecked with gold, tiled floors, and a maple table surrounded by chairs. He ordered me to sit as he started rummaging around in cabinets, and I did as I was told. I smiled as I noticed a plate of cookies covered in plastic wrap.

"Cookies! Did you bake me cookies?!"

He shut the cabinet door with a bit more force than necessary. "You can't eat cookies this early. I'll get you coffee."

I had an inkling he baked cookies because of my prior visit, and it made me feel good to know he was expecting me to return—and that I did.

"What are you smirking for?"

"Am I?"

"You know you are."

"I was just trying to remember the last time I had a cookie for breakfast."

"Now, don't you even..."

He trailed off as I lifted a corner of the plastic and took one off the plate. I took a bite, letting out a sound of delight as I chewed. There wasn't another cookie in the world as heavenly as Mr. Carter's—and that was saying a lot, considering I was a big fan of my mother's baked goods, and knew my own way around an oven.

He walked over to the table with two mugs of coffee in one hand and a pitcher of cream in the other. After setting them down on the table, he looked at me with a frown and took a seat.

"All right, missy, what do you want?"

"Again with the accusations! Can't I stop over just to say hello?"

He looked at me pointedly. "Not this early, you can't."

I poured some cream into my coffee and gave it a stir. "Well, okay, I'll just cut to the chase then, since you've obviously got me figured out. We're going to reopen the bakery."

He paused with his coffee cup to his lips and held it there for a moment before placing it back on the table and looking at me. I wasn't sure if he was about to bark in opposition or call me crazy, so I dunked my cookie into my coffee and took a bite, trying to maintain a look of confidence.

Silence. His frown deepened as he watched me dunk, then he raised a bushy silver eyebrow. "We?"

I let a tiny spark of excitement settle inside my stomach.

When Meredith arrived about an hour later, it was to find that Clara had already joined me in Mr. Carter's kitchen. She looked uncertain at being in his home, but the sight of the two of us eased her worry, replacing it with what I knew to be hope. She pulled out one of the chairs and nearly collapsed into it.

"Tell me," she implored breathlessly. Her eyes roamed from my face to Clara's, who was sitting with her gaze locked on the coffee cup in front of her.

Mr. Carter wandered over with another mug for Mere, then he leaned back against the counter and looked on. She looked like she was teetering on a fence, and whatever I said would decide which way she fell: into unbridled excitement or extreme disappointment. It was probably best not to keep her in suspense.

"We're going to reopen the bakery."

Hesitation. She was really wobbling toward excitement now, but we were similar creatures, Meredith and I, both unwilling to fully believe until we were absolutely certain.

"We?"

Mr. Carter let out a snort of amusement at her response, the same one he'd uttered earlier. I glared at him. I guess I'd done a great job making everyone think there was no way I'd stay in Riverdale. Heck, then again, there was a part of me that didn't think I ever would either.

"Yes, 'we.' You're going to help. So is Clara, and Mr. Carter obviously. And, well... me."

She had only one foot on the fence now. "How are you going to open a bakery when you're in Georgia?"

"I'm not. Going to Georgia that is. At least not right now."

That was all it took; she hopped off that fence onto the side of excitement. In the next instant Meredith pushed herself out of the chair with such force it went sliding across the room. I heard Mr. Carter utter "holy Jesus" in surprise. She threw herself at me and enveloped me in a breath-stealing hug.

"I. Am. So. Happy! Tell me this isn't a dream! I'd hoped—I'd thought—after you came back from visiting Doris—Oh Belles, are you really staying?"

I tried to tell her I was, but the hug was so tight it was a miracle I was able to grab a breath, let alone speak. A moment later, Mr. Carter piped up to save the day.

"She was going to, but if you don't let go of her, the only place she's gonna end up is the hospital!"

Meredith released me at that and stood looking like she'd just won the lottery. "Belles, details!"

I laughed. "Well, go and fetch back your chair and I'll tell you!"

She looked over to where her chair had landed beside Mr. Carter, and with a sheepish look, she walked over and retrieved it. "I'm just a bit excited," she explained.

"You think?" he grunted.

She sat back down and looked at me expectantly. "Okay, go."

I laughed again. "All right, well, as you know, Clara needs a job and a place to stay. But she has a preference for Riverdale." I paused and smiled at Clara, who smiled in return before returning her gaze downward.

"Smart girl," Mr. Carter interjected.

"Right. So she likes Riverdale, and she's going to have a baby, which obviously makes things a bit more complicated. Now, this town isn't exactly big, so when I was thinking things over I realized there's really only one place that might need some help—The Apple Blossom Bakery." I paused dramatically and lingered over the idea until Meredith nodded me on excitedly.

"We're going to bring the bakery back to life, which will make a lot of people in town happy, including myself and I know you, Mr. Carter." I grinned in his direction. "Along with giving Clara a safe place to care for her baby. And no matter how much he may grumble, I know Mr. Carter will secretly be thrilled to have two young ladies living under his roof."

"Hogwash. Had two ladies living here once, and both of 'em left me." The reference to his wife's death made my heart ache, but I looked at him curiously at his mention of *two* ladies. Had Mr. Carter had an affair? Perhaps Riverdale had some secrets after all... but figuring them out would be for another day.

"Mr. Sourdough, don't get cross with me. You're making Meredith nervous." I could tell by Meredith's expression that even in her grown age he still intimidated her, like most others in town. A slight blush tinted her cheeks.

"Anyway, Mere, Mr. Carter has lovingly agreed to let Clara and me, and the baby once it arrives, stay in this wonderful house and aide him in

95

fixing and reopening the bakery—making it as marvelous, if not better, than it was before."

Mr. Carter let out a snort. "I don't know about all that. It was pretty damn good before."

Meredith was literally on the edge of her seat. An inch more forward and she'd be on the floor. "I cannot believe this is happening. What about Georgia? What about hating Riverdale? And what's wrong with Clara?"

Clara, who had barely raised her gaze the entire conversation, snapped her head up, and the both of us could see she had been silently crying.

"Oh my goodness! This is no reason to cry!" Mere was out of her seat in a flash again, moving to the other side of the table and wrapping her arms around the girl. I was right behind her, and the both of us enveloped her in a hug.

"What's wrong, Clara?" I asked worriedly.

"I'm so sorry. I just can't believe this is happening either. It's so perfect!"

Over Clara's head I saw Mr. Carter raise his eyebrow and then shake his head, his arms crossed in front of him. "This what I gotta expect all the time? I forgot how emotional you women are."

Meredith looked slightly affronted, but I just tried not to laugh. "Mr. Sourdough, be a dear and get us a tissue?"

"Hmph." He grunted again but walked out to find a box.

"I'm glad you like the plan so much, Clara," I soothed as I sat back down.

Meredith released her a moment later. "Good things happen to good people," she said. "Sometimes they just take a while."

Clara gave us both a feeble smile. "I'm glad they're happening here, with all of you."

We smiled back at her and Mr. Carter returned, dropping a box of tissues on the table. Clara took one and dabbed at her eyes, while Meredith comfortingly patted her free hand on the table and refocused on me.

"Okay, so Georgia..."

"Georgia isn't going anywhere. Technically, it's not even official— well, I mean, the offer is, but all the paperwork is sitting at my parents' house blank as the day I first got it. I was supposed to mail them down days ago, but I kept getting distracted." I chose to leave out how I couldn't find the focus or interest to sit down and take care of it. "And besides," I said after a moment's pause. "Georgia came to Riverdale!" Clara and I grinned at each other, remembering the incident at Sunday dinner, while Meredith looked on confused.

"So you're willing to put all that aside to stay in a town you don't like?"

"Not like Riverdale? That's damn near impossible." Mr. Carter was like a sports announcer, adding a bit of input to everything that was going on. I gave him a loving glare.

"I don't dislike Riverdale. Sure, it seems like that sometimes—"

"All the time."

"Okay, all the time, but it's just that... well never mind, it doesn't matter right now. I've still got a lot of catching up to do with everyone anyway, and two weeks isn't nearly enough time for that."

Meredith let out a squeal of excitement. "This has to be a dream." Clara nodded in agreement. "Life is amazing, fantastic, wonderful. Can we start right away?"

I was about to say yes, but Mr. Carter piped up before I had the chance.

"Now ladies, can't get too hasty. Before you get to work on that bakery, we need to make sure everything's squared away upstairs so Belle and Miss Clara have a place to sleep."

"Can we at least look at it?"

"What, the bakery?"

Meredith nodded enthusiastically, and Clara looked up at him with an expectant smile.

"I don't see why you would want..." When his gaze went from Meredith to Clara he trailed off and looked at her curiously. "Doesn't matter to me," he finished a moment later. His tone had altered slightly, and he continued to look at Clara as though searching for something in her. It was an odd expression—I wasn't sure what it meant.

The three of us got up from our place at the table and followed him to the door that led to the bakery kitchen. I smiled inwardly as I watched him walk. Maybe it was just my imagination, but I could swear he already had more of a pep in his step. I hoped that was the case.

When we entered, we were surprised to find it was stainless and spotless. At my mention of its cleanliness, Mr. Carter replied gruffly, "Just because the bakery wasn't open doesn't mean I don't take care of what's mine." I supposed I shouldn't have been surprised. This place had meant— no, *still meant*—the world to him.

We walked through to the bakery, and as I looked around that spark of excitement began tickling the inside of my stomach. It smelled a bit musty, just like the first day I was there, and it was dark; the only light illuminating the room was an oil lantern hanging on the wall beside the kitchen door that Mr. Carter lit upon entering.

"An oil lamp?" Meredith commented incredulously.

"Glad you know what it is," he grumbled. "Turned off the electricity in this part, no need for it... I'll call today and get it back."

"Ah," she replied, before biting her lip and turning away. Poor girl. I knew she was hoping for a straightforward answer from him, but she'd be waiting a long time for that one! I didn't think he'd ever given a plain, boring, sarcasm-free answer in his life. I smiled at the two of them then looked at Clara as she wandered around dreamily, pausing to look at the old photographs that adorned the walls, occasionally raising a hand to rid one of a cobweb.

I walked over to one of the windows and flung open the shutters that were blocking out the signs of day. Streams of sunlight poured into the room, eager to swallow up the darkness. The light also highlighted the dust that had settled on top of everything and was floating through the air. I raised an eyebrow at Mr. Carter, and he shrugged in response.

I cleared my throat. "All right then, who's up for some cleaning?"

Clara and Meredith raised a hand, and as I went to open the rest of the windows they marched in search of supplies, and Mr. Carter's suggestion that we ready the bedrooms first was completely forgotten.

The week swept by like the dust we cleaned up on that very first day, and the progress we made was amazing. The three of us were acting like a bunch of schoolgirls. We'd decided not to tell anyone what we were doing, and acted like the entire town didn't have a clue—which, of course, they did. By the time Meredith walked over to pay Mr. Palmer a visit for some fresh paint on Wednesday, word had spread like wildfire. We pretended not to notice. She came back with three cans of paint: two for the bakery and one for the nursery we planned to surprise Clara with. Meredith had told him it was for another bathroom, but he didn't believe her for a second, and insisted on giving her the paint for free.

I had fully expected to invest some of my own money in Apple Blossoms, because I knew Mr. Carter had enough to get by but was by no means wealthy. I had worked out an entire business plan in the evenings when we'd retired to our rooms, always exhausted from the day's work but too excited to sleep. I was discovering, however, that I wasn't going to need as much as I thought.

The paint wasn't the only thing we'd gotten for free. That same day Jeremy came over after work—he and Meredith were seeing each other quite regularly now, so of course she insisted we let him in on the "secret." He'd taken the tables and chairs I wanted refinished to one of his friends, and although I'd told him to come back with a price estimate, he later informed me his friend had said not to worry.

Then, on Friday, I went over to the general store with Clara for enough ingredients to get us through until we got in touch with some local suppliers. Suzanne Walters would hear of nothing but giving me everything for my "insatiable cravings" half price. The sense of community here was continuously amazing me.

There wasn't much else we needed. Since I knew Clara enjoyed gardening, and we didn't want her around the paint or cleaning supplies, we placed her on landscaping duty while we took care of inside. It worked out perfectly. We'd work on painting the bakery walls a pale canary yellow to contrast the newly polished dark wood counters and the floor, then sneak upstairs to work on the nursery. Even Mr. Carter was in on it.

He'd do work towards the front of the bakery while we were upstairs, and warn us when Clara started wondering where we were. Then there were times he'd claim to have a headache and head upstairs for a "nap," but I knew he was working on the nursery as well. It was apparent he was thoroughly excited about everything that was going on, yet he always managed to keep hold of his sourdough persona.

I was now certain that it wasn't my imagination; his step had reacquired its pep. He played an active role in the preparations, and heartily agreed with all of the suggestions I made. The bedrooms he gave Clara and I were more than perfect. Hers looked on the backyard and conveniently had a door that joined it to the room we were making the nursery.

As for me, although I'd always have a place at my parents', they understood my desire to be near Clara as her pregnancy neared the end, so I made the temporary move to Mr. Carter's. my room was to the front of the house and looked out towards the street. There was a desk in front of one of the windows, and I was in grave danger of turning into Doris. I'd already caught myself getting distracted by the happenings outside. I could see half the park, Doris' home across the road, and Riley's office next to it.

My eyes drifted to all three of those places more than once, but I never saw anyone at the latter, most likely because I was rarely up there until after dinner. I imagined Riley would leave the office early to spend time with Alexis, and the image of him with her nauseated me, to my great frustration. I wished my stomach would listen to my head when it said, "I don't care."

Opposite to the lack of a visual on Riley was Doris, who I'd catch a glimpse of just about every day. When I was upstairs in the evening, I'd see her reading in the parlor, a single light on next to her chair. I always had the urge to walk over and sit with her, a book of my own in hand.

She looked so fragile sitting there all alone. It was a contrast to the Doris I'd see and hear about during the daytime.

Yesterday, for instance, she attempted to steal Clara. She was sitting on the porch as always, when she sent over one of the neighborhood kids to get Clara, who was planting a row of tulips in front of the bakery. I'd told her about Doris so when the summons came, she obliged and walked across the street. Doris tried to squeeze details out of her about the bakery, then proceeded to try and get her to work on her own gardens. It worked too—partially. Clara told her she'd stop over whenever she had the chance, and eventually, she managed to get away and return to the bakery.

"Belle? I think you've mixed that enough, don't you?"

I'd let my thoughts wander. I looked down at the batter for the Baileys Brownies I was making and saw that it was indeed mixed enough. I smiled at Clara, who was standing by the oven waiting for a batch of Rum Cookies to be done. It was now Sunday. The three of us had been so wrapped up in giving TLC to Apple Blossoms that we hadn't even realized Monday was Memorial Day. Mr. Carter brought it up while discussing an opening date, and we realized the holiday would be the perfect opportunity to give the town a taste. We planned to set up a table out front and provide samples of all the new treats the bakery would offer—and there were quite a few new additions. I'd be making all of the goodies I sold in college, and while Mr. Carter was a bit skeptical about their reception, he was all for giving it a shot, especially since we could have a test run. Clara was also bringing some additions of her own in the form of a few southern recipes like chocolate popcorn, sugared peanuts, and fudge. Along with that she had a bunch of pies to add to the mix such as Buttermilk, Kentucky—which was a delicious combination of chocolate and walnut—and Bourbon Pecan.

As a result of our last minute plans, the atmosphere in the bakery quickly switched from one of steady excitement as we went about fixing things, to a quiet urgency as we began baking. And the baking made the entire thing seem real. We'd already finished a few batches of Amaretto cookies, tropical cheese bars with coconut rum and pineapple, chocolate popcorn, and sugared peanuts. The rum cookies and Baileys brownies were all we had left to make, and it was only one o'clock.

It was just Clara and I, since Mr. Carter had gone to church and Meredith was off with Jeremy. Clara thought they were having lunch together, but really they were getting things for the surprise baby shower we were going to throw after the parade. The nursery was done, but she still needed quite a few things for the baby. And while I had only invited my family and a few friends, I knew word would get around and plenty of others would show up too, so it was a great way for some of the other residents to get to know her.

Apart from a lingering concern that being in Riverdale meant I might be missing things elsewhere, I was undeniably excited about the next day—and reviving the bakery. It was going to be outrageously busy the next couple of days, especially since the official reopening was set for Wednesday. Mr. Carter had let it slip that was when it first opened nearly fifty years ago, so it felt like perfect timing. Of course, that meant there was a lot to do in the next couple of days. Before then there was Memorial Day, the baby shower, and Sunday dinner at my mom's. She refused to let us out of it, despite my informing her I was up to my elbows in cookie dough.

"Well, dig them out and wash them up," she'd said. "Dinner's at seven, and family comes first, especially over cookies. I don't care how good they are."

The sound of Meredith's laughter in the front of the bakery caused me to look up. I placed my third pan of brownies in the oven and walked out of the kitchen just in time to see Jeremy and Mere wave good-bye to Riley. My stupid heart did another one of those skips. They walked in with their arms full of balloons and gifts wrapped in blue and pink paper. Meredith was about to burst, but I pressed a finger to my lips to let her know Clara was in back. I gave her a questioning look as she handed me the gifts.

"We ran into Riley at the store in Harwinton... he came to lunch with us when we were done shopping. Right, Jeremy?"

Jeremy shook his head in agreement, looking slightly puzzled at what seemed like Meredith's random need to explain. Guess he didn't understand the unspoken language of best friends.

"That's nice, but I don't really care." I didn't, did I? Maybe I did. Okay, I clearly did. Again, dumb. Why couldn't my emotions, physical reactions, and logical thinking all line up? "Well, up for helping Clara and I with the last few batches of goodies?"

Meredith nodded enthusiastically then looked at Jeremy.

"I've never been handy in the kitchen. I'll leave you ladies to it." He walked over and gave Meredith a kiss, then gave me a warm smile before heading out.

They were really something. I looked at Mere and she blushed endearingly.

I laughed. "Let's get to work. I promise I won't pester you about your precious Jeremy."

It was a lie. After all, what are friends for?

10

Monday morning began bright and sunny. I came downstairs to find Mr. Carter sitting at the table. Coffee mixed with the scent of something delicious and extremely familiar teased my senses.

"What's that smell?"

He nodded in the direction of the counter where a plate lay covered, waiting for an investigator such as myself to remove it. And so, I did just that, unveiling a tower of generously iced sticky buns, just like I used to get as a child. I grinned from ear to ear.

"Sticky buns? Oh, you shouldn't have!"

"Figured might as well start this off right. Know how much you like those."

That had to have been one of the sincerest statements I'd ever heard him utter. I took a bite of the warm bun and sat down at the table. "The only thing sweeter than this sticky bun is you, Mr. Carter."

"Bah. Don't go confusing salt with sugar."

I smiled warmly at him. "Never, Mr. Sourdough, never. This is even better than I remember." I took another bite.

"Ain't nothing special about it." He crossed his arms as though what I said didn't matter, but he couldn't keep the pleased expression off his face. "Parade starts in about an hour. Where's Clara?"

"I think she's still sleeping, which makes sense. She's been working hard and needs her rest."

He nodded in agreement. "Shouldn't be working so hard. It's not healthy for either of them."

His acknowledgement of the baby made my heart melt. "How do you like her?"

"I don't think much about you girls one way or the other... always causing trouble, no matter how old—"

"Come on, I'm being serious!"

He raised an eyebrow at me. "All right then, I like her just fine. She reminds me of... well, never mind." Once again I had the feeling there were some things about him I didn't quite know. "Haven't had much of a chance to really talk with you, Annebelle..." He paused as though contemplating whether to continue or not. "Well now, I know this may not be my place, and you've got your family to talk to and all... but you've got me wondering about those fellas you were with in the city."

My look of content started to change to a scowl.

"Don't get that look on your face. You know there ain't no secrets around here so don't act like I just peeked in your diary."

I wiped it away, suddenly realizing this was a good opportunity to get some info out of him. "If you'd like to know about 'those fellas from the city' then I'd like to know about whatever it is you're not telling me."

"I don't have any idea what you're—"

"Then I don't know about any fellas."

Our gazes met for a moment and held. Then he nodded in concession.

"Only person I ever knew more stubborn than you and I was..." His eyes moved toward the doorway and he paused. I looked over as Clara stepped into the room, wearing one of the sundresses we had purchased on our expedition. The cornflower blue color was bright and springy, and the empire waist style flattered her figure. Her black hair was left loose and wavy upon her shoulders.

"Good morning!" she offered up brightly.

I turned from her to Mr. Carter and saw that he was looking at her strangely once again. He felt my gaze and the expression vanished. "Raincheck," he muttered then stood up. "I'm going to set up the table outside. Bring those newfangled desserts of yours when you're ready." He nodded in Clara's direction then headed out front.

"Did I do something?"

"No, no, of course not." I got up to bring my mug to the sink. "He's just getting crabbier with age. Don't take it personally. Have a sticky bun—they're delicious. Meredith will be here in a minute so we can bring everything out. Enjoy breakfast and join us when you're ready."

She nodded, still looking a bit upset, so I reassured her once more. "I promise you didn't do anything. I've known him all my life, and *I* don't understand everything he does. Smile, you look beautiful!"

She did as I said, and her glow returned with the smile. As she walked over to the counter I left for the bakery, and Meredith arrived a minute later. While she brought platters of our goodies outside to Mr. Carter, I snuck upstairs to make sure everything was set in the nursery.

The walls were the color of sky on a bright summer's day. The trim was a lovely mahogany that matched the floor. The room was still relatively bare, but there were sheer curtains on the windows and an old rocking chair in front of them—a gift from Jeremy and his friend, the same one who'd worked on the chairs for the bakery. A teddy bear from Haley and Vanessa was currently occupying it, embracing a bunch of balloons from Tyler, and a music box from April.

Next to the rocking chair was a hope chest I'd found at an estate sale in uptown while at school. I'd fallen instantly in love with it, bought it, and sent it home, never really knowing what I'd do with it. I now knew it would work perfectly for toys once the baby was older, and at present, it held some newborn clothes my sister's kids had never worn. My family was quite enthusiastic about the town's latest addition and was constantly giving me things to add to the collection of "Clara's baby stuff" or offering advice and support. I really was lucky to have them.

I smiled at the thought of them all and how great the nursery had turned out, then walked back downstairs and outside to where Mr. Carter, Clara, and Meredith were putting the finishing touches on everything. Well, that is, Mr. Carter was settling himself into a lawn chair about to light up his pipe, Clara was arranging a vase of flowers on the table, and Meredith was sending a message on her phone, to Jeremy no doubt. She was another one I was extremely thankful for. Despite all the work I knew she had with the vet, she had taken time off this past week to help with the bakery endeavor. And even though she'd be returning to work fulltime after the opening, she'd promised she'd be by to help whenever she had some time. I knew that wasn't likely to happen with Jeremy around though—I was sure she'd want to spend that time with him, and I didn't blame her.

I walked up beside her and she grinned when she saw me. My eyes roamed up the street to where Riverdale's residents were beginning to line up. Some families were already seated by the edge of the road, while others were talking merrily with one another. Their occasional gaze in our direction confirmed what I already knew—their curiosity had been peaked, and it wouldn't be long until they wandered over.

I could just make out Derek and Jules up by Quality's, and I tossed them a wave when they glanced our way. Tyler, who was seated on Derek's shoulders, started waving furiously in return, and April began jumping up and down trying to see me through the crowd. I laughed as Jules attempted to keep hold of her hand as she tried to pull away, while keeping a firm grip on the baby in her arms.

"What are you laughing at, Belles?"

I turned my smile back to Meredith. "How crazy Jules is for having all those kids," I stated, shaking my head.

"Three? Oh, come on now, that's nothing! I swear I remember a time when a certain girl I know wanted no less than ten."

I looked at her in amazement. "I don't remember that! I remember a girl who always wanted to go explore the world and never wanted anything tying her down—like kids, for instance!"

"Are you joking? If you're not, your memory is already beginning to go."

What was she talking about? I was the girl who always made Barbie the independent woman with the pink convertible... wasn't I?

"Well, if she ever mentioned ten children she must have been crazy. It's a good thing she became more sensible."

"Is it though?" Mere raised an eyebrow at me as I readied myself for a reprimand about my priorities, but it never came thanks to the arrival of our first customer

"I knew you'd take my advice, Annebelle. I suppose all that education didn't completely wipe away all common sense." I grinned and turned toward the sound of Doris' voice.

"Your advice? Hmph. Shoulda known this wasn't of Belles' own accord. If I'd have known you brainwashed her into all this there's no way I'd have let it go on." I couldn't tell whether Mr. Carter was serious or not, but he looked about ready to get up from his chair, so I stepped over and planted a comforting but firm hand on his shoulder.

"You just keep on smoking that pipe, Mr. Carter. You give Doris, wise as she is, way too much credit. I wouldn't have stuck around this place if it didn't suit my needs as well as Clara's. All Doris did was save me the trouble of finding some other solution..." I felt him tense up beneath my fingers. "Oh, and of course, I wouldn't have done it if it didn't mean I'd get to live under the same roof as you. And you *are* my favorite, Mr. Sourdough."

"Bah! That's a bunch of hogwash, Annebelle. Don't insult me." He scoffed at my words, but I felt him relax. I was beginning to see that Mr. Carter had an inability to see himself as a good enough reason for... well, a lot of things, including my staying to help at the bakery. I was determined to figure out why but knew this wasn't the time, so I turned my attention back to Doris who was shaking her head at the two of us.

"Doris, I'm happy to see you've made your way over. It wouldn't be fitting for anyone but you, as one of our wisest and most loved residents, to try one of our new recipes first."

Mr. Carter let out a laugh at the distinction I'd given her, and I gave his shoulder another squeeze in reply.

"It's good to see you, Mrs. Clark." Clara smiled brightly at her, and Doris' expression softened. It seemed as though Doris had a new favorite in town.

"Call me Doris, dear. Now, what do we have here..."

I caught Meredith's eyes over the two of them and stuck my tongue out at her. She bared hers in return just as Doris looked in her direction and saw her.

"Meredith Kinney, will you ever grow up?"

She began to blush.

"I certainly hope not!" Meredith jumped as Jeremy appeared beside her and slipped an arm around her waist. "I like her just the way she is." He placed a kiss on her cheek as her face returned to its normal shade. I could tell Doris was pleased by this situation as well.

"Might I suggest an Amaretto cookie?" Doris took the napkin Clara held out to her and tentatively took a bite. We held our breaths. I knew the cookies were delicious since I'd taken the liberty of sampling one of each kind, but Doris was a stickler for tradition, and although she wanted the bakery fixed up and open again, I was fairly certain she rarely bought anything apart from the butter cookies she liked to serve with her lemonade. I couldn't remember her eating anything more outlandish than chocolate chip oatmeal raisin cookies either.

We watched as she placed the cookie back on the napkin and seemed to chew the small piece she had bitten extra slowly. Even Mr. Carter seemed transfixed, his mouth still on the end of his pipe.

"Well," she finally said. "Isn't that nice." We let out our breaths, and Mr. Carter nodded as if he knew all along she'd say that. He returned to puffing on his pipe, a smug look on his face. "Of course, it's nothing to the butter cookies, which I certainly hope you'll be making, but these are quite a nice addition. What else will you be offering?"

Clara and I smiled at each other and she began to explain the rest of the treats to Doris.

Moments later April and Tyler rushed up, followed shortly by the rest of the family. And that was it. Apparently, the rest of Riverdale saw it fit to make their way over after seeing Doris had made an appearance. None of them cared that it was still early, or that a Baileys brownie or tropical cheese bar hardly fell under the "healthy ways to start your day" category. We offered up sample after sample and received praise after praise. Everyone was positively bubbling over with excitement at having the bakery open full time again.

Mr. Carter sat in his chair, trying to look unaffected. He kept his traditional scowl firmly on his face, nodded when he was acknowledged, and offered up a gruff statement only when called for—but I knew he was ecstatic.

Despite the town's small size, the treats kept disappearing off the table. Clara, Mere, and I were kept busy right up until the start of the parade—and we put Jeremy to work as well. We sent him in for new platters when necessary and made him run to the general store for more napkins, milk, and cups when we ran low. He was a big help, but we also knew some of the treats that vanished ended up in his stomach, so we figured it was best to keep him busy.

There was a line in front of our table on more than one occasion, and only when we began to hear the sound of fifes and drums did the crowd thin out and return to their lawn chairs and respective posts along the street. The three of us let out deep breaths and looked at each other in wonder as the parade started to approach from the direction of Harwinton. Mr. Carter continued to act like he'd expected the treats to be a success all along, until I reminded him of his earlier doubts.

"I thought you didn't think our 'newfangled' ideas would be any good, Mr. Sourdough?"

"Bah! If I didn't think they'd have any merit I wouldn't have let you three waste your time or my electricity making 'em! Nah, I knew they'd do just fine. New ideas work all right as long as you mix 'em well with the old." He nodded again and inhaled his pipe tobacco. "All those folks who asked about the recipes that used to be here woulda been mighty upset if you'd told 'em we wouldn't offer them no more. I doubt they'd think those coconut tree whatchamacallits were half so nice if you said there wouldn't be any bread for buying." He nodded again.

I shook my head, knowing it would be useless to argue with him, and better to simply be happy at how well everything was received.

"Well, if you're a quarter as busy once you open as you have been this morning, you all are gonna be quite occupied." Jeremy took a bite out of what was probably his fifth brownie, his arm once again around Meredith's waist.

Meredith didn't seem the least bit uncomfortable with his display of affection, and, considering how much she blundered and blushed that day at the gas station, it was quite a change; she was like a flower that finally got enough sunlight to bloom. They seemed so natural together, so comfortable. I thought back to high school and how Meredith and I wouldn't have thought in a million years that the two of them would date.

"I don't know if I can handle that!" Clara sunk down into a chair.

"Well, you're not always going to be pregnant, Clara."

She placed a hand on her stomach. "No, you're right. Before long I'll be the kind of tired that comes from being up all night, changing diapers, and never getting any rest as opposed to being tired from having a little person moving around inside me."

"Oh please, you'll do fine. You're going to be a natural at the mom thing and multitasking. I can tell," Mere assured her.

"I agree. Besides, there won't be a rush of people like there was just now. Well, maybe when we first reopen but not forever—and you made it through today!"

She looked at me warily. "I know, but..."

"Don't you worry about a thing, Clara. You're doing great, and now we get to relax and enjoy the parade along with everyone else."

She gave me a feeble smile and I suddenly realized that, stupidly, I hadn't taken into account the fact she was probably thinking about her fiancé an extra lot since it was Memorial Day. I decided it might be best to keep her distracted by hinting at the surprise we had waiting.

"Oh, and by the way." I glanced at Mere and Jeremy. "Once the parade is done, we may or may not have a surprise for you."

"You do? What is it? You've already done so much for me, Belles—you all have!" The feeble smile turned into a grin and a questioning gaze.

"Oh don't worry, I promise it's nothing big. I mean it's not a car or anything."

"What is it?"

"Like I'm telling you."

"You really won't tell me?"

"That's what I just said isn't it? You can go right ahead and try and figure it out but we're not telling you. Now, we'd like to enjoy the parade if you don't mind," I grinned.

She looked from me, to Meredith, to Jeremy, to Mr. Carter, but we had turned our attention to the girls in front of us twirling batons in the air.

We watched as the traditional parade participants passed: bands, reenactors, Boy Scouts, Girl Scouts, horses, local politicians, representatives of each military branch, etc. I had to admit, while I still enjoyed the festivities they had been much more fun when I was younger, and it was acceptable for me to run out and grab some of the candy the firemen tossed from their big red trucks. Now I just got to watch. Although, I had to admit they weren't bad on the eyes, and I laughed and waved as Mark Nichols, another classmate, whistled at me from his gleaming red chariot.

I was about to turn to Meredith and joke about perhaps pursuing something with a local fireman, when my eyes landed upon Riley standing across the street. He was looking back at me. And as soon as our eyes met he began walking over—straight through the middle of the parade. I couldn't look away; it had always been hard for me to break eye contact with Riley. Whenever we talked—whenever we looked at each other—it was like our gaze got locked in place. It was like we got lost in each other's eyes and couldn't find our way out.

I didn't want to be looking at him. I didn't want him to be crossing through the middle of the parade like an idiot to come see me either but before I knew it he was standing in front of me. I didn't say a word. Just like the plenty of other frustrating moments I'd been having lately, I cursed myself for standing there like a mute while the parade, the people next to me—the entire world apart from Riley and me—started to disappear like they had at my graduation party and on so many other occasions when we used to be together. I didn't like it one bit. What was wrong with me? I was doing a terrible job being angry at him for being with Alexis, and being angry at myself for even thinking I *should* be angry at him for being with Alexis—because I really shouldn't be, not if I truly didn't care about him anymore. It was all so confusing.

It felt like the two of us were going to stay lost in each other's eyes forever, but minutes—or had it been only moments?—later, Jeremy dragged us back to reality.

"Riley, how's it going? You just couldn't wait to come over when it was safe, could you?"

Riley broke the gaze first, and the daze started to dissipate. "Nope, if what I've been hearing about your desserts is true, they're worth getting run over by the band for." His eyes started to move toward mine again, so I quickly began rearranging some of the platters on the table. I couldn't get lost again.

"Would you like to try some?"

"Thanks Mere, I think I would."

I looked up and saw Clara hand Riley a napkin piled with one of each item. Apparently she'd anticipated Meredith's offer.

He nodded gratefully at her. "You must be Clara."

She held out her hand in confirmation. "I am. And you must be Riley."

I looked over at her in wonder at her forward reply. Just like Meredith, Clara was changing right before my eyes. She was no longer acting like the shy, fragile doe of a girl I'd found in the library. She was starting to come out of her shell, and I could tell she'd be a welcome part of the community before long. The intrigued expression on her face told me she knew, at least partially, the history between Riley and myself— it was yet another sign she was starting to become integrated into Riverdale: people were filling her in on the town's gossip.

"So how do you like Riverdale?" He asked her.

"Oh, I love it! I don't see why anyone would ever want to live anywhere else!"

"I agree. I may have left for school, but I always knew I'd come back. I can't say everyone here agrees with our sentiments though."

My eyes flew up, and I was about to offer a retort when Clara realized how I'd take what she'd said and tried to backtrack. "Oh, well, everyone's different, and there *are* plenty of places I'm sure are just as nice."

Riley laughed. "Sure there are. Still, there's no place like Riverdale. You don't have to change your sentiments for Annebelle's sake. She knows there aren't too many around here who understand her dislike for this place, although..." His attention returned to me, and I could tell by the twinkle in his eyes he knew his words were making me upset. Of course, the fact that he was *trying* to get a rise out of me made me more frustrated than angry. "I'd like to at least try and figure out the reasons, which is why I was hoping she'd agree to go out to dinner with me if I asked in front of an audience."

The audacity. I looked at everyone else, wondering why they weren't upset at the fact that he was trying to date two women at once. Were they secretly so upset at my wanting to live elsewhere that they didn't give a damn Riley wanted to take me to dinner while dating Alexis? They didn't seem the least bit affronted.

I let out a laugh in disbelief. "First of all, there are plenty of towns just like Riverdale, and I don't plan on going to any of them. I want something different. Second of all, I must not hate it here as much as everyone thinks because I'm still here, aren't I? And about to reopen a bakery no less! Thirdly, if you think I'd feel the slightest bit of hesitation in refusing your offer for dinner in front of some of my dearest and best friends—both old and new..." I looked at Clara and smiled. "Then you don't know me at all! Unfortunately, I *am* going to have to decline. I don't have time to go to dinner with you."

My refusal didn't faze him and his smile only widened. "Annebelle, Annebelle, Annebelle. The only person who knows you better than I do is probably your wonderful mother, although I'm pretty sure I can dig up some stories even *she* doesn't know."

I didn't doubt it, but I wasn't about to give him the satisfaction of admitting that. "I made them up."

"Oh did you now? So you mean to tell me that time beneath the bleachers after the Thanksgiving Day football game was made up? Because I'm almost positive your mom doesn't know about *that*." I remained silent. "I was there."

He winked at Clara and I could tell he'd won her over. Yep, Riley was loved by everyone, and I was the dumb girl who broke up with him and was crazy for doing so. Never mind that my decision helped him become the attorney he was today! The plan had worked almost perfectly—except for the fact that he'd also turned into a player. Oh, sure, there was also me, and the fact I remained rather discontent despite my belief moving to the Big Apple would solve all that, but that was beside the point.

"Why don't you stop by the bakery opening day? I'm sure Belle will have some time to spare in the afternoon. The two of you could go to Amy's or support the bakery by skipping a meal and having dessert!"

I looked at Clara open-mouthed for having the nerve to encourage him. Meredith and Jeremy laughed, and Mr. Carter let out a grunt of amusement from his chair. Riley beamed at her and I wasn't sure how I felt about the two of them getting along so well. "That's a great idea Clara. You can't refuse that one, can you Belles?"

I crossed my arms in front of me. "Just because I'm going to be working across the street from you..."

"And living," he interjected with a grin.

"*For now*. That doesn't mean you can start stalking me."

"I wouldn't dream of doing that—what kind of a person do you think I am? I just happen to love baked goods, but maybe you forgot..."

"I didn't forget a single..." I paused, realizing I was going to make him think I thought about him more than I did. Or, well, as much as I actually *had* been thinking of him lately, but was trying not to. "Oh, would you go away? You're frustrating me and I've got work to do. The opening isn't for two days, so you can go cause trouble elsewhere until then."

"I'm looking forward to our date but—"

"It's not a date."

"Right, well anyway, although I'm looking forward to eating biscuits with you on Tuesday, I think I'm gonna stick around here for a bit. You're all great company, these are delicious..." He popped a chocolate chip hazelnut liquor cookie into his mouth. "And I was invited to stick around for Cl... well, to socialize after the parade."

I glared at Meredith and Jeremy, wondering which of them invited him to the baby shower. Neither looked the least bit sorry, and Riley walked behind the table and started conversing with them. The parade had passed, and I could hear the mayor beginning his speech from the center of the green.

Although we all loved Mayor Ames, his speeches weren't exactly enthralling, so I wasn't surprised when some of the residents started returning for more samples. I purposely kept myself busy helping them, leaving the others to converse. On more than one occasion I could feel Riley looking at me, and I knew everyone who came over was taking note of the fact he was standing there with us. And then, of course, I knew when they went home later they weren't going to say it was because of Clara. And so spins the gossip mill.

Shortly after, the 21-gun salute echoed through the air and I fought the urge to cover my ears. Riley would have undoubtedly commented on it. He always made fun of the way I couldn't stand gunfire or the sound of fireworks, yet positively loved the latter. I'd spent many a Fourth of July near the river with him, dealing with the noise for the colorful display in the sky.

As soon as the shots ended, the crowd began to disperse. I handed over the last piece of Kahlua pie and turned to Clara. "I guess we can call it a day—and a successful one at that! Want to help me bring what's left into the kitchen?" I saw my family start to make their way over, and I glanced knowingly at Mere; she was going to bring everyone in through the main door to the house and usher them up to the nursery while I distracted Clara.

"It's definitely been a success!" Clara picked up two of the platters, nearly empty now, and followed me in through the bakery.

I squinted as we went indoors away from the bright sunlight. As my eyes slowly adjusted, I was again proud and amazed at the work we'd done to the bakery. It looked fantastic, and apparently Clara felt the same way.

"It looks great in here, Belles. I can't believe how quickly we were able to get everything ready."

I walked behind the counters with the freshly cleaned glass that would soon be filled with all our creations, and into the bakery kitchen. "I know. I guess we know what we're capable of now."

"No kidding." She set the platters down and began rummaging for something to store the remaining cookies in—everything else had been eaten. "We're capable of pretty much anything I'd say!"

I started moving the leftover rum cookies into the container she handed me. "I agree."

"So..." she began. I had a feeling I knew what was coming, and I wondered how long I needed to keep her downstairs before heading up to for the shower—the sooner the better. "You and Riley used to date?"

"Mmhmm." I pressed the top on forcefully.

"What happened?"

"Nothing. We broke up with each other—I went to school in New York and he went to school in California, and, you just heard Riley—he plans to settle here, while I'd like to live somewhere else."

"Hmm 'we' broke up? The way everyone..." she paused as I glanced at her sternly. "Well, the way it seemed to me, it didn't appear like it was a mutual decision."

"Do you have evidence to back that up?" She remained silent. I knew she wouldn't say it was because other people told her it wasn't mutual, especially since she knew I wasn't a fan of people sticking their noses where they didn't belong. "I didn't think so."

"Well, he seems like a really great guy. Why are you so adamant about keeping your distance?" She carried the empty trays to the sinks.

"I'm not." Now it was her turn to look at me sternly. "Okay, well, maybe I am. It's just that, he may seem great but..." He moved on and turned into a snooty attorney player. I thought this but couldn't bring myself to slander him to anyone. "Just because someone seems great doesn't mean that they are. I mean, take my college boyfriend for example. He..." I hesitated, not sure how open I wanted to be with her, especially since I hadn't even talked about this with Meredith—and she was my best friend!

"Don't stop, Belles. Remember when I told you all about myself on the way to Harwinton? When I asked about you, you said you'd share another day. Make that day today. You can trust me. And I'm here for you, the same way you were for me." She was looking at me so earnestly that I couldn't say no. In fact, I felt like finally telling someone. I took a breath.

"Okay, well, he seemed really great. I mean, with him I never had to wonder whether he liked me or not. He always made sure I knew. He introduced himself to me, asked me out, always complimented me... he was straightforward about his feelings, which I thought was great."

"Riley didn't let you know how he felt?"

My brow furrowed. That was *so far* from the truth. "No, no, of course Riley did. But that's not what this is about. The two of us were on opposite sides of the country at this point. And, Rick... he seemed great, and all my college friends thought it was wonderful that he was so attentive, and I did too—at first. But then he started to get... overbearing. And jealous. I've always been friendly, and I liked going out with my friends and meeting people—having a good time. But he started getting mad when I went out, or making it his business to always know where I was or what I was doing... or even what I was wearing!"

I stopped to see if she was uninterested in what I was saying, but her look was nothing but attentive, so I continued. "I'm not the type of person to be okay with that, especially because of the independence factor and all. But because he was so nice to me, I let it slide. I changed how I dressed and acted, I stopped spending time with my friends as much, I didn't come home for visits... and when we were in public it all seemed worthwhile because things were so great. He treated me *so well* when there was an audience." I paused, my mind drifting back to some of the days I'd tried to wipe from my memory. I was so good at it that I'd nearly fooled myself. "But then I'd do something to get him mad, and he'd turn into a completely different person."

Clara's eyes began to widen. "Did he hurt you?"

"Never on purpose..."

"What do you mean 'never on purpose!?' Of course it was on purpose! It's not like someone else came in and made him do it, did they?"

I knew she was right, and my response was the type of thing I'd have said back when I was still with him, defending him to my friends after they started to see him for who he really was... but not now. I shouldn't be saying that now. I'd gotten away. I was moving on. I'd left him—and everything related to him—behind.

"Ugh, you're right. I'm sorry. I haven't talked about this with anyone from here, and when my college friends would bring it up after they noticed the changes, that's pretty much what I'd say... but I know there's no excuse for how he acted. I think, looking back on things, that's why it was so scary. When I was in it, I couldn't see the relationship for what it really was... I couldn't see *him* for who he really was. ...It never got too bad though."

She looked like she was about to scold me again, so I clarified. "I mean, it could have been much worse. It was mostly an occasional shove, grabbing hold of my wrist just a bit too tight, or yelling at me."

"That's bad enough."

"He proposed to me."

Her eyes were now doublewide. "He *what!*"

"Yeah." I let out a laugh. "Ironically that's what finally brought me to my senses. He proposed to me in our apartment shortly before graduation—when it was just the two of us of course, and he was being ridiculously sweet. But I didn't answer right away. I tried picturing our wedding, our future—the house, the kids, the pets... and I couldn't see it. I don't mean I saw it and I didn't like it—I just couldn't see it. My mind went blank. Then, when I didn't answer right away, he became furious." I paused as the memories came back and a shudder ran through me. "He grabbed me and threw me against the glass coffee table. It shattered, and since it was my shoulder that hit it, I got cut up there pretty bad. There's a scar now." I reached a hand over my right shoulder and rubbed there lightly. Although the injury had healed, talking about it made it ache.

Clara looked like she was about to cry, and suddenly I felt foolish for choosing that particular time to share. All I was supposed to do was keep her downstairs until everyone had time to get to the nursery, and here I was spilling my secrets and making her upset.

"But I'm fine now!" I tried assuring her. "I mean, what scares me the most is the fact that if he hadn't gotten so upset at my hesitation, who knows what my answer would have been in the end. I wasn't myself, so even though I can't see a future that involves a husband and kids... maybe I would have said "yes." Then who knows where I'd be today."

To my embarrassment I felt my eyes start to water, and Clara embraced me in a tight hug. "Annebelle, I'm so, so sorry! I know what that's like... I mean, kind of. My mom was always ending up in relationships with guys who treated her terribly. It's hard for those who aren't in the relationship to understand why someone would stay with such abuse—most of the time it's even hard for the person who's *in it* to understand why they stay. But you got out of it, and that's what matters. I don't think you're giving yourself enough credit. It takes a lot to get out of those situations, but you're a strong woman Belle. You're always looking out for others and fixing things and doing what's right. You saved me, you know?"

I pulled away and looked at her.

"No, don't try and deny it because it's true, you really did, and I'm the one who'd know it."

"It's just a ruse. I'm really not that strong at all."

It's funny how roles could change; all of a sudden Clara was the certain one and I was the fragile one lacking confidence.

"Oh, I think you are. Probably more than you realize. So even if he hadn't gotten mad, I don't think you would have said 'yes.' And you know, I don't think you should look too much into the fact that you couldn't see a future as a wife or mother. I mean, you couldn't see all those things in a future with *him*, but I think that's just because he wasn't the right one. When I saw my mom in all those relationships, I swore I was going to stay single all my life. The only thing to come from all she did that you might say was a good thing was me—and I never met the loser who was the catalyst for *that* accident." She laughed. "But that's how certain I was that there weren't any decent men out there. Then I met Jackson and everything changed. I knew, almost instantly, that I wanted to be with him forever. You'll know when you find that."

The look on her face said more than her words. She was thinking of Jackson, and I could see just how much she'd loved him. It made my heart ache that she had lost it, but she was so unbelievably lucky to have had it for even a short while.

"At least I've got a piece of him to keep with me always—something I would have never thought I'd be able to handle if it weren't for you and everyone in Riverdale. I can't believe the baby will be here in less than a month." Her hand rested lovingly on her stomach, and I remembered the baby shower.

"The surprise!" Clara jumped at my sudden exclamation. "Sorry, I didn't mean to startle you, but I nearly forgot!" I took her by the hand and began leading her through the door to the house. "Come with me!"

"Belle, wait." She halted in her tracks. "Are you sure you're all right?"

I smiled at her in earnest. "Yes, I'm fine. I feel better just having told someone. It's in the past now, and I want to focus on the present—which is all about you. And the future—which is all about that baby! Besides, that ridiculously long confession was really only to prove my point—just because someone *seems* great doesn't mean that they are."

I tugged on her hand again and she followed me up the stairs. I didn't want to think about the past anymore—about Rick.

"Right," she agreed as she walked behind me. "But I don't think Riley is like that at all, so I don't think that really works in proving a point."

I knew she was right. Riley would never hurt me, and comparing someone who was manipulative and abusive but pretended to be a gentleman with someone who actually was a gentleman—or, at least, had been before deciding to try his hand at dating more than one girl at a time—didn't really work. I wasn't about to say that to her though. Nor was I going to tell her that I *had* seen my future, just like she said I would, with someone else. Except... when I'd seen it back when I was still in high school, it scared me so much I ran away from it as fast as I could. So now that image was in the past as well. I wondered if you could see your future that vividly with more than one person. Perhaps I should think about picturing a future with Mark Nichols...

I pushed open the door to the nursery and my thoughts about firefighters and futures, pasts and past decisions, were pushed aside as Clara entered the room and a chorus of "surprise" rang out.

11

The baby shower had been a combination of laughter and tears,which was, I supposed, highly appropriate considering the emotional state of the guest of honor. Clara started crying the moment she realized what was happening and took note of the room around her. She deemed the nursery perfect, and swore she couldn't have dreamed up a better room for the baby. Plates of light hors d'oeuvres made by my mom and Aunt Arlene were passed around as the guests conversed with one another. Those who already had children reminisced and shared tips, while those without children—apart from my nieces, that left Meredith and I— smiled and nodded, and kept busy popping tiny cucumber sandwiches into our mouths. The men in attendance grouped together in the corner of the nursery closest to the door, and there they remained until it was time to open gifts.

At that point, I received a few surprises along with Clara. The second present she received after the nursery itself was the rocking chair, which she sat in immediately. As she rocked back and forth holding the teddy bear from the twins, Jeremy informed her it was a gift from Riley and him, but he emphasized that most of the credit for labor belonged to the latter, and I came close to choking on a cucumber.

Riley, it turned out, had made a hobby out of fixing up old furniture in the years since I'd seen him, and he was the friend responsible for repairing and refinishing the tables and chairs in the bakery. I supposed I should have guessed. At some point over the last six years the two men had become good friends, and I don't know why, with Riverdale being the size that it was, I didn't assume I'd know who the "friend" was. This was a far cry from Manhattan, and one person's social circle was likely to be the same as the next. I wasn't sure how I felt about Riley being a part of Operation Apple Blossom. The part of me that disliked him— well, *tried* to dislike him—resented the help. But the rest of me liked that he'd found the time to refinish everything in between work and dates with Alexis. In my mind, that meant he thought us more important than her, which of course, we were—but I liked the idea of him thinking that too. Was that childish? Maybe.

After the rocking chair, Clara received a knitted blanket from Doris; more clothes from Jules, Kate and my mom; a carrier and car seat; a literal mountain of diapers; and other necessities I'm sure I would have remembered if I'd paid more attention, but most of it had been focused on Riley. I tried staying in whichever part of the room was furthest from him, and at some point I realized he thought my blatant attempts to stay away were funny. On more than one occasion I'd look over to find him gazing back with a raised eyebrow and an amused expression on his face. He'd start stepping around the guests to get closer to me, and I'd begin moving around the room in the other direction. I supposed I could see the humor—it must have looked like we were doing some elaborate dance around the nursery. I thought he'd get the hint and eventually give up, but he kept at it, and finally caught up to me while I was at the punch bowl.

"This nursery isn't that big. I'm surprised you didn't knock something or someone over careening through the crowd like that," he stated playfully.

I took a sip of my punch before replying, "Same to you."

"You sure are trying awful hard to keep away from me."

"That's because I don't like you."

He smiled his gorgeous smile, and I knew he didn't believe me. I couldn't blame him, since I didn't even believe myself.

"Ah, so the truth comes out. You sure have an odd way of showing it. After all, you were the one who practically tackled me with a hug at your party, remember?"

"Oh please. It was just a hug and I was only being polite. Plus, I didn't know how foul you'd turned out at the time. I know better now."

He paused for a moment, and I could tell it was because he wasn't sure if I were serious about the "foul" part or not. His hesitation made me wonder if maybe *he* was upset at the way he'd turned out. Maybe he was starting to realize the problem with being a womanizer.

"You don't like how I turned out?"

"Do *you* like how you turned out?"

He let out a breath of air and ran a hand through his hair. "Some days I wonder if becoming partners with my dad was the right decision. I mean, how will I ever be able to live up to him? But most days I think I ended up all right, especially considering..."

I laughed, deciding he didn't have a conscience after all.

"What's so funny?" He'd looked momentarily affronted.

"Nothing at all." It figured. "Considering what?"

"Just... well, everything that happened between us. It really—"

Before he could finish we were interrupted by Jules, who asked if she could put Ryan, who'd fallen asleep in her arms, down on my bed. Afterwards, Doris exclaimed how outrageous it was that the one thing Clara hadn't received was a crib. In response Mr. Carter, who'd kept to himself for most of the shower, piped up and gruffly informed us there was one more gift. He walked out of the room, grabbing Riley as he passed. A slight murmur of interest rippled through the crowd, and I was left wondering about the gift and the rest of Riley's sentence.

Only the former was answered a moment later when the two men walked back in holding a beautiful cradle with a ribbon tied around the center. All of the women gasped at the sight of it, then began ogling it all at once. The commotion made Mr. Carter mighty uncomfortable, and he brushed off all the compliments about what a lovely gift it was.

"It was gathering dust and taking up space in the attic. I was thinkin' to burn it, but figured Clara might get some use out of it first. Those new baby beds are mighty expensive," he stated, and Clara started crying once more. What an emotional day.

It was a wonderful gift, and the enthusiasm of everyone in attendance, including Mr. Carter, was quite endearing. I knew I wouldn't have to worry about Clara even if I were to leave tomorrow, but I wondered if I was the only one curious as to why Mr. Carter had an old cradle in his attic...

"Would you knock it off? Every time you yawn I do too!"

My thoughts were close to becoming dreams as I fought against falling asleep while standing. "I'm sorry, Mere. I didn't realize I'd have such trouble waking up this early." My hand flew to my mouth as what was probably the tenth yawn escaped. "This is going to take some getting used to." I idly watched as the mixer perfectly blended the ingredients to form dough. If I were still in college, I'd probably be heading to sleep right now after a night of studying—or partying—not starting my day.

"You girls complaining already? Ready to quit? Knew this hobby of yours wouldn't seem fun for long." Mr. Carter pulled a sheet with four loaves of fresh bread on it from the oven. They smelled divine.

"Mr. Sourdough, this is not a hobby! I'm just not adjusted... I need coffee ASAP."

"It's here, it's here!" Clara came waltzing in from the house kitchen with a tray of fresh coffee. She was grinning from ear to ear and more awake than anyone should be at this hour. I was amazed, especially considering she was quite pregnant. Weren't pregnant women supposed to sleep all the time and be cranky?

"Who gave you happy pills this morning?"

She laughed as she handed me a steaming mug. "How could I not be happy? This is so exciting! We're opening today!"

Mr. Carter looked over at her and shook his head in what I knew to be an admiring manner. "Looks like Clara has baker's fever."

"What's that?" She inquired.

"It's what makes a baker do what he does. It's what makes 'em get up every morning, put a dozen different loaves of bread in the oven, and be happy doing it. It's a fever."

"What, are you two related or something?" I joked. "Give Merekins and I a chance, will you? We have baker's fever too, we just need a break-in period!"

"Um, I'm going to have to disagree. I do *not* have baker's fever. I'm excited about the bakery and happy to help, but I like sleeping until the sun is at least visible on the horizon. I'll stick to being a vet."

"Okay, never mind, Mere does not have baker's fever. Just let me drink my coffee and I'll be good." I took a sip and let out a moan as the warm liquid slid down my throat. "I feel better already."

"Placebo effect," Meredith muttered. "Caffeine doesn't hit your system that fast."

I grabbed a piece of dough from the bowl and tossed it at her.

By the time the sun rose, not only had Meredith and I completely woken up, but we managed to successfully make it through our first morning of baking. Granted, it couldn't have been done without Clara and Mr. Carter. There was no doubt I loved baking, but when I made my creations at school it was usually on my own schedule and sometime during the afternoon. It didn't seem half as fun when it was still dark outside, but neither Clara nor Mr. Carter seemed to mind. They worked with a quiet determination mixing, kneading, rolling, baking, repeating—up until the bakery was filled with fresh loaves of bread, warm rolls, muffins, and of course, sticky buns.

I hadn't expected Clara to take to the position of baker so quickly and enthusiastically, but I was happy to see it happen. I left the two of them to their work while Meredith and I began setting up the front of the bakery. We brought out the pies we'd made the day before—Kahlua pudding, buttermilk, lemon meringue, and bourbon pecan—and placed them beneath the counter along with the cookies and brownies—traditional varieties mixed with some of the new additions. We set bowls of sugared peanuts and chocolate popcorn on the tops, opened up the blinds to let the sun pour in, and stepped back to admire the result. The bakery had been renewed with the work we'd put into cleaning it up, but up until this particular moment it had looked more like a model bakery than one that would actually be used.

We grinned broadly at each other before hollering out for the other two to come and take a look. They walked out of the kitchen wiping their hands on their aprons, looking hot but happy, and came to stand next to us to examine The Apple Blossom Bakery on opening day.

Clara pressed her hands to her cheeks in astonishment as she looked around wide-eyed. "It looks just like a picture!"

Mr. Carter nodded in agreement. "Looks mighty fine. 'Bout as good as it did when we first opened, I'd say."

My smile widened at his approval. I took in the open admiration on his face, knowing full well he'd return to being Mr. Sourdough in a moment or two.

"Let's make it one!"

"One what?" I inquired.

"A picture! I'm going to get my phone." Clara walked excitedly into the back as the three of us looked at each other and stifled a groan. I for one, was sure I didn't look my best, not after being up for hours and working in a kitchen with three large ovens.

Meredith voiced my concern. "I'm not taking a photo. I look a mess."

Clara returned a moment later waving her phone in the air. "All right you three, go stand behind the counter!"

Mere suddenly saw an escape. "Oh no, I don't think so Clara. You did more baking than I did, and I'm only temporary help. I'll take the picture, and *you three* get behind the counter." She swiped the phone from Clara's hand.

"But..." she began in protest.

"Nope, either we're all in the photo or the three of you are, and since the picture won't take itself and there's no one else to take it, it looks like—"

A knock on the door stopped her midsentence. We turned around, wondering who was here before we'd even put the sign out, and saw Jeremy grinning from the other side.

I unlocked the door and let him in. "Looks like you're gonna be in the photo after all. Nice try though, Meredith. Great timing, Jeremy, mind taking a photo of us?"

His gaze swept over the bakery, and his eyes took on the look of a kid in a candy store. When he focused on Meredith, the look remained—

heightened, even. "It looks, and smells, heavenly in here. And it'd be my pleasure."

Meredith flashed a look of condemnation in Jeremy's direction, showing she had no intention of relinquishing the phone, but when he stepped over to her and placed a kiss on her mouth, the look vanished and she released it without hesitation.

"Good morning, beautiful," he said admiringly.

My smile once again widened, but for a different reason. My cheeks were beginning to hurt and it wasn't even eight.

"Morning," Mere responded in a slightly dreamy tone. He turned her around and pushed her in the direction of the counter where Mr. Carter and Clara were already standing. She walked over to them and I followed suit. I stood between Meredith and Clara, slipping an arm around each of them. Mr. Carter was on the other side of Clara, and she did the same to him. I bit my lip to keep from laughing at Mr. Carter's look of hesitation as her arm slipped around him, then he responded by placing his arm over her shoulders. There was something about Clara that made everyone—even someone as defensive against newcomers as Doris, and as cross as Mr. Carter—love her. My guess was that it was due to a combination of her southern charm, sweet attitude, and a sort of innocence that made you feel like she needed protecting. Either way, Mr. Carter had a soft spot for Clara just as he always had for me, and I wasn't even envious of the thought that perhaps it meant my place at the counter might be lost to her.

"All right, on three..." Jeremey commanded. "One, two..." I didn't need to force a smile on my face since one had been there all morning. "Three!"

After he snapped the picture I looked at the clock, noted it was five after eight, and reached under the counter for the flag that read "Open." I turned to Mr. Carter and held it out. "Well, Mr. Sourdough, what do you say we get this show on the road?"

He took hold of the flag and walked out the front door to slip it onto the pole beside the entrance. Seeing him head over to once again open the bakery that had been his livelihood for so long—a bakery he'd probably resigned himself to never reopening—was a bit emotional. I held my breath to keep the water that had gathered in my eyes from spilling over as tears. I looked over at the other women and found their faces to be as full of emotion as I imagined mine was. Meredith caught my eye and we let out a laugh, then Clara joined in as she took notice as well. With the laughter, the tears that threatened dissipated. Mr. Carter unfurled the flag then turned and walked back in. He gave the bakery another once over then nodded at the group of us.

"Well, all right then. Looks like The Apple Blossom Bakery is open once again."

Jeremy was, of course, our first customer. As soon as Mr. Carter stepped behind the counter, he asked for a sticky bun and a blueberry muffin then settled himself on one of the stools to enjoy his fare.

"I'm gonna stay here all day," he announced as he delved into the gooey bun.

"Don't you have to work?" Meredith inquired.

"Not anymore I don't. This is too good." He took another bite. "I quit."

She laughed and took a seat beside him with a muffin of her own.

"Did you quit too?" I joked.

"I'm taking advantage of my 'temporary help' status and becoming a patron for the moment," she responded.

I shook my head, grabbed a piece of her muffin, and looked over at the door as our next customer walked in. "Good Morning, Natalie," I said as I realized it was Sarah's daughter.

"Hi Annebelle, mom sent me over to get a loaf of bread and some muffins. My grandparents are back now too, and I guess they love the butter cookies and the rum ones my mom got for them from the parade the other day. Mom said if I didn't come over now they'd probably be gone."

"Hear that, Mr. Carter? Looks like the town's expecting us to sell out today."

"Hmph. I'll believe it when it happens," he muttered.

"Always so negative." I shook my head disapprovingly.

"Do you think we'll be able to stay open until four as planned? What kind of muffins would you like, sweetie?" Clara asked. Natalie walked over to make her selection, grabbing a handful of sugared peanuts from the counter.

"We'll find out soon enough... Lucy! It's so good to see you!" I waved as Lucy Stevens—now Lucy Truman—stepped inside. "I can't believe I haven't run into you before now. Meredith and I were talking about your infamous breakup with Bobby not too long ago."

Lucy laughed as she walked over. Her attire told me she was on her way to work at the town office. "What a waste of a shake."

"That's what I said!" Meredith exclaimed before popping the last bit of muffin into her mouth.

Jeremy shook his head, clearly remembering what a jerk Bobby had been—and still is, apparently.

"What can I get for you today?"

"Actually, I have no idea. I just had to stop in. I can't believe it's open again—it looks great!"

"Thanks! It was a group effort." I smiled in the direction of Clara and Mr. Carter. "Why don't you take a look at what we have, then let me know if something strikes your fancy, and if you don't see anything today, come back tomorrow. We're going to keep things interesting by making different types of cookies and pies each day, but we'll keep the bread selections pretty constant."

"Sounds great! I'm positive I'll find something I want though, which is unfortunate news for my hips." She started to look over our offerings, and I once again turned my attention to the door as two more figures walked in.

"I can't tell you how great it feels to walk through that door, Benjamin." I smiled at Mr. Palmer and Ms. Ferris, still amazed at the two of them being together.

Mr. Carter reached across the counter to shake hands with Mr. Palmer. "Good to see you walk through it, Jethro."

I greeted Ms. Ferris with a hug and answered her inquiries as to why I hadn't borrowed any books when I stopped by that first Sunday. I explained how the storm had caused me to leave before deciding on any books, but after a look at Clara, I conveniently left out the part about discovering her there. Ms. Ferris would be appalled, and even though it would only be in a concerned sort of way, I figured I'd spare Clara the embarrassment.

"I hope you've got butter cookies like you said you would," Doris said as she walked through the door. "I've got a plate on my porch that's been without them for much too long."

"Morning, Doris, we certainly do!" I exclaimed. Clara greeted her moments later and offered to package up a bunch.

"Annebelle Roth, it's good to see your degree being put to good use." I looked toward the door as Eric Valentine and his wife Olivia walked in wearing workout clothes. Eric was another classmate of mine, and he met Olivia on our senior trip to Daytona Beach.

"And it's good to see you were good on your word and convinced Olivia to give Riverdale a shot. Been running?"

"She's a smart woman, she knew a good town when she saw it." I kept silent. "And yeah, we like to run nearly every day, but we only ever get to go together when the little ones spend the night at their grandparents. And we couldn't run by here without stopping in on opening day, so we figured we'd get some carbs."

"We're going to conveniently forget about the sugar and all that," Olivia chimed in.

"Well, you two will be better off here than I will. I haven't gone for a run in weeks!"

"Oh, you run??" Olivia asked interestedly. "You should join in on the town 5K!"

"Since when is there a race in Riverdale?"

"Olivia and I started one up a few years back. We pick a different place or cause to raise money for each year. It's in September."

"I'd love to, assuming I'm still in town."

"You can't go a single day without talking about leaving, can you?"

I followed the sarcastic tone of my brother's voice and smiled when it led me to him. "Nathan!"

"Morning, sis." He walked over to the counter and started looking over the treats. "I promised the girls I'd stop over and pick them up some things. They tried to convince Kate and I to bring them to school late so they could come."

"Well, we'll be open until four, so you could always bring them by then."

"They have dance after school. Anyway, think you'll have anything left by then?" He looked toward Mr. Carter who was ringing up Mr. Palmer and Ms. Ferris. Doris was in line behind them, still chatting with Clara, who was packaging up a few pieces of pie for Eric and Olivia. I laughed and waved as two more people walked in. "Maybe not." I grabbed a piece of parchment paper and one of the boxes we were using to package things. "What would you like?"

"Put together a mix of cookies, will you? And make sure to put in some of those Baileys brownies for me."

I nodded and got to work.

"So..." I glanced up to find him eyeing me.

"What is it?"

"The bakery looks great."

"Thanks." I raised an eyebrow. "And?"

"Does all this mean you plan to stick around?"

"I don't know, Nathan. Riverdale can't be the only great place in America."

"It's not," he said matter-of-factly, "But there's no place like Riverdale, Belles. I traveled when I was enlisted. I traveled quite a bit and ended up in some awesome places, but you seem to have forgotten that."

"I didn't forget, but you came back."

"Yeah, I did, because after a while I realized those places were missing something, and I figured out what it was—family. What are you trying to prove anyway? That you're successful because you left? That you're more educated? More worldly? You don't have to go live in some city down south to prove that. We already know how great you are." Nathan paused, rested his arms on the glass counter, and looked at me thoughtfully as I closed up the box and wrapped string around it like Christmas ribbon on a gift.

"Look at Clara," he continued. "she's been wandering around like a lost soul, looking for something—anything—to make her feel like she's found a home. And you know why she's so lost? She doesn't have any family. She doesn't have that lighthouse to look for when she can't find her way. So go—move away, do all of the things you want to do. But at the end of the day, when you picture 'home,' what do you think you'll see? I bet you'll see a place that looks like Riverdale, and I guarantee you're not going to find that in some other state or some other country. Riverdale is Riverdale. There's no place like it. It's where your family is. And that's what makes it special." He paused again. "Take what I've said or leave it. I'm not going to bring it up again. It's your call. I just think you're searching for something that's right in front of you."

I shook my head uncertainly and handed the box to Mr. Carter to ring up. "Thanks for the monologue Nathan," I said. "But I've got to get back to work."

He nodded as I headed back to the end of the counter and greeted Mayor Ames, pushing all my brother had said aside.

"Shouldn't you be at the town hall?" I smiled at him.

"I'm out on business—attending the reopening of one of Riverdale's gems, The Apple Blossom Bakery." He winked at me and I grinned in return.

"That's as worthy a use of our tax dollars as I've ever heard. If you're trying to get yourself a free loaf of bread with the compliments, you might just succeed."

"My wife would like that loaf of bread for sure, but I'm going to pay for it the same as everyone else. And I've got my eyes set on that meringue pie, too."

"One slice?"

"I'll take the whole thing."

12

The rest of opening morning went by in the same manner as the first hour. Residents continued to arrive in a steady stream to support the bakery, and by the time the lunch hour was over, the items we had to offer were relatively slim. I could tell Mr. Carter, despite keeping up his signature gruff countenance, was a bit in awe of it all. I knew he was happy, if not in a state of disbelief, at the fact that the bakery was open again. And Clara was just as happy as she had been at four in the morning, if not a bit exhausted.

After sitting with Jeremy in the corner half the morning, Meredith helped by cleaning off the tables of the people who decided to eat their treats in-house. Quite a few chose to do so, and I knew it was more than would have stayed in the past—Mr. Sourdough did a good job getting people in and out. Apart from me, there hadn't been many who'd stick around for a muffin and a scowl from him when I was growing up. I had a feeling a bit of feminine energy had softened the atmosphere, and I wondered if this was what it had been like while his wife was alive.

When the clock hit 2:30 my mind was already on the evening ahead which—big surprise—included baking for tomorrow. The four of us also began discussing how everything went and any changes we felt needed to be made. Meredith suggested we offer some drinks, especially when people wanted to stay and eat something in the morning. I didn't think it was a bad idea but planned on running it by the diner to make sure she wouldn't feel like we were stepping on any toes. My mind was swirling with thoughts like cinnamon swirling through those sticky buns. I was so distracted I completely forgot about the meeting planned with a certain individual until I heard the tinkling of the door being opened. I looked up from my place behind the counter where I stood talking with the others.

"Riley! Hey!" Clara said, enthusiastic as always.

"Hi, Riley. You look nice. Doesn't he, Belles?" I subtly kicked Mere behind the counter and remained silent, although I had to admit he did look nice in pressed khakis, a button-down, and tie.

"Thanks, Mere. I've been busy at work all morning. This is the first chance I've had for a break, and unfortunately it can't be long. I have a meeting with a client in half an hour."

"Have you had lunch?" Clara inquired.

He shook his head negatively.

"What!" Clara said, appalled. "The two of you should go eat at Amy's then, and forget about staying here and snacking on cookies."

I was about to tell him I'd rather not, or suggest he go ahead and we meet up some other time, but when he made eye contact with me, I noticed how exhausted he looked. He didn't seem up for any banter, so when he asked if I'd join him, I nodded in agreement and stepped out from behind the counter.

Of course, I didn't forget to toss a glare at the girls before leaving. I followed him out of the bakery and walked beside him toward Amy's. Conversation was kept light, with Riley commenting on the steady flow of people he saw entering the bakery and asking how the day went. When he entered the diner Amy greeted Riley enthusiastically as she saw him, and when I stepped in behind him her excitement doubled.

"Annebelle Roth! I can't believe it!" She wiped her hands on her apron the same way Sarah had when she'd seen me, rushed over, and embraced me in a giant hug. She was an older version of her daughter. Her salt and pepper hair was up in a bun, her cheeks had the same flush Sarah's had, and her big eyes sparkled. She looked back and forth from Riley to me and her grin widened. "I heard you had quite the opening day. You must be starving. And Riley, I know you're always working hard. I'm surprised you found the time to get in here!" Without a moment's hesitation she grabbed two menus and waltzed over to the booth in the corner—our booth—the same one Sarah had kept Alexis and him from eating in. Riley caught my eye, and I knew he was wondering if I wanted him to say something to Amy and have her seat us elsewhere, but I just shrugged and slid onto the seat.

"The usually, Riley?"

"That'd be great, Amy, thanks."

"And for you, Annebelle? Up for a burger?"

"I'll just have a BLT today, thanks."

Amy looked momentarily taken aback. Nearly every time we'd come in over the years I'd ordered a burger with golden fries and was usually able to finish more than Riley. "Well, that's quite a change. What about to drink? You're not going to say water with lemon, are you?"

I laughed. "I'll have a shake—half chocolate, half strawberry."

She seemed much more pleased with that response and hurried away to place our orders.

"There's *one* thing that hasn't changed."

I smiled at Riley. "There's a lot that hasn't changed."

"Could have fooled me."

"Well, it's not like you've been around me enough to notice what's different or not."

"You won't exactly *let me* be around you."

Would this be the right time to call him out and let him know I wasn't about his games? Knowing that he even played games now was infuriating enough, but even more so was the fact that I liked the idea of him *wanting* to be around me, even though he wanted to be around another girl, too.

He took note of my hesitation. "I'm not trying to start a fight with you, Belles."

"Good, because I don't feel like fighting."

"I just want to talk."

"All right, let's talk."

He nodded. "Tell me about college."

"I can't just sit here and ramble on, you have to ask me something."

Amy walked over and dropped off our shakes—Riley's usual was chocolate with extra syrup. I took a sip of my own and waited.

"How was it?" he asked.

"It was good."

He looked at me with an expression I had seen often back in the day; it was like a parent who was about to scold their kid for eating cookies before dinner.

"Okay, okay. I had fun. The city is great, but I told you that before. It's always busy, always... alive. You can find something to do at any time of the day or night. You'll see new faces everywhere you go... new people to meet. But you were in LA, I'm sure you know what I mean."

"I do. But I didn't think of the 'new faces' I saw as people to meet. I just thought of them as strangers—a sea of strangers. It was a lot different from here, where you can walk down the street and know just about every single person. In fact, it was..."

"The opposite," we said in unison.

However, I didn't think the fact that we both thought the cities we'd gone to for college were opposite to Riverdale meant the same to both of us. Or at least, I wasn't going to let him think it did. I was assuming he didn't like that it was so different, while I did... that is, most of the time. There were days when I didn't like the sea of the unknown and craved the familiarity of Riverdale, but I shrugged those days aside, attributing the feeling to homesickness and considering myself simply anxious about venturing into the world.

"Exactly." He nodded. "I guess I'm just a homebody underneath it all. I always knew I'd come back to Riverdale. And you... " he paused and looked at me curiously.

"What?"

"I don't know, I always pegged you for one, too. But apparently you couldn't—and can't—wait to get away."

I shrugged and took another sip of my shake.

"Did you date?" he asked next.

"Did you?"

"Some."

He probably dated dozens. "Me too."

Amy walked over and placed our meals down with a smile, then left us to converse.

"Cali girls are a lot different from the girls here."

"Better?"

"Maybe to some, but not to me." He locked his gaze with mine and remained silent for a moment, like he was trying to say something without words. "How were those New York guys? As wild and free as you like them?"

I broke eye contact and thought about Rick. Well, he was certainly wild, that was for sure. But I never went out searching for a guy who was "wild and free," so I was a bit confused as to where Riley would get that idea. In fact, I never really searched for *any* guy. Rick just sort of... happened. My eyes wandered around the diner and discovered Amy peeking out from the kitchen area, glancing toward us while talking on the phone. I'd bet my life she was telling someone that Riley and I were sitting here together, just like the old days.

"Yeah, I guess they were."

"Why didn't you stay with any of them?"

"How do you know I'm not seeing someone?"

He leaned back against the booth and eyed me while he picked up a fry, dipped it into his honey mustard sauce, and popped it into his mouth. "I suppose I don't." He chewed it slowly for a moment. "I wish you'd take down the stupid wall you put up between us."

"There's no wall."

He suddenly looked agitated. "The hell there isn't. We've always been open with each other. We've always been able to talk to each other about anything and everything. You never used to need me to ask questions, you used to ramble just fine. But now... now you're acting like we're nothing more than acquaintances and I'm someone you need to be suspicious about."

"Eight years is a long time. People change."

"You just told me there's a lot that *hasn't* changed."

"Well, maybe I was exaggerating." I looked down at my sandwich and no longer felt hungry.

"Jesus, Belles, I don't believe that. I wish you would just tell me."

"Tell you what?"

"Everything! Beginning with why you suddenly realized I wasn't good enough for you and broke it off the way you did." I looked up, expecting to find him ready to yell at me, but instead I found him looking rather hurt. Of course he wouldn't scream at me—this was Riley, not Rick. I was momentarily stunned at the absurd idea he had that I didn't think him good enough. I had to set him straight.

"I—" His phone began to ring, interrupting me.

"Damn it." He pulled it out, then glanced at me apologetically. "I have to get this."

I nodded my consent.

"Hi." He was silent as he listened to the voice on the other end. I couldn't make out what was being said, but the high-pitched, female voice was familiar. He reached into his pocket again and took out his wallet. "Alexis, just calm down all right?"

Instantly, I wished I'd told him not to pick it up. My stomach twisted into uneasy knots.

"I'll be right over." He hung up, then took some money out and dropped it on the table. "I'm really sorry, Belles. I've got to go...we'll finish this soon, okay?"

I wanted to tell him that it wasn't okay—that he shouldn't talk to me about being open when he wasn't being open with me about his relationship with Alexis. I wanted to tell him he better not think we were going to make a habit of keeping this corner booth warm together. But instead I just looked at him as he stood up and headed for the door.

"Riley, you can't be finished already?" Amy hollered over.

"No, but I've got to meet someone. Wrap it up for me, will you? I'll grab it on my way home tonight."

"You got it, honey."

He pushed open the door, glanced back and gave me a half smile that, despite everything, made my stomach flip... and then walked out. I watched him for a moment as he headed up the street, then stared down at the uneaten sandwich in front of me, wondering what Amy would make of the situation.

———————

I thought about lunch with Riley a lot the remainder of that week. I didn't see him again, except for those times I caught sight of him heading into his office or driving off toward home or Harwinton. But in between batches of cookies and pies and other work at the bakery, which remained as busy as it had been on opening day, I wondered why it mattered to him that I'd put up a wall. I wondered what he saw in Alexis and how on earth he could possibly think I broke everything off because I didn't find him good enough, despite all the times I'd said otherwise. Was it so hard for him to see that I thought he was *too* good? That I didn't want him to get stuck in Riverdale and never reach his potential? That *I* didn't want to get stuck in Riverdale? Was I wrong in thinking he needed, and deserved, to get away? I didn't think he'd come back once he left. I thought he'd see how great the world was and stay away—but he came back, just like Nathan had, and so many others. Were Riverdale's residents stuck because they chose to be?

Truth be told, I didn't mind it here as much as I tried to convince myself I did, and the things I claimed to dislike—the fierce loyalty, the love of tradition, how everyone knew each other, and the difficulty of keeping a secret—could actually be seen as charming if you looked at them the right way. After the people in town started to get to know Clara for instance, they came together and welcomed her with open arms, getting excited about the baby right along with her. When word got out that we were working on the bakery, everyone helped in their own little way, determined to bring a piece of Riverdale's history back to life. I didn't think either of those things would have happened in the city. So why was it, despite this knowledge, that I still felt like I needed to leave?

It wasn't until Sunday morning, when Mr. Carter came upon me reclining on a lawn chair in the backyard, that my thoughts were diverted to another topic.

"I'm mighty surprised at just how well those new recipes have taken."

I turned to look at him and smiled. "Are you really?"

"I knew they'd do just fine eventually, just didn't think they'd take so fast."

"Are you happy with how things are turning out?"

He took a seat in one of the chairs beside me and puffed on his pipe. "Suppose I am."

"Good. Clara and you make a great team."

He nodded. "She's a special lady."

I could tell he was in rare form—his rough countenance had been temporarily placed aside.

"Course, who knows how long she'll stick around. She'll probably up and leave soon after you do, if not the same time." His tone became slightly resentful.

"I don't think so. She loves it here and was pretty adamant about staying in town. Besides, she doesn't have any family, so where would she go?"

"Hmph, family don't got nothin' to do with it."

"That's not what Nathan says. He says that's why he stayed in town. Seems like that's why Riley came back too. Most everyone stays around."

"Not you—and all your family's right here. And not my Molly either."

"Well I'm here now, aren't I? And we're only two ex... wait, who?" I was positive his wife's name had been Clarissa.

He puffed silently on his pipe for a moment. "Never finished that conversation we started in the kitchen a while back."

I pulled the chair to a sitting position and gave him my full attention. "No, we didn't. Who's Molly?"

"I know you think there aren't secrets in this town, and everyone talks about everybody else's business."

It was true, I did.

"But the thing with small towns is, sometimes a situation comes along, and it makes a person so sad that the people don't talk about it. There ain't no gossip. No spreading it around." What was he talking about? "That's what happened with Clarissa. And with Molly." I was about to object—I'd heard great things about Clarissa before—but he continued on. "You say people don't leave this town, and maybe that's true a lot of times, but it ain't true all the time. Molly left."

"Mr. Carter, I'm confused. Who's Molly?"

He took another puff from his pipe and paused. "She was my daughter."

The baby cradle. I looked at him speechless. Mr. Carter had a daughter?

He let out an empty laugh at my expression. "You look like you just caught sight of a ghost."

"Well, you never... I never..." I was having trouble forming a coherent sentence. "You have a daughter?"

He nodded slowly. "I did."

"What happened to her?"

"She left."

"What do you mean, 'she left?'"

"Just that. Woke up one morning and she'd gone."

"Where'd she go?" I inquired.

He shrugged in reply. "Ain't got any idea. She was a wild one. Always wantin' to explore and see new things—reminds me of you in that way—and wouldn't you know, the both of you left!" He laughed the empty laugh again. "Can't say I know exactly why she did it. Maybe she just wanted to see what was out there. Maybe it was 'cause she didn't know how much I loved her. Lord knows I did, but I never was one for showing it."

I nodded, knowing that to be true, but at the same time I was still able to tell when Mr. Carter liked—or didn't like—someone or something even without any showy affection. How could his own daughter not see that? "But what about your wife? What about Clarissa?"

"Clarissa had nothin' but love in her bones—enough for me, the bakery, the baby, and just about everyone else in town. That was her way. But even that wasn't enough to keep Molly around. She was gone a day after turning eighteen. Broke Clarissa's heart—she was never the same."

My own heart ached at what that must have been like. "And yours too, I'd imagine."

"Hmph. After that, Clarissa and I put all we had into the bakery. That was all we had left—apple pies and each other."

"How is it I never heard about her?"

"Told you. There are times when the folk in a small town know it's best to just leave well enough alone. Was a long time ago now... Molly left, oh, about fifteen years before you were born, I'd say."

"What about my mom? Did she know? I mean, if she grew up here, everyone must have known her!"

"Of course they did. But like I said, no one talked about it. And with time, people move on."

"Why didn't you look for her? What if she was kidnapped?" My mind jumped ahead and I started to think about searching for her online.

He shook his head and my planning halted. "She wasn't kidnapped. Left a note. An' I could feel it—she'd just gone. Told you she was wild... but she was sweet too. And she reminds me of Clara in that way—the sweetness. Guess Molly was a bit like the both of ya, but Clara mostly, I'd say."

The odd way he would look at Clara at times suddenly made sense. "Is that why you're telling me all this?"

He responded with a half nod. "Some days she looks just like her. I even swear I can see bits of Clarissa in some of what she does."

I started to wonder if maybe his age wasn't getting to him more than I'd thought. "Mr. Carter... do you think Clara is actually Molly?"

He let out a genuine laugh and looked at me as though I were crazy. The lucid look in his eyes made me feel silly for asking such a thing. "Annebelle Roth, I'm getting up there in age, but I ain't gone yet. Clara isn't Molly, that's impossible. I just... Alls I'm sayin' is she reminds me of her. One of those uncanny resemblances."

I nodded in understanding. "So why *are* you telling me this then?"

He shrugged. "I know you catch me lookin' at her funny at times, and I knew you'd be wonderin' bout that baby cradle."

I smiled. "You know me well."

His eyes took on a distant look again. "I can't tell you how long after Molly left I blamed myself for maybe not bein' all that I could to her... spendin' more time with her and sayin' 'I love you' and all that. Sometimes I still wonder if she'd have stayed or not. You always comin' to the bakery growing up, that helped. I liked havin' you around, and there weren't many I could stand. There *still* aren't too many. I do better by myself." I didn't totally believe that, but I kept silent. "You never listened, you're such a sassafras. You just hung around, eating those sticky buns. And it made me not think about Molly, or miss Clarissa so much."

The fact that my being in the bakery had actually meant something to Mr. Carter made me feel a bit weepy.

"Then you up and left too." His gruff tone returned with that last statement, and I looked at him in surprise. "I was mad at you for leaving for some time, you know. Then I figured it was bound to happen. 'Course you wouldn't stick around, you got a lot goin' for you. I know a couple of biscuits and some scowls from me weren't incentive to stay."

His hesitation towards me when I'd first returned, and his extra gruff attitude suddenly made sense; when I left it was like Molly leaving all over again. I couldn't help but feel terribly sorry for doing that to him, despite it being unintentional.

"After you came back, first I was glad to see your face, then I got to thinkin' 'what was the point of comin' back just to leave soon after?' And that got me upset all over again. I'd be a whole lot happier if you'd just say you'd stay in town and not keep goin' and comin' like a traveling salesman."

I wasn't sure whether to laugh, cry, yell, or apologize. "I can't say that right now Mr. Carter. But if it makes you feel any better, I don't have a set date to leave just yet."

"Hmph. So you're just gonna up and surprise us then?"

"No, not at all. I promise I won't leave until I make sure everything's set here in town."

"Things ain't ever gonna be set, so guess you just have to stay then."

I found it extremely endearing that he wanted me to stay, but even though, I could admit, aspects of town were starting to grow on me, I wasn't convinced it was where I was meant to be. "I'm not going to tell you I'll stay in town, Mr. Carter. I've got to figure myself out, and I just don't know if I'll be able to do that here."

He glared at me, and I knew our moments of sentiment were coming to an end. "Fine, you just go ahead and scurry on out of town." He got up from the chair. "Better head on in to the kitchen. Don't want Clara or that Meredith makin' a mess of things."

"Mr. Carter?"

He halted and turned back toward me.

"I'm sorry about your daughter."

He grunted in reply. "Can't change the past, and I don't think I'll ever get to know why she left. Never could understand you women. I still don't." Then he disappeared inside.

It was somewhat comforting knowing I wasn't the only one confused about things.

13

Routine fell over Apple Blossoms after that first week. We chose our official hours, tweaked our offerings and added coffee, tea, hot chocolate, and a couple of other beverages to the menu after approval from the ladies at Amy's. Along with the basics—Mr. Carter's bread, rolls, biscuits, baguettes, and muffins—we decided to continue with a selection of cookies each day and pies to be sold by the slice (entire pies could be ordered ahead). For the most part, the kind of pies we offered would be dependent on the season so our fruit could come from local farmers. At present I was enjoying the strawberry and rhubarb pies we'd recently added while looking forward to blueberry cream cheese in mid-July and raspberry-peach come August.

Sunday dinners happened at my mom's as usual, and before I knew it, I'd been to three and it was the last week of June. With almost a month behind us, we were feeling like quite the bakers. Meredith had returned to work at the vet, and a lot of her free time was spent with Jeremy. I'd get texts from her almost daily about something sweet he'd done, and I couldn't help but think of how our roles had switched. In high school, I was the one telling her about the things my boyfriend did, and she'd fawn over how adorable they were. Now, it was the other way around. But that fact didn't upset me. On the contrary, I thought it was how things should be. If anything, she deserved to be treated like royalty more than I did. She was such a wonderful person.

I stuck two spoons into the bowl of dough I'd just mixed up, scooped out a heap, and placed it on the waiting cookie sheet. It was extra quiet in the bakery this evening. Clara was due any day now, and with quite a bit of convincing, I was finally able to get her upstairs to rest—she'd be baking right up until labor if I let her. I knew she was extra determined to work hard because of her circumstance. Despite getting along with everyone and truly integrating herself in town, I knew to some extent she still felt like an outsider who had to prove her worth. I wondered how long it would take for her to feel like a Riverdale resident instead of a visitor.

I placed the sheet of cookies in the oven, wiped my hands on my apron, and walked to the front of the bakery. The front room felt and looked completely different than it had when I'd first returned. Even when there weren't any customers, Apple Blossoms still felt... alive. It was a good feeling. I grabbed a towel from behind the counter and began wiping down the tops. After being hounded endlessly by Doris, Mr. Carter had gone for an evening of bingo at the church. He'd tried using the bakery as an excuse not to go, but I assured him things would be fine and ushered him out the door. It would be good for him to get out now and then, and I hoped he'd do just that now that Clara and I were around. I had an inkling he'd been at home far too much over the years.

A deep roll of thunder sounded from outside, and I looked to find the sky had turned a dark gray. The branches on the trees out front were swaying in the wind, and I walked over to open one of the windows. It'd been humid lately, and there was nothing quite like a sudden downpour accompanied by a breeze to cool things off.

As if on cue, rain began to fall as I raised the glass. I inhaled the fresh scent it created, then wandered back to the kitchen to take care of the cause of another aroma heading my way—the Ebony and Ivory Cookies I was baking. They were one of my favorites—traditional chocolate chip kicked up a notch with the addition of white chocolate chips and some extra spices. I took them out of the oven, placed in another sheet, then halted at the sound of banging on the bakery door. I hurried out, instantly worried something was wrong, but that worry disappeared as I saw Meredith standing in the rain. She was soaked, but grinning from ear to ear, and as I unlocked the door she came rushing in.

"Belles!" She threw her arms around me and gave me a hug, and I shrieked in surprise at the motion.

"Merekins, you're soaking wet! Get off!" I laughed and tried pulling away.

She released me and took a step back, her grin still in place.

"What is it?"

Her grin widened.

"Meredith, *what?*"

She held out her hand. I felt butterflies in my stomach even before I glanced down, knowing what I'd find. I grinned along with her as I took hold of her hand and looked down to see a diamond sitting on her ring finger. The sudden clap of thunder that vibrated through the air drowned out our screams of excitement. It was probably for the best, since an outsider would likely think a murder had just taken place. This time I was the one to go in for a hug, not caring the least bit she was wet.

We jumped up and down like schoolgirls, and I felt like crying out of happiness. "Mere, I can't believe it! You're getting married!"

"I know!" She choked out, and I realized she really *was* crying, which made me laugh. I hugged her again, then stood back and gripped her by the shoulders.

"This is so exciting! I'm so happy. Tell me how it happened." I grabbed her by the wrist and pulled her over to the counter, pushing her down onto one of the stools. I sat beside her and gazed at her wide-eyed, my chin resting on my hands.

She laughed at my expression. "You look like a kid on Christmas morning."

"Oh please, this is better than Christmas morning! Tell me!"

She wiped away the stray tears that had fallen and smiled at me. "Well... after work today he came to the vet and picked me up because we'd made plans to go out for dinner."

"Mmhmm."

"But he said he wanted to show me something first."

"What was it?"

"I'm getting to that! Remember that day at the gas station when you first got back?"

"How could I forget! Paint for the bathroom."

She rolled her eyes. "Exactly. And we went to the gas station..."

"And I *knew* there was going to be something between you two!"

"You did not!"

"Oh please, I'm your best friend, of course I knew. You were fawning over him and he kept giving you the once over."

She blushed prettily. "Whatever. Anyway, remember how he told you he was saving up for some land near Spring Meadow?"

I nodded. "About the same time you spilled gasoline all over yourself?"

"Yeah that. I was just so surprised he was planning to buy land! Well, he brought me there. And it's not just 'some land,' it's the old Miller place."

"The Miller place? You mean with the fields we used to ride horses in? And the white house you always wanted?"

"Exactly. The Miller place with those beautiful fields and that beautiful farmhouse and that big old barn." A dreamy look appeared in her eyes as she thought about it. "I love it there, I always have. And can you believe it, that's the 'land' he means to buy! So, he took me there and walked me out to the middle of the hayfield on top of that hill. You know the one—you can see all the property from there and the river off in the distance..."

I nodded, remembering it to be a beautiful spot.

"Then he told me how he meant to buy it and that he'd been negotiating with whichever of the Miller boys is still around—Jim, I think—over in Cypress. He told me he's nearly there, and that he's always wanted that spot and couldn't picture himself living anywhere else." She paused and toyed with the ring on her finger.

"Would you please continue!"

"He told me he always knew he wanted to live there, have a small farm and, once he found a woman he wanted to marry, raise a family."

"Once he *found* a woman?"

She laughed again. "When he said that, I thought that meant he didn't love me—that he hadn't found that woman yet. I swear my heart dropped out through my feet. I started to turn away from him, to look out over the meadows hoping he wouldn't notice I might just cry, but he grabbed my hand and turned me back toward him. That's when he got down on his knee. And he said..." She halted again, and this time I was certain it was because she really *would* cry. "He said that he'd found her. He told me that he'd actually found her years ago but had always been too shy to try and catch her."

I smiled so wide I thought my cheeks would split.

"He asked me if I'd help him make his dreams come true—he asked me if there was any way he could become a part of my dreams, too. Then he asked me if I'd be his wife."

I jumped up from my stool and gave her another hug, which was accompanied by a shriek of joy. This time there was no thunder to cover it up. "That is absolutely perfect! Then what happened?"

"Well, I said 'yes' of course. And then we kissed. And then... well, then it started to pour!" She laughed, and I began to right along with her. "So we ran down the hill hand in hand and hopped into his truck and headed on over, because of course, you were the first I wanted to tell, especially since you're going to be the maid of honor and all. I mean, if you want."

"If I want! What are you, crazy? Of course I do! I'd be honored! We need to celebrate... where are we going to celebrate? Where's Jeremy?"

"Somehow I knew you'd say that. Jeremy's across the street telling Riley."

I felt the butterflies in my stomach again, and this time they weren't out of excitement for Meredith.

"We were thinking about a couple of celebratory drinks at The Tavern. Will you come with us?"

"Oh please, like you have to ask! Let me just shut off the oven. I'll finish the cookies later." I headed toward the kitchen then paused and looked back at her soaking ensemble. "Merekins, you wanna borrow some clothes?"

"I was hoping you'd say that."

She followed me into the kitchen where I put the remaining dough in the fridge, pulled out the cookies that had just finished, shut off the oven, and headed upstairs. I began rummaging through my closet while Meredith explored my drawers for something suitable. I grabbed a couple dresses and tossed them at her.

"Try one of these."

She obliged, asking as she moved to put on the first, "Where's Clara?"

"She's probably sleeping. She's been working way too much for someone who could go into labor at any time."

"I can't believe she's going to have her baby soon. That's so exciting."

"I know it. I'll go look in on her and see if she's awake." I left Meredith to get dressed and walked over to Clara's door. A soft knock garnered no answer, so I carefully opened the door and peeked inside. She was curled up on the bed, fast asleep beneath the covers, and I thought it likely she'd sleep through the entire night. The door to the nursery was wide open, and I could admit I was rather anxious for its inhabitant to arrive. I smiled at the thought, grabbed a piece of paper from her desk and placed it on her nightstand after scribbling a note. I returned to my room to find Meredith lying on my bed in a cream-colored cotton dress with cap sleeves, eyeing her ring.

"Great choice!" I assured her. "You look gorgeous."

I returned to the closet to select one for myself and settled on a peach colored halter. As I pulled it over my head, Meredith's phone started ringing from her purse. She sprung up to grab it.

"Hey, Jer," she answered. "Mmhmm. Okay, we'll be right down." She hung up. "The guys are waiting in the truck out front."

"Okay." I zipped up the dress as far as I could then turned so Meredith could finish it up.

"You look great, too" she told me, as I started to pull my hair back and secure it with bobby pins.

"Thanks, Merekins. There are sandals in the closet if you want to grab a pair."

She started searching through my shoes while I finished with my hair.

"I feel like we're in high school again, about to go out on a double date or something," Meredith stated as she pulled out a pair of gold sandals.

I laughed, undeniably excited. "Except for the part where you're *engaged*—not dating—and Riley and I aren't a couple."

She fastened the sandals on her feet then stood up. "Well, you certainly could be if you weren't so stubborn."

"Are you being sarcastic right now? There's no way I'd ever be girlfriend number two."

"What?" She looked at me with a confused expression. Her phone rang again. "Hello?" She listened but continued to look at me oddly. "I told you we're coming!"

I shook my head at their impatience, grabbed my purse and headed for the door.

"We'll be right there. Yes, we're on the stairs right now. Oh, you can? Well we're about to be... They can see the light from the street," she informed me and rolled her eyes. I flipped the switch. "There—it's off now, see? Now we really are on the stairs. Okay, I love you, too."

"Did you really just say 'I love you' when we're going to see him in fifteen seconds?"

She blushed again. "Shut up, Belles."

I pulled open the front door, and we stepped out into the rainy evening. Jeremy's red truck was waiting beside the street and as we ran over, Riley stepped out of the passenger side to open the door to the cab. When Meredith reached him, he gave her a tight hug and said "congratulations" before she hopped into the truck. Then he looked at me, smiled, and grabbed me for a hug as well. I hadn't been expecting one, so the sudden feel of his arms around me caused the butterflies to move about in a tizzy and my skin to erupt in tingles. "You look amazing," he stated matter-of-factly before releasing me.

I gave him a shaky smile. "Thanks, you too." I hopped up beside Meredith.

"I'm not crazy, right? This does feel like high school, doesn't it?" Meredith draped her arm over the front seat so Jeremy could reach and hold her hand.

The guys laughed. "I guess so," Jeremy responded. "Or at least a high school that *could* have been. But you and I weren't dating then... and, well..." He glanced at Riley. "Now *they* aren't dating and we're engaged."

"Don't forget the fact that you and I didn't talk nearly as much in high school as we do now." Riley added.

"That too," he agreed.

"So really, what they're saying Mere, is this isn't like high school at all," I concluded, and they laughed.

"Well, whatever, I still like it."

"I don't blame you, Miss Fiancée. I don't think it's half bad myself!" I looked into the side mirror and saw Riley smiling at me. "So, any wedding ideas?"

Jeremy and Meredith nodded at the same time.

"Oh! I wasn't expecting you to actually say 'yes' already! Care to share?" I implored.

"We want to get married this summer."

I raised an eyebrow at how soon they were planning.

"And have it at the Miller place," added Jeremy. "Everything should be set in July... and I'd like us to be married before we live together, so..."

"You know me, Belles. I'm traditional, but I don't like big celebrations and neither does Jeremy. So we thought that would be—"

"Perfect," I finished. "And it is!"

"Of course, we only talked it over for a minute on the way to see you two, so there are still a million details to work out—but you'll help me with those, right?"

"Oh, you know I will! I can't wait."

Jeremy raised Meredith's hand to his mouth and kissed it, then turned up the radio at her request.

———

We stepped inside The Tavern and asked the hostess for a secluded table in the back of the restaurant. There was still a pretty good chance we'd bump into someone we knew, and there seemed to be an unspoken agreement between the four of us: we felt like enjoying our little celebration completely uninterrupted before anyone else caught news of the engagement.

As Jeremy and Riley pulled out our chairs for us (making it feel like it was in fact a double date) and we sat down, I took a look around. The Tavern was in no way a fancy establishment by Manhattan standards, but it was still quite nice with dark mahogany wood walls, gleaming floors, burgundy accents, and a large fireplace at one end that made shadows dance around the room. The hum of the other patrons' voices mixed with the soft jazz music that was playing, and the delightful smells of food wafted over to us from the kitchen.

"Welcome to The Tavern, my name's Marissa and I'll be taking care of you tonight. Can I get you something to drink?" I looked up at the young waitress who had wandered over and smiled, thankful it wasn't anyone we knew. I was about to rattle off the name of a cocktail, when Riley piped up from across the table.

"Actually, can you bring us a bottle of champagne to start? We've a reason to celebrate tonight."

"Of course, Riley, which kind would you like? We have—" I raised an eyebrow at the use of his name. Another girl who knows him? I should stop being so surprised.

"Moët Impérial will be perfect, thanks Marissa."

The waitress nodded and headed off.

Moët? He really had turned into a high-class act—not that he hadn't always been underneath it all—but champagne? Most of the guys in town would have simply offered up a cheer with a bottle of Bud.

"Riley, you didn't have to order champagne. We could have just as easily celebrated with a beer." I smiled at my point being proven so soon.

"Jeremy, you just got engaged. That's not the same as the Giants winning the Super Bowl. This definitely calls for champagne."

Marissa returned with the bottle and showed it to Riley. "Would you like me to open it for you?" He shook his head no, and she set it down accompanied by the ice bucket. "Will you be having anything to eat tonight?"

"I think we just need some appetizers to go with our drinks. How does that sound?" The three of us nodded in agreement, and I couldn't help but admire the way he took the lead—I liked that. It didn't feel controlling in the same sense as Rick, just self-assured. "How about you bring out The Tavern Plate for us?"

"Sure thing." She headed off again.

"You seem to be well acquainted with this place—even the waitress knows you! Do you bring a lot of your dates here?" I knew it probably wasn't a good thing to ask, but I couldn't resist.

He raised an eyebrow at me the way I had at him minutes ago. "No, actually, but I have meetings with some of my clients here. And I worked with Marissa's mom on her divorce settlement."

"Oh." It was a good thing the lighting was dark, because I was sure I was blushing. I watched as Riley expertly popped open the bottle of champagne without shooting the cork halfway across the room— something I'd probably do—and filled each of our flutes.

"How many dates do you think I go on anyway?" He asked as he handed Jeremy and Meredith their glasses.

I shrugged. "I don't know." Our fingers touched briefly as he handed me my champagne, and, as always, they instantly started to tingle. "A lot."

He let out a chuckle as he raised his champagne. "All right." He looked from Meredith to Jeremy. "Here's to you two. Congratulations on your engagement. I couldn't imagine anyone better for each other." Our flutes clinked together, and as we lifted them to our lips, I looked across to find Riley looking at me over the top of his glass. He winked as he took back the champagne, which led me to take mine back as well. So much for sipping. Why was he toying with me? As the delicious liquid starting gliding down my throat, I began to feel more relaxed. A few more of these and I wouldn't care. I put down my empty glass and turned to Meredith.

"Let's talk wedding, shall we?" She grinned and required no further prompting. Soon we were planning out the big day with the guys, who added their occasional comedic commentary between bites of appetizers. I looked over more than once to find my glass had been refilled, and as we continued to sip and laugh, I felt myself getting more and more excited. Taking my maid of honor duties quite seriously, I took out a pen and notepad from my bag and started jotting down notes: August 8, afternoon, ceremony at the church, lavender and cream, joint reception/housewarming at the Miller (soon to be Larson!) place.

"I know you said you don't like big celebrations, Merekins, but you do realize that's not likely to happen with the reception, don't you? I mean, the entire town's going to show up."

She took a swig of her champagne and rolled her eyes in an adorable manner that had Jeremy leaning over to kiss her. "I know," she admitted, grinning from ear to ear and not looking the least bit perturbed.

"Well, in the scheme of things, it still won't be too, too big since Riverdale isn't huge to begin with," added Jeremy.

"At least they can't come along on the honeymoon," I added, which she gasped at the mention of.

"Honeymoon! Do we get to go on a honeymoon?"

Jeremy laughed. "I think we can probably work that out."

She shrieked in excitement, and I jotted down "choose honeymoon destination" with extra exclamation points to capture her exuberance. Our conversation continued to revolve around wedding and post wedding plans as we finished off the champagne and switched to wine. Eventually the guys' talk changed to other topics, but Meredith and I kept on track, getting increasingly bubbly from the bubbly and extra romantic from the wine. The effect it had on Meredith became apparent when, after talking about how great Riley and I would look walking down the aisle together, she sighed and exclaimed in only a slightly slurred tone, "Can't you two just start dating again?"

I nearly choked on my drink. A brief silence followed, and I found Riley looking at me as though waiting for me to say something. My liquid courage urged me to call Riley out as the player he'd become.

"There's no way Riley and I are dating. I refuse to be girlfriend number two. Actually, I refuse to ever date anyone who would want a girlfriend number two!" I thought I sounded quite logical, and had firmly made my point, but it was answered with yet another silence and a confused look from the others.

Meredith stared at me. "Okay. What? You mentioned something about this before we left and I was confused then, too. What are you talking about 'girlfriend number two?'"

"I thought I was being pretty clear," I replied. "I'm not going to be the second girl, and I don't get why you're encouraging it! That's not fair to me *or* Alexis, and even though I don't like her one bit, I still wouldn't want her to get cheated on. And I know you've known Riley a long time, too, but you've known me longer. I don't get why you would ever try and tell me to be with someone who obviously wouldn't treat me the way I deserve to be treated, seeing as he thinks it's okay to date more than one person at a time now. It doesn't make any sense. And I don't even get how you could do that Riley. I mean, you're a gentleman in so many ways... but this? Not very gentlemanlike." I paused and took a breath, well aware that my tangent didn't make me sound as sober as I was trying to seem.

I looked from Meredith to the guys to find Jeremy chuckling and Riley looking at me with the same expression as Mere, tinged with disbelief.

"Dating... Alexis?" he finally said.

"Yes. Alexis. Her lifelong dream come true!" I reaffirmed.

"Belles, I'm not dating Alexis." His tone was gentle, and while a part of me wanted to tell him I thought he was lying just for the sake of saying so, I knew instantly that he wasn't.

"You're not?"

"Of course he's not you idiot!" exclaimed Meredith incredulously. "What kind of a guy do you think he is?"

I threw her a look and Jeremy instantly shushed her, still chuckling to himself.

"No, I'm not. Whatever gave you that idea?"

"Um, well, let's see, you're always with her, you're always coming to Harwinton, and when she calls you go running to her like you'll die if you don't see her."

Jeremy's chuckle turned into a full-blown laugh, and this time it was Meredith who shushed *him*, despite clearly trying not to laugh herself.

"Belles, she's a client."

"Exactly! She... she's what?" Once again I was glad it was dark in the restaurant because I was certain my cheeks were red, and not just because of the alcohol.

"She's a client. She's trying to get full ownership of her salon, but her partner, who's not exactly the nicest person, isn't making that easy."

"Alexis isn't exactly the nicest person either," mumbled Meredith.

"True, but she's paying me to represent her. So if it seems like I go running to her, that's because it's my job to—within limits."

I was feeling sillier by the moment. "That day at Amy's..."

"Her partner was throwing a huge fit at the salon, that's why I had to rush. I didn't want her doing anything that might jeopardize the proceedings. I didn't say anything because I know you don't like her..."

I looked down at my empty wine glass, suddenly wishing it were full so I could drown myself in it. "Oh."

"Belle, did you seriously think he was dating Alexis all this time?"

"Shut up, Meredith. No one exactly said otherwise! And Alexis definitely made it seem that way the day the two of them were at Amy's."

Meredith laughed. "Okay, okay. In your defense that *B* did, but I just assumed—and I think everyone else did too—that there was no way you'd think Riley would date her. I mean, you've known him for how long?"

"People change." I mumbled.

"In some ways," stated Riley. "But like you said before, they stay the same too."

"Phew! Well! I'm glad that's all cleared up!" Meredith reached for her glass and noticed it was empty. She pouted as she picked it up. "Oh boo. Let's order some more wine and celebrate again."

"I think we've celebrated our engagement enough for one night," Jeremy said.

"I don't mean celebrate our engagement silly, I mean celebrate Riley and Annebelle dating again. And our first double date!" She let out a hiccup as she finished her sentence, grinning from ear to ear.

"This isn't a double date," Riley and I said in unison. I looked at him, and even though I had said it too, my heart dropped a little at how quick he was to refute her statement.

"Anyway, I think we should probably get on home, don't you? We'll have plenty more celebratory opportunities in the near future."

"You're right Jer, let's go... can we sleep at the Miller Place?" She gazed at her fiancé with dreamy eyes.

Jeremy laughed. "It doesn't belong to us yet."

"So what. Let's sleep in the barn. I wanna sleep with you in the barn. We don't have to tell anyone." She looked from me to Riley "Shh, don't tell." She looked at each of us again. "You two are *so* cute together."

Even though I was feeling quite stupid at my own assumptions about Riley, I couldn't help but laugh at my usually sweet and shy but now quite drunk and brazen best friend. I was feeling a bit tipsy myself but I tried not to show it, and managed to stand up without knocking anything over. But when I realized we hadn't paid, I spun around so fast I seemed to beat my own vision and lost my balance. Riley grabbed my elbow to steady me, and the tingles started up again.

"You all right?"

"Whoa. Yeah, I just spun around too fast—I realized we haven't paid yet."

He held on for a moment, then released me. "It's taken care of."

"But how? The check wasn't even brought over."

"I put it on my tab."

"They have that here?"

He chuckled. "Not really, but when you're here as much as I am, they make exceptions. Kind of like that 'reserved booth' at Amy's."

We shared a smile at that, then Meredith's voice called out, "Come on you lovebirds, let's go have a slumber party in the barn." She continued to go on about that sleepover right up until Jeremy stopped in front of the bakery. When she looked out the window and saw where we were her pouty expression came back. "Oh double boo. We're not having our slumber party, are we?"

I leaned over and gave her a hug. "Not tonight, Merekins. I'll talk to you tomorrow. Love you."

She hugged me back but continued to pout. "Fine. You and Riley can have a slumber party, and Meremy, I mean, Jeremy and I, will go have one, too."

I laughed at the name she'd accidentally said. "Meremy! That's like one of those names given to celebrity couples—Meredith and Jeremy put together!" I got out of the truck as Riley opened the door, continuing to laugh.

"Please, spare me the name, Belle," pleaded Jeremy. "Meredith, you wanna come up front?" He patted the seat beside him, but Meredith just sprawled out in back.

"Nope, I think I'm just gonna take a nap before our slumber party." She flung an arm across her eyes, and Riley shut the door.

"Have fun," he told Jeremy.

"Gee thanks," he responded, chuckling.

Before he drove off, Meredith's voice could be heard from the back: "Thanks for the champagne, Riley. You two are a perfect couple."

And then they were gone. Riley and I stood silent in the dark for a moment. The rain had stopped, and the storm had succeeded in removing the humidity. The night air was cool and fresh. The only light came from a nearby streetlamp; the only sound from a chorus of crickets.

"I think she means you and the champagne." I finally said.

"What?"

"You and the champagne—you make a perfect couple." I cringed at the comment, thinking after it was too late how dumb a statement it was. I was nervous. How could I be nervous? This was Riley!

"I'm pretty sure she was talking about us."

"Yeah, well she was drunk. So, thanks for that."

"Thanks for what?"

"Getting my best friend drunk."

He laughed. "You're welcome."

"That was half sarcasm. But really though, thanks for the drinks and all tonight. That was nice of you."

"You're welcome again. So... you really thought I was dating Alexis?" He was standing in front of me now, and the pace of my heartbeats picked up a notch.

"Yes, I did."

"That's completely ridiculous." He lifted his hand, traced a finger along my jaw line, then tilted my face up toward him. "I wasn't attracted to her in high school, and I haven't been attracted to her since."

A part of me felt like stepping back out of his reach, and if it'd been earlier in the day I would have without a moment's hesitation. But the drinks, coupled with the celebratory mood of the evening and the knowledge he wasn't dating Alexis—it made me stay exactly where I was.

He bent his head a moment later, gently touching his lips to mine in a feathery kiss. Tingles shot from my lips all the way down to my toes. It only lasted a moment, but in that time the kiss felt both familiar and new. Familiar because of all those years we'd spent together, and new because of the time that had passed since then; it was more than eight years ago. Like he'd said—like I'd said—we were different, yet the same. We'd experienced things—more of life, other people—and we could feel that. I couldn't deny that I wanted to wrap my arms around him and discover all the things that were different—to make them familiar—but I kept my hands firmly by my side. He pulled away and stepped back.

"Completely ridiculous," he reiterated. "Night, Belles. I'll talk to you tomorrow." He turned and crossed the street toward his office and his car, becoming nothing more than a silhouette in the dark.

"Night," I replied faintly, not even sure he could hear me. I turned on my heels and headed into the bakery, locking the door behind me. The world was still spinning, and now I wasn't sure whether it was from the kiss, the champagne, or both—just like I wasn't sure whether the fact that he wasn't dating Alexis, that he was available, that he kissed me, and that I liked it, was good or bad. I walked through the kitchen, idly noticing either Clara or Mr. Carter had finished the cookies, then went through the living room and up to my room where I tossed myself on the bed, kicked off my shoes, and closed my eyes.

14

The sound of my cell phone woke me from deep sleep to pounding headache. I groaned at the piercing noise and at opening my eyes to find the room filled with blinding sunlight. I quickly closed them again and felt around for my phone.

"Hello?" I practically growled.

"Oh good. I'm so glad you're in as much pain as I am."

"Meredith?"

"Who else would it be? Are you still in bed?"

"What time is it? Ugh, what's wrong with me? I feel awful. Am I dead?" I was starting to whine.

"You should be one to complain. I feel like I got hit by a semi, and now I'm surrounded by the constant barking of dogs."

The events of the previous night slowly came back to me. "Champagne, I hate you."

"Yeah. Champagne and wine. Never again. Look, if I'm up and miserable you have to be, too. Get up and go downstairs. There's an old guy and a very pregnant girl running the bakery right now."

I rolled over and tossed back the covers, surprised to find my dress still on from the night before. "I think I was drunker than I thought."

"Are you still in your dress?"

"How'd you know?"

"I was too."

I laughed halfheartedly. "I thought you were going to have a slumber party?"

"Yeah, well, I fell asleep in the back of the truck. Jeremy carried me up to my room."

"So much for that."

"Tell me about it. Oh, and, the town knows about the engagement already; Jeremy told the guys at work this morning before I'd even made it to the vet. You know how that goes. So now I've had to plaster a smile on my face, too. Do you know how difficult that is when you're hungover?"

"Yes. You just made me smile. It sucks."

"Exactly. It's almost eleven-thirty. Get up!"

"Fine, bossy." I ended the call and got up to shower, heading downstairs twenty minutes later feeling better, but in desperate need of some coffee. I entered the bakery to find everything under control, although I shouldn't have expected anything less; Clara and Mr. Carter knew what they were doing.

"Good morning sleepyhead," Clara chimed when she saw me. I smiled as I looked at her, noticing the dark circles under her eyes had faded since I'd insisted she rest yesterday.

"Morning Clara, how are things?"

"Wonderful!" she said in a singsong voice. "And that's so exciting about Meredith!"

"Isn't it? How'd you find out?" I waved at Mr. Edwards who was sitting in the corner with his three kids eating goodies, then reached under the counter and took out a cinnamon raisin bagel.

"Riley was here this morning." She laughed as she looked at my selection. "Came in early... for a cinnamon raisin bagel actually."

Figures.

"He told me you all had quite a bit of champagne."

I nodded and pointed to my head. "Hence the constant throbbing."

"Think you're still in college or something? Partying like you're on spring break." Mr. Carter scolded. I turned and gave him a feeble smile.

"Ha. Ha. Very funny," I said sarcastically. "That was hardly the case. We just had a bit of champagne."

"Hmph. Wine, too, from what I hear."

"Yes, and wine. Trust me, you don't need to chide me. I'm in enough pain. This headache is the worst." I sliced the bagel and placed it in the toaster, then poured myself some coffee, leaving it black and bringing it immediately to my lips. "I wish you'd gotten to come, Clara, but I didn't want to wake you—you needed the rest. God that's good." I said of the brew.

She nodded in agreement. "I know. It wouldn't have been nearly as fun for me anyway—I couldn't have taken part in the champagne toasts. We'll just have to celebrate again as soon as this little one decides to arrive." She patted her stomach fondly.

"I hope it's soon. I can't wait to snuggle them!" I took the bagel from the toaster, spread cream cheese on both sides, and eagerly took a bite. "Soo, Mr. Carter...mind if I just kept to the back today?"

"Of course not," he grumbled. "Don't need a hungover helper bringing down the mood in the place anyhow."

I gave him a smile then headed to the kitchen to work on some of tomorrow's baking. I was in the zone before I knew it, swaying between methodically putting together batches of brownies and cookies and, I had to admit, daydreaming about Riley and the kiss we shared. I still wasn't sure what the best course of action was when it came to the two of us, but one thing was for certain—he wasn't two-timing anyone. And the more I thought about it, the more I felt ridiculous for even assuming he'd do such a thing.

Closing time came suddenly, and I cleaned up the kitchen while Clara and Mr. Carter tidied up the storefront. After they were done, Mr. Carter headed upstairs to freshen up for evening cribbage at the church, and Clara came in to help me finish.

"How was it today?" I asked her as I handed her a cloth for the countertops.

"Busy like always. I can't believe all the customers we get from out of town."

"I know. It is rather impressive. I'd really only thought about making sure the bakery stayed alive and well for everyone in Riverdale, I didn't think it'd become a local sensation."

I loaded up the dishwasher with the rest of the dishes that were lying around.

"I think it has a lot to do with those recipes you incorporated. They're such a hit!"

"It's not just that, I think it's about the variety—my recipes, your recipes, Mr. Carter's classics. It's a perfect mix of everything delicious! That article in the paper didn't hurt either."

"Isn't that the truth." She tossed the cloth into the laundry bag and tied it shut. When she started to lift it, I stepped over and took it from her, glancing at her baby bump.

"I don't think so, missy." She smiled at me and headed toward the door to the house. "So, tell me, are you glad you ran out of money in Riverdale?" I asked as I flipped the light switch on the wall and followed behind. "Or do you secretly regret the day you became a baker?"

"Oh no, never! I'm so happy here. I mean..." She paused, and I looked at her curiously.

"What is it?"

"Oh, nothing." She'd stopped in the middle of the living room, so I did as well. I dropped the laundry bag and crossed my arms in front of me.

"Clara, you know you can tell me anything."

"I know. It's just... well... do you ever regret the day you found me in the library?"

"Of course not! I'm so happy you're a part of our lives. Everyone here loves you. You're as much a part of Riverdale now as the rest of us."

She smiled feebly at me. "It makes me really happy to hear you say that. But Belle, there's something I have to tell you."

My mind went back to the beginning, to everyone warning me I knew nothing about this girl and saying she might be a criminal. I prepared myself for her admittance that she was actually on the run, but I knew even if that were the case, I'd help her. There had to be a good reason for whatever it was she'd done.

"What is it?"

"I didn't end up in Riverdale because I ran out of money."

"What?" I said, not sure what to expect.

"I mean, I was nearly out of money, but I came here on purpose."

I looked at her, confused. "What do you mean, you came here 'on purpose?'"

"Just that. I planned on coming to Riverdale all along."

I walked over and sat on the arm of Mr. Carter's big red chair. "But why?"

"I was looking for family."

My heart melted. She'd been such a lonely girl. She'd lost her mom, never knew her dad, her fiancé died... she had no one, and so she'd gone in search of it, just like Nathan had alluded to. "Well, I'd say you found it. Practically the entire town has adopted you. That baby of yours is going to have more aunts and uncles than we can count!"

She gave me another smile. "I know, and I'm so unbelievably thankful for that. But you're not getting it." She walked over to her purse on the sofa and began rummaging around inside it. When she found her wallet, she pulled out what looked to be a folded piece of paper. She walked back toward me and held out her hand. "I came here looking for *family*—this is why I came to Riverdale."

I took the paper from her, realizing it was actually a photograph. I opened it and gazed down at the picture. It was old, black and white, and full of creases from being repeatedly folded and opened, looked at, and carried around. In the picture was a woman standing in front of a big stone building, smiling at the camera. She was in a simple, pretty dress.

Her hair was done up and she carried a bouquet. I assumed it was her wedding day. She was beautiful, and although something about her was oddly familiar, I wasn't sure who she was. The building, on the other hand, I knew quite well. Even if I hadn't recognized the structure as a whole from passing it nearly every day, I would have known it from the words etched into the stone above the doors. It read "Riverdale" and underneath that, "Est. 1675." It was the town hall.

"Where did you get this?"

"I found it in my mother's things when I was very young."

"Do you know who the woman is?"

She nodded in response. "She was my grandmother."

Family. Clara had family—actual family—in Riverdale.

"I went to the library and looked up pictures of town halls in places named Riverdale until I found the right one. That's how I knew where to come. I just wanted you to know. Obviously, I didn't find her. But I'm happy with the family I discovered instead. And I'm glad you don't regret coming upon me that day."

I smiled at her then looked down at the picture again. I had a nagging feeling I'd seen it somewhere before. I stared at it for a minute, then suddenly I remembered. I looked up at the wall behind Clara where there hung three small black and white photographs—photographs I hadn't paid much attention to since seeing them one of the first times I came to visit.

"Clara..."

"What is it?"

"I know who she is."

Clara paled significantly. "You do?"

I stood up and pointed behind her, then walked to the television, reached over it, and took the photo off the wall. It was in better condition than Clara's copy, but it was identical to the one she'd shown me. We both stared down at the two images in wonder.

"How did I never notice this before?" she asked herself. "Who is she?"

"Clara, that's Mr. Carter's wife."

Her gaze flew up to meet mine. "Mr. Carter's wife?"

"Yes. That's Clarissa. His wife."

"If that's his wife... and she's also my grandmother... then Mr. Carter is..."

She paused before finishing, and I could see her eyes were beginning to tear.

"Your grandfather," I finished in a whisper.

A sudden creak on the wood floor had us both looking toward the stairs to find Mr. Carter firmly bracing the banister.

Neither one of us knew what to do, so we stood motionless. Clara was looking at Mr. Carter and Mr. Carter was staring at Clara. My own gaze kept moving between the two. It was as though a spell had been cast, turning everyone to stone. It was so quiet I could have sworn I heard the tiny ticking of Mr. Carter's wristwatch from across the room. He was the one who finally break the spell.

"Damn it, I knew it." He stated quietly, and then crossed the room in three of the biggest strides I had ever seen him take. He enveloped Clara in a giant hug and at that, her tears began to flow freely and she let out a sob, wrapping her arms around him in return. I felt like I just might cry along with her, so I turned on my heels and walked back into the bakery kitchen to give them some time alone. Mr. Carter was Clara's grandfather. Clara was Mr. Carter's granddaughter! I felt like laughing at fate. What a funny, unbelievable thing it was. I looked down at the framed photo, which I was still carrying. I laughed quietly, then placed it on the counter and pulled out my cell to text Meredith. "CLARA AND CARTER ARE RELATED!!!" it read. I hit send and waited for a response. I couldn't stand still. I walked out to the front of the bakery, shaking my head and grinning. I'd never had the urge to tell someone something so badly. Where was Meredith? I looked out the front windows and caught sight of Riley walking across the street. I unlocked the door and shouted over to him.

"Riley! Get over here!"

He gave me a surprised look then came over. "How'd you know I was headed this way?"

"I didn't... you were?"

"Yep." He held up his hand and handed me a bouquet of tiny white flowers. "It's lily of the valley. There's some growing behind the office. Nothing spectacular, but I thought you might like them. There's a nice meaning behind them, too."

I forgot all about the news I'd been so anxious to share as I took the flowers and smiled. "They're beautiful." I looked up and gazed into those honey brown eyes, sure that I was about to dissolve right where I stood. "What meaning?"

"Luck in love... the return of happiness..." He took a step toward me, and I was certain he was going to kiss me again. Just like the night before, I wasn't going to back away. But then my phone vibrated in my hand and I remembered what had just happened.

"Oh!" I exclaimed. "You'll never believe this!"

Riley startled slightly at my sudden excitement, and the intimate moment passed. "What is it?"

I looked down at my phone and saw Meredith had responded "HUH?" I grinned at Riley. "Clara and Mr. Carter are related!"

His reaction was identical to Meredith's. "Huh?"

"Did I speak a foreign language? I said..."

"Annebelle!" Clara's voice drifted out from the living room. The hint of panic in her tone had me turning on my heels and rushing inside, with Riley right behind. We entered the house, and I found Clara in the same spot in front of the sofa, one hand clutching her stomach. Mr. Carter had a firm, steadying grip on her elbow. I took in her expression; her face was a mixture of nervousness and excitement and I knew. It was time. I turned back to Riley.

"Help Mr. Carter bring her outside," I ordered. Then I bolted up the stairs to the nursery where we'd put together a bag of items for this very occasion. I grabbed it, then took out my phone again. I ignored Meredith's response to my first exciting statement and typed out another message before racing to the car. "CLARA'S HAVING HER BABY!!!!!"

15

Throughout history, July 1 has been a day of little importance. Well, the Battle of Gettysburg began on this day in 1863, and the world's first international telephone call took place on this date in 1881. And, okay, plenty of other historical moments have occurred as well, but up until now, I didn't give July 1 all that much thought. Now it was one of my favorite days—a day I wouldn't forget—the birthday of Clara's baby boy, Everett Carter Cunningham.

From the beginning I knew Everett—Rett for short—would never find he was lacking in the love department. During Clara's labor, Meredith and I were present in the hospital room holding her hand, encouraging her. Periodically one of us would rush outside to update everyone in the waiting room who was sitting anxiously. Jules, my mom, and Jeremy came as soon as we'd alerted them, and Riley and Mr. Carter had stayed ever since we'd checked in at seven the previous night. Mr. Carter barely said a word the entire time, understandably in a state of shock and overwhelm at becoming not just a grandfather, but a *great*-grandfather. I was still pretty astounded myself. A day can certainly change things, and I couldn't help but think of a phrase I'd heard: "never mistake fate for coincidence." Clara had been a bit preoccupied giving birth to think too much about the fact that she'd actually found the family she was looking for, but it didn't take long after the baby was born for her thoughts to return to that wonderful discovery.

"I want him named after both of them," Clara had declared as she gently ran a finger along her newborn's cheek.

"Both of who?" Meredith inquired as she stared transfixed from beside the bed.

"Jackson and Mr... my grandfather."

Chills shot up my spine as Clara called Mr. Carter "grandfather," while my heart ached for her and the one person who should have been present but wasn't—her fiancé.

"He has Jackson's eyes" she whispered, followed by a sniffle.

I peered over the other side of the bed and caught sight of the bluest eyes I had ever seen as the baby looked up at his mama curiously.

"They're beautiful."

"Are all newborns this quiet?" Meredith wondered aloud.

One of the nurses laughed from the other side of the room where she was cleaning up. "I can say with firsthand knowledge they are not."

Clara smiled proudly.

"Should I let in the others?" the nurse asked, and Clara nodded.

Moments later everyone walked in and shuffled around the bed. I stepped back so there'd be room and looked on as each person grinned at the sight of the baby and commented on how calm and handsome he was.

"I wish my kids had been this pleasant from the start," remarked Jules.

"So do I," added my mom.

"Hey! I thought you said we were angels?" I exclaimed with a laugh. She remained silent as I shook my head, pretending to be hurt.

"I certainly hope ours are like your little one, Clara." I looked over at Jeremy and found it completely endearing that he brought up having kids with Meredith. I smiled as he wrapped an arm around his blushing fiancée.

"I don't think that's likely to happen with you as the father," Riley chimed in. I looked over at him and grinned.

"What are you talking about? I was the nicest. Ask my mom. God bless anyone who has *your* kids, though."

I suddenly felt various pairs of eyes on me, so I quickly turned the attention back to Clara to keep from blushing. One kiss and people were already jumping to kids??

"How do you feel, Clara?"

She looked up from staring at the baby and smiled warmly at me. "Tired, admittedly, but so completely happy. I can't even tell you." She looked at Mr. Carter then, who was standing a little bit away watching the scene unfold. "Mr. Carter?"

He looked at her and nodded his head in acknowledgment. I had an inkling he was keeping quiet because he was at a loss for words.

"Would you like to hold your great-grandson?"

The chills came back again, and everyone watched as he stepped beside the bed. Clara lifted up her baby and held him out toward Mr. Carter while formally introducing him to everyone. "I'd like you to meet Everett Carter Cunningham," she stated as she placed the baby in his arms. Mr. Carter's eyes flew from Clara to the baby, then to Clara and the baby once more. I thought it quite possible he just might cry, right along with the rest of us. My mom was holding a hand up to her heart, Meredith was resting her head on Jeremy's shoulder, and Jules was clutching her throat as though she'd just seen the sweetest thing in the world. I scanned the room for tissues, feeling my own eyes start to water.

By the time Clara was released a couple of days later, a good portion of the town had already made their way to the hospital to catch a glimpse of the newest resident, and I was sure it wouldn't be long until everyone else had as well. We'd returned home with our arms full of balloons and bouquets of flowers, which we placed throughout the bakery, and ushered Clara upstairs to rest with her bundle of joy.

Everything felt so perfectly complete now that Rett was present in the nursery. He continued to be the happiest baby I'd ever seen, gazing quietly around with big eyes in between naps and feedings. An air of serenity enveloped Clara as she cared for him, a small smile constantly on her lips as she gazed at her baby, rocking gently in the chair Jeremy and Riley had given her. The place was positively filled with love, and each time I walked upstairs to ask if she needed anything, I felt as though I could stay there forever, looking on at the beautiful scene created by mother and child. Of course, staying upstairs wasn't an option, not with the bakery to tend to while Clara—the second most dedicated baker apart from Mr. Carter—was rightfully preoccupied.

On top of that, Mr. Carter was the most distracted I'd ever seen him, and I knew this also had to do with the two individuals upstairs. A bit of his roughness seemed to have vanished when he'd held his great-grandson, and I wasn't sure it would ever return. He appeared much more contemplative and content, and he instantly took on the role of doting grandfather—and great-grandfather. It was a side of him I had never seen before, and I had an inkling he was determined not to let what he considered a mistake with his daughter—not showing just how much he cared—happen again. He went upstairs more frequently than I and would come back with a detailed report each time. I just grinned as I stood up to my elbows in flour and unsalted sticks of butter.

The bakery had been closed for two days because of the birth and would close early on the Fourth of July. As a result, I was working hard to make enough goods to satisfy the cravings people would inevitably have after a few days without an Apple Blossoms' treat. Along with that, we had to make various Fourth of July themed items like star cupcakes, flag frosted cookies, and several custom orders of the American pie combo: a two-pie special featuring a delicious blueberry cream cheese and a mouth-watering strawberry pie.

By the time the dinner hour rolled around, I managed to take care of a good lot of it, but still had a feeling I might be there all night making sure things were ready. I probably would have worked straight through if Riley hadn't knocked on the door shortly after five. I peered around the corner from the kitchen, dusted off my hands, and headed out front when I saw who it was. I was conscious of the fact I looked a mess with pieces of hair escaping from my hair tie, cheeks flushed from the oven, and flour all over my apron. There wasn't much I could do about it though, so I planted a smile on my face as I unlocked the door, ignoring the hammering in my heart.

"I figured I might just find you here."

I let out a laugh. "Where else would I be?"

"That's my point. This place is like Willy Wonka's—you go in and you never come out."

"There's a lot to do."

"I don't doubt it. Where's Carter?"

I tried to tuck some of my stray hairs behind my ears. "Upstairs with Clara. He can't get enough of them, and I can't say I blame him."

"Neither can I. It's incredible the way they ended up finding each other. They were both without family, and now look at them!" He rested his shoulder on the doorframe, eyeing me, and I wondered how long we'd stand in the doorway talking. "Of course, the present state of things means you must have your hands full with this place."

I shrugged. "I can handle it."

"I know you can. You can handle just about anything. And if I remember correctly, you're one to keep on going 'til you finish a job— frequently at the cost of one or all of your meals. Eaten anything today?"

"Do bits of cookie dough and pie filling count?"

"No chance. Got time for a bite at Amy's?"

"I…"

"Actually, I don't know why I phrased it like that. It wasn't supposed to be a question. Let's go get some dinner at Amy's."

I was about to protest, using my appearance as an excuse, then decided against it. Instead I reached behind and untied my apron. "Sure," I replied. I tossed the apron over a nearby chair and stepped through the door.

"That was easy."

Another shrug. "I don't feel like arguing. I think I'm still too happy about the baby." We started walking side by side down the sidewalk, the warm summer air cooled by a gentle breeze.

"In that case, I better ask you out on our second date right away. Will you go to the fireworks with me?"

"Is this a date?"

"Sure it is. It's late though—I'd planned on asking you out Monday when I brought the flowers, but you know what happened then."

"You did?" He nodded and my heart fluttered. "Well, yeah, labor is a surefire way to get a date put on hold. Thanks for helping by the way— you know, bringing her there then staying and all."

"No worries. I'm glad I happened to be there—Clara's a great girl. We've had some nice conversations," he said.

"Yeah. She's said the same about you, too."

"I'm a great girl?"

I nudged him playfully in the shoulder. "You know what I mean."

He held open the door to Amy's and I walked in. The diner was in full swing with the dinner rush but as we entered, Amy caught sight of us and waved, then nodded in the direction of that oh-so-familiar booth. Despite how busy it was, the spot was empty.

"What are the odds," Riley commented as he led the way smiling. I greeted a couple of familiar faces as we walked through, then slid onto the seat across from him.

"No kidding. What, did you call ahead or something?" I'd said it half sarcastically—after all, what Alexis had said the first time she'd tried to steal their booth was true: Amy's didn't take reservations. But Riley's silence told me he actually had and I laughed, amused. "You really did, didn't you?! How'd you manage that one? And what if I'd told you I couldn't come??"

He grinned back at me. "Amy likes me—and you. And that's why I phrased it as a statement, not a question."

We paused as a waitress came over and took our orders, returning a few minutes later with our drinks. I excitedly took a sip of my strawberry-chocolate shake.

"You'll never stop getting those will you?" He shook his head at me.

"Probably not. Why? You want me to?"

"Not for the world." He laughed. "So… you didn't answer me before, and I'm hoping it's not because you're trying to avoid turning me down. Fireworks?"

My mind automatically began searching for reasons to say no, but I quickly stopped that train of thought. I knew they wouldn't really be reasons after all, just excuses. And the truth was, I liked spending time with Riley, especially now that I knew he wasn't dating Alexis—and I was dumb for ever thinking he would. But apart from that, I'd started to realize the distance I'd put between us also had to do with everything that happened with Rick. There was *nothing* similar between the two of them, but a situation like that... well, Riley was right when he said I had walls up, and it was no longer simply due to some teenage idea that we had to go off and see the world. It felt so good to lower them... if only a little bit. "Sure," I answered.

"Really?" He sat back against the booth and raised an eyebrow at me. "Wow, that was easy too. I think more people you know need to have babies. I can't wait for Jeremy and Mere to have one now—they make you so... nice!"

I laughed but wasn't sure whether to be insulted or not. "Oh, I'm not nice the rest of the time?"

"Well, in general you're a nice person, but you like to put up your guard a lot. More so now than you used to. And that makes me wonder why..." He paused for a moment like he was giving me a chance to offer an explanation, but despite the feeling of openness slowly returning between the two of us, I didn't feel like ruining the meal by talking about Rick. When I didn't say anything, he continued. "Then, of course, you just like giving people—me in particular—a hard time."

"You've got that right. It keeps things interesting."

The waitress returned and placed our food in front of us, and as the smell of my burger and sizzling fries hit my nostrils my stomach began to growl. Suddenly feeling famished, I picked up the burger and took a giant bite. Riley chuckled and I looked at him, daring him to say something about my eating habits.

"There she is," he stated as he took a bite of his own.

"What?" I mumbled.

"The girl who likes to eat. I knew she was in there somewhere."

I rolled my eyes as I chewed and swallowed. "Whatever."

"Uh-oh, I think the warm, fuzzy feelings Rett's birth gave you are wearing off."

I simply smiled, enjoying the banter between the two of us. We continued on like that as we ate, slipping in a comment or two between bites—half of them sarcastic, the other half friendly and light.

"Would you two care for some dessert?" The waitress interrupted.

Riley looked at me and waited.

"Umm, no, I couldn't possibly eat another thing."

"No banana split?" he asked astonished.

"I'm not 16 anymore." I laughed. "I can't eat nearly as much as I used to, and my hips can't handle it either."

"Don't be ridiculous, Belles." He turned to the waitress. "We'll share a banana split. Go easy on the walnuts and put an extra scoop of strawberry."

"Got it," she noted then walked off.

"You remember just how I like it," I acknowledged appreciatively.

"Of course I do. Okay, look, I'm just gonna put this out there—I don't think we've forgotten a thing about each other. We spent a lot of time together, you and me."

I knew I hadn't, not that I was going to tell him that—but he hadn't either? Why did everything he say have to give me butterflies as though I actually *was* still sixteen? "You can put out to whomever, whenever you want," I said, trying to be funny but once again inwardly grimacing at my attempt.

He let out his deep, hearty laugh. "Did you just call me a man whore?"

I smiled angelically. "I would never!"

"Good. That wouldn't make any sense anyway since I said 'put *this* out there' not 'put out.'"

I started to pout.

"But we'll pretend it works," he added.

"Guess I do remember some things. I mean, the pout still works!" I said.

"Only some things? I'm hurt. But yes, the pout still works—only because it's so cute."

I felt my cheeks start to warm at his words, and I was glad when the waitress brought over our dessert. She placed it in the middle with two spoons, and as I looked at the delicious concoction my stomach magically had enough room for me to dive right in. I picked up a spoon and dipped it into one of the scoops of strawberry ice cream, bringing it to my lips covered in marshmallow and whipped cream.

"Mmm, delicious," I stated as I enjoyed the bite.

Riley followed suit and stuck his spoon into the scoop of chocolate. "I knew you wouldn't talk about that 'my hips can't handle it' crap once it got here," he stated.

"Oh, shut up." I went back for a second bite. "So what were we talking about?"

"Before or after you called me a man whore? Which, might I add, is far from the truth."

"Before."

"The practice. Although we pretty much covered everything. But it does bring me to the topic of you and your career."

"What are you, my dad now?"

"Far from it, I'm just curious..."

"What?"

"Well, when are you gonna admit you're staying in Riverdale?"

The question caught me off guard, and I stopped with the spoon halfway to my mouth. "I'm not. I mean, I don't... do we have to talk about this right now?"

"We're being frank, aren't we? I'm just wondering when you're gonna finally admit you love it here just as much as the rest of us."

His assumption, which in many ways mirrored that day in his room oh-so long ago, didn't scare me like it had then. And even though I felt like I *should* get mad at him for it, I wasn't. But what that meant I wasn't quite sure. "I do love Riverdale, but I'm not settling here, or anywhere, until I find what I'm looking for."

"What are you looking for?"

I remained silent.

"You don't even know, do you?"

"I'll know when I find it."

"How does that make any sense?"

"It just does. Don't act like you don't know what I'm talking about."

"No, you're right, I guess I do. But I've always known what I was looking for so I knew when I had it. You, on the other hand, seem to be confused."

"What are you talking about?"

He shook his head. "Nothing. So you're gonna take the job in Georgia after all then?"

"Maybe." Honestly, I hadn't given the position in Georgia even half a thought since making the decision to hold off on going. "You're giving me a headache. You should probably bring me home, especially if you want that second date. I wouldn't want us to get sick of each other."

"Not possible," he muttered, but slid out of the booth. I followed, and we walked over to the counter to pay for our meal then headed outside and back toward Apple Blossoms. The conversation on the way back was significantly less than on the way there, as both of us seemed lost in thought. What did he mean by saying he knew what he wanted and when he had found it? The success of the practice? And I wasn't confused, I was just open to different possibilities. Wasn't I? I'd know when I'd found what I was looking for. I'd feel it. Right? It made sense to me. Sort of. What *did* I want?

"Stop frowning. You'll get lines."

I turned to look at him just as he bent his head and placed a kiss on my forehead where my brow had knit together. The frown instantly vanished.

"That's better. Thanks for coming to dinner with me."

"No, thank..."

He held up a hand. "Don't. It was my pleasure. Maybe I'll see you tomorrow? But if not, fireworks on the Fourth. Don't forget."

I tapped a finger to my brain. "Got it. Fireworks on the Fourth." I quickly walked up the driveway before I had the chance to make a fool of myself with another awkward comment. How was it, that after all these years, it felt like I was going out with him for the first time? Only, it was different now. For one thing, we weren't young and stupid. And at least one of us had figured out—and apparently had—what he wanted.

16

"Clara, your baby was the best marketing move Apple Blossoms ever made."

Clara laughed as she slipped the tiny white onesie that read "American Baby" in red and blue letters over Everett's head. "What do you mean?"

I sat back in the rocking chair and looked on admiringly as I began moving to and fro. "We were in no way lacking customers before, but I swear we had twice as many as usual yesterday. He sure is a well-loved addition, and he's only been in the public eye for a day!"

Yesterday Clara had felt rested enough to come down to the bakery with the baby in tow; she'd placed him on the counter in his carrier as she stood behind it talking with customers, and on more than one occasion someone asked if they could take the baby home with their cookies.

"I'm so happy, Annebelle." She pressed together the snaps on the bottom of the onesie then slipped a pair of matching red pants on Rett's tiny legs.

"You've got a lot of reason to be, and knowing you're so happy makes me happy right back!"

She lifted Rett up, kissing him on the cheek before turning him toward me so I could see. "I'm glad. If you feel half as happy as I do right now... the only thing that could possibly make me any happier would be if... well..." She paused and I knew she was thinking of Jackson. "Never mind. How does this little guy look?"

"It's okay to miss him, Clara." I stated before taking in Rett's appearance. "And he looks good enough to eat!" I stood up and straightened my summer dress. "You ready?"

She nodded, and we went downstairs to find Mr. Carter in the living room looking rather smart in a pair of khakis and a plaid button down.

"Mr. Carter—looking good!"

"Hmph, think I didn't know how to use an iron?" He grumbled at me, then turned to Clara and Everett and smiled.

I shook my head. "I see you'll forever be Mr. Sourdough to me. You're lucky I'm not more sensitive."

"May I?" he said to Clara, then held out his hands for his great-grandson. She handed him over with a grin. "Can't change on you now, Annebelle. Been the same way too long for that."

"I'm glad to hear it. I admit, I'm rather fond of you just as you are." It was true, I always had been. I doubt I would have made half as much of an effort to stick around the bakery if he was just a sweet old man selling cupcakes. I liked the challenge and had always loved him as Mr. Sourdough, but I was glad he'd found more reasons to smile.

"Well, ladies and little gentleman, ready to head to the river?"

I nodded at Mr. Carter, and we followed him outside and through the yard to where the hedges lining his property broke apart and revealed a tiny path. On the other side, another path wove behind the buildings on Main Street and led right up to the clearing beside the river where the annual picnic had been held for as long as I could remember. The distant sound of '50s music floated over to our ears as we walked. We waved at Amy and Sarah as they headed out from the diner with their families, and I caught sight of Mr. Palmer linking arms with Ms. Ferris beside the hardware store.

We rounded the final corner before the clearing and dozens of blankets spread across the ground came into view. The music was louder now, and I could tell even from a distance that everyone was in a lively, happy mood. Kids were dancing and shrieking with joy in front of the bandstand. Families were laying out their afternoon picnic fare. Groups of friends and neighbors stood together talking, their kids occasionally running up to grab onto a pant leg for protection as they were chased in a game of tag. It looked like a scene right out of a Rockwell painting, and I was suddenly quite ecstatic to be there. I hadn't been to a Fourth of July picnic in Riverdale since the summer after high school.

As we stepped out from the trees, it took all of ten seconds for Meredith to catch sight of us. She hollered out my name and waved frantically from her place on the ground where she sat with her parents and Jeremy. Heading in her direction, we were intercepted by Haley and Vanessa who came scurrying over, throwing themselves against me.

"Auntie Belle! We missed you!" exclaimed Vanessa, and Haley nodded in agreement.

"You missed me?" I laughed. "But you saw me yesterday at the bakery!"

"We know, but we missed you anyway."

Haley looked up from where she had pressed herself against me and smiled. "We missed the baby, too."

"Aha! The truth comes out!" I pretended to be upset and tried to push them off of me. "You don't miss me at all! You just want the little guy!"

"No, no, no, we don't!" They laughed as they tried to hold on.

"Lies! Well... either way, come on over to see Meredith with us, and I'm sure Clara will let you have your time with Blue Eyes over there."

"I certainly will! If his poppy will give him over that is." She smiled at Mr. Carter, who looked gruffly down at the girls. They looked up at him with wide eyes, half expecting him to turn them down.

"Hmph, suppose I could do that, long as you little whippersnappers don't try and run away with him."

"Yay!" They jumped up and down in anticipation and released me so we could continue walking.

"Oh, and April wants to hold him too, but she told us to get her only once you got here. She's been reading over by those oak trees," informed Vanessa.

"All afternoon!" added Haley incredulously.

I glanced toward the grove of oaks, expecting to find April sitting against one of the trunks engrossed in the pages of her latest novel. But instead, I saw her leaning against a tree talking with a tall, somewhat lanky and unfamiliar boy, the book forgotten on the ground beside her. Ah, young summer love. I supposed it was only a matter of time before books took second place to another "b" word. I was definitely going to have to talk to Jules and figure out who that boy was. I smiled to myself as we approached Meredith's blanket.

"Should we go get her now?" inquired Haley.

I quickly shook my head. "No, how about you two spend some quality time with Rett first, then you can go and grab your cousin. Besides, we could use your help spreading the blanket and all."

"Okay," they said in unison, taking the picnic basket I'd brought from my hands.

"Belles!" Meredith stood up as we approached. "So glad you're all finally here!"

"Finally? It's not even that late!"

"Well no, but my mom wanted to get here extra early so we'd get a perfect spot for firework viewing. We were here while the band was still setting up!"

I looked down at her parents and smiled. "Hi Mr. and Mrs. Kinney—good to see you as always."

"You, too, Annebelle dear. And I don't see why Meredith's complaining—she certainly won't be when the show starts and we can see everything clear as day."

"I'm not complaining mom, just stating a fact." She rolled her eyes at me and I laughed.

"I don't know how you deal with these two, Mr. Kinney—they're a handful."

"Coffee in the morning and a nice brandy in the evening, Annebelle. It makes all the difference." Mrs. Kinney smacked him playfully on the arm, and he winked at me in return.

"Charles has already started preparing me for the life I've got ahead of me," Jeremy said with a grin. "He gave me a fine bottle of brandy as an engagement present."

Mirroring her mom, Meredith smacked him on the shoulder, but followed it with a kiss on the cheek. "Oh hush up! Anyway, we saved a place next to us for you and Mr. Carter, Clara. Belles... I would have saved one for you too but..." She paused, and I raised an eyebrow. "Ahem, well..."

"You're gonna be with Riley!" finished Vanessa.

I looked down at her, surprised, as the others started chuckling. Haley brought a hand to her mouth and started giggling behind it. "What?" asked Vanessa. "I heard mom on the phone with grandma. Isn't that what you're talking about?"

I rolled my eyes. "Aren't you two here to help with the blanket?"

"Oh yeah!" Vanessa and Haley took the basket from my hand and retrieved the blanket, then began spreading it on the ground beside Meredith and her family.

"Where is Riley anyway?" Clara asked.

"Maybe he got caught up at work and can't make it," I muttered.

"Nope, he'll be here," Jeremy said. "I spoke to him about an hour ago."

"Ah." There were the butterflies again. "Well I'm gonna go find the rest of the family and say 'hi.' I'll be back."

"Okay." Clara and Mr. Carter settled down on the blanket, with Haley and Vanessa instantly surrounding them and gazing at Rett. I wandered off and began making my way through the crowd of blankets and people, stepping carefully around excited kids and dogs.

"Annebelle, hi sweetie." I smiled at my mom as I found her standing with Ryan in her arms, chatting with Jules.

"Hey, Mom. Hi, Jules." I planted a kiss on Ryan's cheek. "Hi, chubster." He gave me a toothy grin. "You're not the littlest baby anymore!" He looked at me happily, completely unaware.

"Well, he'll always be *my* little baby!" countered Jules.

"Speaking of your babies... who's the boy April's talking to?"

"The...?" She pressed a hand up to her forehead to shadow her eyes and scanned across the crowd toward the oak trees. "Oh, that's Dave. They're just friends."

"That's what they all say."

"Ugh, I know." She sighed. "But I'd rather believe that than think my baby girl is interested in anything apart from her books. It's easier that way." I shook my head. "He's a nice boy, though. He comes over sometimes after school and they do homework together."

"Do we know his family?"

"No, they moved here last year—from Minnesota, believe it or not, but I haven't met his parents yet. If they keep hanging out like this, I'll definitely have to though."

"My, how time flies." I turned to my mom. "Where's dad?"

"Down by the river with Tyler and Derek. They brought their fishing poles along."

"Of course they did." I inhaled deeply and sighed. "It's so beautiful out." Jules and my mom looked at me oddly. "What?"

They shook their heads quickly. "Nothing," answered my mom. "You just seem a lot more content than you did when you first got back."

I thought for a second. "Well, I suppose that's because I am. I mean, things are more relaxed here than they are in the city for one thing... and there's a lot I don't have to worry about here." I paused and wondered if they should know about Rick, but decided against it once again as I saw Doris and Aunt Arlene make their way over.

"Belles." I looked at Jules. "We know there's something you're keeping from us." I saw my mom open her mouth to speak but Jules raised a hand. "We're not going to pressure you tell us." My mom relaxed at that, obviously assuming Jules was going to try and push the issue. "Just know that whatever it is, we're here for you."

It meant a lot to hear them say that, and I resolved to let them know soon.

"Annebelle, why, I thought you'd be off somewhere with Riley!"

I placed the smile I always saved just for Doris on my face and turned to greet her. "He's not here at the moment."

"Ah, of course. I'm sure you'll be with him as soon as he is. It's so nice to see the two of you going on together again. I caught sight of you with him at Amy's the other day. I nodded to myself and said 'now that's just how it should be.'"

My aunt stood beside Doris, shaking her head in amusement. I stepped over to give her a hug. "Hi Auntie."

"You two always looked so well together," Doris continued.

"Riley and I aren't dating, Mrs. Clark. We're just friends."

"That's what they all say," Jules said with a laugh, mirroring my earlier assertion.

"Oh, well now, I didn't say you were dating, and if you'd like to call it 'friendship' you go right ahead. There are so many terms for it these days I can't keep up."

"It *is* rather frustrating," encouraged Arlene as she smiled at me mischievously.

"Have a seat, Doris." My mom motioned to one of the lawn chairs that was set out, and Doris settled herself down then looked up at me.

"Plan on staying a while?" she inquired.

"What?" At first I thought she was referring to staying in town again, but at my question, she waved a hand at the blanket on the ground.

"Sit down, you're blocking the sun."

"Oh!" I lowered myself onto the blanket, and the others did so as well. My mom placed Ryan down in front of her, and he immediately started crawling in my direction.

"There he goes." She laughed as she started rummaging around in the picnic basket. "Sandwich anyone?"

We all answered in the affirmative, and as she placed them on plates for each of us, Jules poured glasses of cool lemonade. I picked up Ryan and began to shower him with kisses.

"I must say, Annebelle," Doris said as she took a sip of her drink. "I'm quite glad you took my advice and decided to bring back the bakery. It's wonderful to see it so lively again, and from what I can see it's been bringing quite a few people in from out of town."

I nodded and smiled, too stubborn to say outright that her suggestion had been a good idea. After all, who's to say I wouldn't have eventually thought it up on my own? Even if I hadn't gone to see her that day, I would have made my way to see Mr. Carter at some point, and after realizing the bakery was practically closed for good, I would have wanted to help. Wouldn't I? At least, I'd like to think I would have. Then again... if I was completely honest with myself, I'm not so sure that'd have been the case. When I first got back my walls were up just as Riley had alluded to, and I could think of nothing but getting out as fast as possible. Frankly, I was completely selfish, looking at everyone with a disdainful eye and thinking only of starting a life far away from Riverdale. And why? For what?

"Annebelle?"

I turned to Doris. "Sorry, what was that?"

She looked at me disapprovingly for not listening. "Well," she huffed. "I was trying to say what a good thing it is that you decided to stay in town after all..."

"This is only temporary, Mrs. Clark. Mr. Carter has Clara, and the two of them will be more than able to handle things at Apple Blossoms as soon as Everett is a bit older. Once that happens, I'm sure I'll be heading some other place." I was once again surprised at my calm response to her comments. I didn't feel angry or find it necessary to instantly refute the idea that I was staying in town—I just told her the truth. It was an interesting change.

"Well, even if that's the case, I'm sure something else will come up that'll take its place... Oh, look who's finally arrived!" Doris nodded her head and the rest of us turned to look. There, across the clearing, stood Riley.

My heart did its little skip at the sight of him—a reaction I was getting quite used to again, but still found rather annoying. His gaze roamed slowly over the crowd of people, and although I thought perhaps it was me he was looking for, the teenage girl he seemed to evoke in me doubted it. I took in his appearance appreciatively as he looked around; he was in a pair of faded blue jeans and a T-shirt—a nice change from the khakis and button downs I saw him in most of the time.

I watched as he found the blanket where we sat a minute later. His eyes seemed to find my mom first, and he smiled. Then they quickly went from Jules, to Doris, to Arlene, to where I sat with Ryan, slightly hidden from view beside her chair. As soon as he discovered I was sitting there, the doubt vanished—he was searching for me. He continued to look at me as he began walking in our direction and my heart flip-flopped again.

"He looks like a man on a mission," commented Doris.

"He most certainly does," agreed Arlene.

"I wonder what he could be after," my mom stated sarcastically, and I felt myself blush.

"I think you better hand Ryan over to me. I have a feeling you won't be with us for much longer" Jules laughed.

I began to protest, clutching Ryan closer to me—he formed a nice protective barrier—but Jules stood up, stepped over, and plucked him from my arms just as Riley approached. It felt like my entire family was scheming to get Riley and I together. Why was I nervous?

"Hello, ladies," he said, smiling at us all. "And gentleman," he added with a nod toward Ryan. His voice flowed over me like warm molasses, and my nerves seemed silly. I began to relax. "Enjoying yourselves?"

"We certainly are," responded Jules. "I, for one, am looking forward to how tired it's going to make the kids! I love summer," she smiled.

"We were wondering where you were before, Riley. Is everything all right?" my mom asked.

He placed a hand in his pocket, shaking his head. "I know, I meant to get here earlier. I've been looking forward to the picnic all week... I just got caught up with some business."

I wasn't sure why his reference to business had me glancing toward the entrance to the clearing, but it did, and right when I looked over Alexis came into view. I instantly started to feel jealous; I had a feeling she was the "business" he was talking about. Even though I believed him when he'd told me there wasn't—and never would be—anything between the two of them, I was positive she felt differently, so it still made me a bit green that'd she'd gotten to see him before I did.

"It's just business," I mumbled, trying to shake away the feeling.

"What was that dear?" asked Doris.

"Oh, nothing."

Doris pursed her lips at my refusal to share, then returned her attention to her favorite. "Things are going quite well at the practice, aren't they, Riley dear?"

"They sure are, Mrs. Clark. Actually, just yesterday I got a call from a potential client in Los Angeles. Apparently one of my professors over there referred me."

I looked up at him, intrigued.

"Los Angeles?" Doris looked affronted. "Surely, you're not thinking of moving away?"

He laughed his deep, rumbling laugh. "Of course not, you know I'd never leave."

She settled back in her chair, looking quite satisfied with his answer, and tossed a look my way that most definitely meant "see that, *Riley* would never leave Riverdale."

"He's moving this way at the end of the year and is looking to make some connections in advance."

"Ah, that's wonderful," she continued. "So nice to see you doing so well. Your father is so proud to have you by his side."

He smiled gratefully at the compliment then turned his attention back to me. "I hope you're hungry. I brought us some things to eat."

I was about to tell him I'd eaten a sandwich, but Arlene spoke up before I had the chance. "Thank goodness. She's been sitting here complaining about how hungry she is since we got here."

Riley raised an eyebrow, looking around at the plates scattered on the ground.

"Not enough food?"

"Not for someone with an appetite like Belle's," my mom said, smiling at me.

"Ha. Ha. Very funny, Mom." Now I wasn't nervous at all and wanted to wander around with Riley sans the comments from Doris and my family. "Want to walk around for a bit? There are some people I'd like to say hello to."

"Let's do it." He reached his hand out toward me and I took hold, feeling those familiar tingles when we touched. He pulled me up and I stepped across the blanket, then began to loosen my grip on his hand. But instead of letting go, Riley held on, and for a moment his strong grasp had me recalling the very first time I'd met Rick, when he'd held fast to my hand in the museum. How different the two holds felt. I should have known.

"Have fun, dear," urged my mom as we walked away.

"Why do I feel like they were all teasing you?" Riley asked when we were out of earshot.

"Because they were." I smiled up at him. Once again, the anticipation of being around him made me nervous, while actually being with him did the opposite. When I was in his presence it felt as it should—like I was talking with someone I'd known practically forever, someone I had a history with.

The two of us wandered aimlessly around for a while, stopping now and then to talk to someone we knew. We made our way to Mr. Palmer and Ms. Ferris at one point, and I was glad I finally had the opportunity to catch up with them. Things were well with Mr. Palmer, and I promised I'd head over to Quality's soon, even if I didn't need anything. His response, however, wasn't exactly what I'd been expecting.

"It's always a pleasure seeing you Annebelle, but I have to admit, you coming along for a pail of paint now and then isn't quite the same as those days when you'd wander around causing a ruckus. You're just going to have to have a kid of your own before long to take your place."

I looked at him wide-eyed, unsure what to say. I became aware of Riley chuckling beside me.

"Don't mind him, Annebelle. He's getting senile in his old age and talks a lot of nonsense. Forget about stopping in at the hardware store and come see me at the library instead. The books miss you."

I smiled warmly at Ms. Ferris, amused at the idea of the books actually missing me. "I'll be sure to do just that real soon. It's been way too long since I've sat down with a good book."

"Well, Belles, you ready to grab something to eat?"

I turned to Riley. "Hungry?"

He nodded in response. "I didn't have time for lunch today."

"You didn't!? Why didn't you say so!" I was appalled he'd let us stand around and socialize while he hadn't eaten since breakfast. "Ms. Ferris, Mr. Palmer, it was nice talking with you as always."

"You too, sweetie. Enjoy your evening!"

I grabbed Riley by the hand and started leading him away while Mr. Palmer began to deny his proclaimed senility behind us. "I'm not senile! I knew exactly what I was saying..."

"I know, dear. I was just saying that. But you embarrassed the poor girl..."

"Do you know where we're going?"

I stopped short at Riley's question, realizing I had no clue. "Umm, no, I guess I don't." I released my grip on his hand. "Where are we going?"

"Allow me." He smiled and grabbed my hand the same way I'd just done, then walked toward the path I'd taken to get here earlier in the day. I didn't mind everyone seeing us as we held hands, even though it contradicted how adamant I'd been at squashing any rumors about us.

"Why are we leaving?" I asked as we walked back around the bend.

"We're not." He winked at me then stopped and pushed aside some of the hedges to the left. A smile lit up my face as I suddenly remembered the alcove beside the river. I stepped through the opening he'd made. There wasn't a path on the other side, but a few broken branches and trampled ground highlighted the area he must have walked down.

"I forgot all about this place. You better go first—I don't think I'll remember how to get there."

He moved in front of me and, taking my hand again, began walking down the hill that led to the riverbank. "How is it you managed to forget so many great memories?"

I thought for a moment. "It made things easier, I guess."

"Made what easier?"

Leaving you, I thought to myself. "I don't know, just... life in general. Going away to college."

We reached the bottom, stepping onto the soft dirt beside the river. He turned left and started walking back in the direction of the festivities. "Or maybe the memories just weren't as great to you as they were to me," he said quietly.

Definitely not true. As soon as I realized where we were going, every single memory—memories of at least four picnics spent watching fireworks beside the river, coming down for a swim, or simply talking and laughing on the river's edge—came rushing back. So, I hadn't really forgotten about this place; I'd just pushed it all aside and tried not to think about it.

"They were great to me, too," I assured him.

He stopped as we reached the alcove—one of only a couple areas on the riverbank that was more than a few feet wide and didn't meet with the hilly incline. Instead, the soft dirt upon which the river gently touched met with a flat grassy area nestled into the hillside; a small cliff with giant roots peeking out from the trees above formed crude walls on three sides. Despite this, it had a perfect view of the sky over the water. There was no better place to watch the fireworks set off from the opposite side of the river. We'd discovered the spot on one of our adventures years ago and had claimed it as our own. As far as we knew, no one else had happened upon it yet, so it still created a wonderful little hideaway.

"Well... either way, I've decided I'm just gonna have to create new memories for you that are simply too amazing to forget." Riley moved to the side, and I took in the sight before me. He'd spread a blanket on the grass, and beside it lay a picnic basket with a bouquet of roses on top. There was a bottle of wine in a silver ice bucket, two glasses, and a full charcuterie board.

He smiled at my smile, which he'd once again managed to make grow wider than I thought possible. I walked over, taking in the spread.

"Take a seat," he urged, and I settled myself down on the blanket. Riley did the same then took to opening the wine. "I figured our alcove getaway could use a little classing up, especially now that you've experienced New York City sophistication."

"Classing up, ey?" I took the glass he handed me. "I don't know, I kind of enjoyed the peanut butter and jelly sandwiches we used to bring."

"Well, that's good, because I brought those too."

I let out a laugh. "You did?"

He shrugged. "I told you I got caught up with work. I didn't have time to make the Croque Monsieur I'd originally planned on." He held his glass out toward mine. "Cheers—to unforgettable memories."

"You make Croque Monsieur?"

"Well no," he laughed, "No I don't..."

Our glasses clinked and our eyes locked as we took a drink. The sun descended further toward the horizon as we sat there talking. I nibbled on different items from the charcuterie in between sips of wine while Riley consumed his peanut butter and jelly sandwich.

"So," he began between bites. "Remember when we talked about my career at Amy's the other day?"

I nodded as I popped a grape into my mouth.

"We never really touched on yours."

"Sure we did. We talked about how I don't know what I'm looking for and you've got everything figured out."

He shook his head at me. "I was just giving you a hard time, the same way your family was earlier. I think you know, underneath it all. I think you're just too stubborn to listen or admit it."

I took a sip of my wine to avoid responding.

"Anyway, I have the answer."

"You do?"

"I do." He took a bite of his sandwich, chewing slowly, a thoughtful look on his face.

"Well, are you going to tell me?"

He continued to chew, and I knew he was purposefully keeping me in suspense. What was he talking about, he had "the answer"? The answer to what?

I let out a sigh, fell back onto the blanket and looked up at the darkening sky.

A minute later, he spoke up. "Consulting."

"What?" I raised myself up onto my elbows and glanced at him.

"You can do business consulting."

"What are you talking about?"

"You can make a business out of helping businesses. Look at what you did for Apple Blossoms. You brought it back to life and made it successful—maybe even more so than it was before. You're good at it, so why not make a career out of it?"

"What? That's crazy!"

"No, it's not. You went to school for business, didn't you?"

"Yes, but..."

"And didn't you like fixing up the bakery, working out the business plans, and all the other stuff you had to do?"

It was true, I did. "Yes..."

"So it's perfect. Loving what you do for a living is a dream everyone has, but not many achieve. I think you have the opportunity to do just that, so why wouldn't you go for it?"

I was transfixed by how excited he seemed at his idea and wondered how long he'd been thinking about it.

"Just think. You could start local and help out anyone around here who wants to work on their business, whether it be by improving advertising, getting online, changing their business plan, organizing, redecorating... whatever. You become their go-to consultant. Then you could think bigger. And when that happens, you'd get to travel for work, so you'd still get your adventure and change of scenery."

I was speechless, unsure what to think or say.

"Look, I'm not trying to freak you out. I don't want you to throw a piece of jewelry at me or anything. I just wanted to put the idea out there. I think you'd be great at it, and it'd solve your dilemma regarding what you should do now that you've successfully brought Apple Blossoms back to life." He paused. "And it'd also solve the dilemma I have regarding how to keep you around."

My heart ached at his referral to the day I broke up with him—although *throwing* the ring was a bit of an exaggeration. My mind began to reel and my stomach flip-flop from the idea he presented and his determination to keep me around.

"You want me to stick around?"

"Don't be dumb, Belles—of course I do. Out of everything I just said, is that the only part you heard?"

"No, I heard the rest..."

"I don't want you make a decision right now either. You're not very good at making decisions in the moment. I just want you to think about it. Can you tell me you'll think about it?"

I nodded. "I can do that. I can think about it."

He seemed relieved. "Thanks, Belles." He leaned forward, briefly brushing his lips against mine. He began to pull back, then seemed to have second thoughts and deepened the kiss instead. My mind, which was already reeling at the idea he'd presented, started to spin even faster; I felt like I was drowning, only I didn't want to be saved. Everything else disappeared again, and the only things that were real were his lips against mine, his hand cupping the back of my neck, and my own hand gripping his shirt as though it were the only thing keeping me from losing myself completely.

So much for restraint. So much for acting like I didn't care about him. Now I couldn't even remember why I'd thought that necessary in the first place! He wanted me to stay in town. He wanted to kiss me. He'd thought of a way for me to stay. Could I stay? Did I want to stay? Did I want to leave? Why did I break up with him again? I vaguely remembered the feeling of being trapped, a worry that he'd be settling if we stayed together—a worry that *I'd* be settling if we stayed together. A fear of never getting to see the world, to experience things... but those feelings all seemed foolish now. They felt like tiny pricks on a finger compared to the goliath waves of electricity the feeling of right now—of kissing Riley Parker—sent through me.

Suddenly, he pulled away and I came tumbling back to reality. "Sorry."

Sorry? Why the heck was he apologizing? "It's fine..." I muttered breathless, unsure what else to say. We looked at each other through darkness that seemed to arrive suddenly. Silence filled the space between us, and I was certain he could hear my heart pounding against my chest. In the next instant, I thought my heart actually had exploded with a loud bang, and I jumped, surprised.

Then, as the sky filled with a burst of light, I realized it wasn't my heart at all—it was the start of the fireworks. Riley laughed at how the sound startled me, and the tense moment that followed our kiss vanished.

"Still scared of the fireworks, I see." He chuckled as he settled down on the blanket beside me.

"No, I just wasn't expecting it."

I laid my head back down to find his arm stretched out behind me. He pulled me against him. I fit next to him like a puzzle piece, and I smiled to myself as we gazed up at the night sky. "You weren't expecting it? You do remember we came here to watch fireworks, don't you?"

I elbowed him gently in the side. "Shut up," I ordered, and we watched the starry sky explode with color.

"Did you have sex on the beach?"

"Meredith!"

"What?! I'm just asking."

"First of all, we weren't on the beach. We were on the riverbank. Second of all, that's gross."

"How is that gross? People are always talking about how great sex on the beach is!"

"And which people are you referring to, Mere?" This from Clara, who was mixing up a batch of cookie dough with one hand, while gently rocking Rett in his carrier with the other.

"Well... I don't know, exactly, but I know I've heard it."

"Right, because potentially getting sand in areas where sand is definitely not supposed to be is really appealing." I laughed as I flipped through one of the wedding magazines Meredith had brought to the bakery.

"Ew. Okay, you're right. When you put it like that... that sounds gross," she admitted as she flipped through one of her own. "So what did you do then?"

"Watch the fireworks."

Meredith glared at me, well aware that I wasn't telling the truth.

"Okay, okay. We may have kissed for a bit..."

"A bit?"

"Yes, a bit. Then the fireworks started. Although..."

"What?"

"He stopped sort of suddenly, and then he said 'sorry.' Think I did something wrong?"

"Oh my God, I doubt it. Maybe he was just nervous."

"Nervous? You act like Riley and I haven't known each other for ages."

"True, but the last time you two were together it didn't exactly end well for him, did it?"

"We're not together..."

Clara made a noise that seemed to say "yeah right," and Meredith groaned.

"What! It's true... it's not like he asked me to be his girlfriend or anything."

"Oh, so we're twelve now?"

I laughed, realizing that did sound rather immature. "Oh, whatever."

"You two are dating. He brought you roses and wine."

"And a charcuterie!!" added Clara.

"What, are you pregnant again?" joked Meredith. "Forget the snack board! The point is, you're together, and it's about damn time."

"Can we please not talk about this anymore? Riley and I are just two adults who enjoy each other's company right now—nothing more, nothing less."

"Does Riley know this?"

"I think he feels the same way. Why else would he have pulled back and apologized last night? He's trying to make sure I don't get the wrong idea."

"I dunno, Belles. I think you're giving yourself the wrong idea by *thinking* he's trying to make sure you don't get the wrong idea."

"I agree with Meredith, Annebelle. Whenever Riley and I talk he always brings you up," Clara said.

Meredith nodded. "And besides, you told us he said he wants you to stay in town! What was his idea, anyway?"

"You want me to stay in town, too. That doesn't mean you love me."

"Of course it does, you idiot—you're my best friend! I swear, Belles, sometimes I wonder how you made it through graduate school!"

I picked up a pen and chucked it at her. "All right, that's enough nonsense. We're not here to talk about Riley and me. We're here to talk about the Meremy wedding."

Meredith whacked her head on the counter as she stood up from grabbing the pen. "Ouch! The what?!"

"The Meremy wedding. Don't you remember saying that the night we celebrated your engagement?"

Clara started laughing hysterically from behind the counter, and Meredith joined in shortly after.

"Umm, no?"

"You said it accidentally, and I told you it was like one of those celebrity couple names. You know, like Brad Pitt and Angelina Jolie were Brangelina. You and Jeremy are Meremy!"

"Oh God." Meredith placed a hand on her forehead, and I couldn't tell if it was from hitting her head or because she couldn't remember saying that.

"Can we please put that on the invitations?" implored Clara.

"Over my dead body," she said. "And make note to keep me away from the champagne. I'd like to remember my wedding, thanks very much."

"Don't worry, Clara, we'll find somewhere to sneak it in on the big day," I assured her.

Meredith glared at both of us this time, and I was glad my pet name had successfully steered the conversation elsewhere. I didn't share my plan to help with the bakery before I'd thought it out—to make sure it was something I wanted to do—and similarly, I didn't want the girls to know the idea of starting a business in town was even circulating in my thoughts. It was, of course, but I'd decided I didn't need to make a decision until after the wedding. That way I could focus completely on helping ensure my best friend got her dream day.

It was relatively quiet at the bakery for a Saturday morning, which we planned on taking advantage of. Meredith came over as soon as we'd opened with her arms full of bridal magazines and clippings. So armed with cups of coffee and cupcakes, we sat at the counter and started flipping through page after page, taking notes and dog-earing the pages with pictures and ideas she liked. Meredith joked that this was more wedding talk than I'd had in my entire life, and she was probably right. A brief image of my independent Barbie handing over the keys to her pink convertible and sitting at the kitchen table with Meredith's domestic diva doll flitted through my mind. But I didn't mind it all that much—I was having fun!

"Where did you say Mr. Carter was?" Mere wondered.

"Some of the ladies from church dragged him off to a few tag sales. I get the impression that now that he isn't such a grump, they seem to consider him an attractive bachelor."

Meredith raised her eyebrows. "Are you serious? How does that make you feel, Clara?"

"What?"

"Knowing your grandfather is on the market and potentially playing the dating game."

Clara laughed. "I think it's good—whatever makes him happy."

"He has a lot making him happy these days, more than I think he ever expected to have." I smiled from her to Rett, who was silently observing everything around him like usual.

"So do I," Clara added quietly, her cheeks glowing prettily as she looked at her baby.

Mere let out a sigh. "There's an awful lot of love going around this town. I think something's in the water."

I rolled my eyes. "No, there's just nothing better to do." Meredith scowled at me, and I laughed. "I'm kidding, I'm kidding!"

"Well that's a nice improvement. If this were a couple of months ago you'd have been 100 percent serious!"

"Oh come on, I wasn't that bad, was I?"

"Belles... every time you opened your mouth you had something disdainful to say, and even when the words you spoke were nice, the tone was still condescending."

I bit my lip. "Ugh. Why on Earth did you put up with me?"

"Because you're my best friend, that's why." She chucked my pen back down the counter at me, and I caught it before it could roll off the edge.

"Well, I hope I'm better now."

"Much!" She grinned. "Which makes me wonder why?"

I shrugged. "I guess maybe I'm learning that being in Riverdale doesn't mean I'm *trapped* in Riverdale." Thanks to Riley.

"Well, duh! You think? It's taken you what, eight years to figure that out?"

"Oh be quiet. Can we please focus on your wedding now? You don't have much time."

"What are you talking about, I don't have much time? The wedding's not until August 8th!"

"Right, and it's July 5th, and you've barely got anything settled beyond the location. Do you realize how fast a month and three days is going to fly by?"

Meredith's eyes grew as wide as saucers and her face grew pale. "Oh. My. God. You're right, we need to focus!"

17

We were finally able to concentrate that Saturday in the bakery and it was a good thing, too. Just as I'd said it would, the month flew by in a whirlwind of dress shopping and decisions regarding bouquets, food, music, decorations, and invitations (which, no matter how much Clara and I pleaded, did not get approval for "The Meremy Wedding" to be printed on the front). Then there was the honeymoon to plan—flights to book, hotels to choose from—along with all of life's regular activities.

Meredith had her veterinary work, and I continued to help at the bakery despite how capable Mr. Carter and Clara seemed to be, even with the addition of baby Rett. He was over a month old now, and he grew more handsome with each passing day. Clara was doing unbelievably well balancing motherhood with the responsibilities of the bakery, and my heart swelled with pride when I thought of how far she'd come. It felt like an eternity, but it was only a few short months ago that she'd been frightened and alone, crying and hopeless in the library. Now she was healthy and happy, with the exception of an occasional glimpse of sadness in her eyes for her lost fiancé. I knew she probably thought of him often with all the wedding preparations going on, but Clara Carter (she'd legally changed her name to that of her grandfather's) weathered it well. She wasn't going to be the wife she'd planned on, but she was still able to be a mother, friend, and granddaughter—for that I knew she was thankful.

Now, she sat in one of the armchairs in the living room, cradling her baby and watching us get ready with a smile on her face.

"I feel like I'm going to puke" said Meredith, who was standing in front of me while I slid the zipper up along the back of her dress.

"Calm down, would you? Everything's going to be fine. Your mom's gone to the church, so she's not stressing you out anymore... what else do you want?" I asked.

"I don't know. It's easy for you to say everything's fine—you're already dressed, and you don't have to stand in front of a church full of people and speak. I hate speaking in public!"

I shook my head at her whiney voice as I spread out the bottom of her chapel train. "It's not really public speaking—you just have to repeat whatever Reverend Thomas says!"

"And don't worry about anyone else," chimed in Clara. "This day is about the love you and Jeremy share, and that's it. You got it?"

"Oh, oh, ohhh, I love you two so much!" You could tell from her voice that tears were on the way.

I quickly grabbed her by the shoulders, spinning her around. "Oh no you don't! No tears until you're at the altar or after. You'll ruin your makeup! You got that?"

She nodded and bit her lip. "You look beautiful, Belles."

I had on a lavender-colored, knee-length, strapless, chiffon dress. My hair had been transformed into a mass of soft curls that were swept into a low, loose ponytail. I loved the dress Meredith and I had chosen, and while I was confident I looked good in the ensemble, it was nothing compared to Meredith's appearance. She wore an elegant, ivory-colored, off the shoulder gown with a sweetheart neckline and a chapel train that flowed gracefully behind her. Her hair was pulled back into a chignon accented with tiny white flowers. She wore dangling pearl earrings and a pearl bracelet—and looked positively stunning.

"*I* look beautiful?!" I scoffed at Meredith's remark. "No, *you* look beautiful, Meredith Kinney. You look like a princess..." I paused, then it hit me. "Oh, oh, ohhh! I just realized you're not going to be Meredith Kinney anymore! You've always been Meredith Kinney!" Now I felt close to tears.

Clara sprung up from her chair and came over to us. "Get a hold of yourselves, will you? You just spent hours in the salon getting your hair and makeup done—you even braved Alexis. You wouldn't want it to be for nothing, would you? You've spent well over a month preparing for this day and everything's come together beautifully. You wouldn't want to fall apart now, after all the hard work, would you?"

Meredith and I looked at Clara in astonishment at her sudden speech. Rett looked up at her while we shook our heads meekly.

"No, Sergeant Carter, we wouldn't." The mood lightened instantly, and the three of us broke into laughter.

"That's better." She turned and picked up the two bouquets that were resting on the coffee table, handing them to us. "Now let's go have a wedding."

"Good thing she's here," Meredith said to me as we headed for the door. "A lot of help you would have been as a crying mess, Annebelle."

"Oh, whatever." I laughed.

Outside, a horse and carriage from Spring Meadow Farm stood on the road in front of the bakery. Ribbons were braided into the horse's mane, and small bunches of purple flowers were tied along the carriage posts. We walked over and the driver, Sam Taylor, who happened to be the owner of the farm, helped Meredith and I in.

"All right, ladies, I'll see you at the church."

"Clara, what are you talking about? Get in here with us."

"No, no, it's all right. The carriage is for the bridal party. I'll take the car over."

"Don't make me come down there and risk ruining my dress and breaking my neck, Clara Carter. Get in this carriage with us before I'm late for my wedding!" Clara wasn't about to argue with that tone, so she stepped over, handed Rett to me, and allowed Mr. Taylor to help her up. And then we were off.

It was a short drive to the church, but riding up the road in a horse and carriage made all of us—not just the bride—feel extra special. We waved at the residents who were standing outside as we passed by the green. Many of them would be at the reception later, but the ceremony in the old church would be intimate. The sound of bells beckoned us as we approached and when we pulled to a stop, Meredith's parents came rushing down the steps, looking as proud as any parent would on their only daughter's wedding day.

"Oh my, oh my. You look absolutely beautiful, Meredith dear." Mrs. Kinney began fanning her face to keep from crying, while Mr. Kinney remained silent as he helped his daughter out of the carriage. Mr. Taylor assisted Clara and I down then went off to secure the horse and take a seat inside.

"Well, princess, are you ready?" Mr. Kinney beamed at his daughter and offered her his arm. His voice sounded only slightly shaky, and I knew he was trying hard to keep his composure.

"Mom, is everyone here?" Meredith inquired.

"Yes, sweetie," she affirmed, stepping over to tuck a stray curl behind her daughter's ear.

"Then shouldn't you head in too so we can get started?"

"Oh! Yes, yes of course." She placed a kiss on her daughter's cheek then reached for Clara's hand. "Come along, Clara."

Clara hugged Meredith, then took Mrs. Kinney's hand and headed inside with Rett.

"All right, best friend, let's do this." I smiled at my best friend since childhood and hugged 'Meredith Kinney' for the last time. Then I followed the sound of the church bells and led the way up the steps.

I walked through the double doors and into the entryway, where I paused and waited for the music to begin. As soon as the sounds began to fill the air, I stepped into the aisle and began walking up it. I looked at the faces of the guests and the lovely decorations; everything had come together beautifully. Lavender and cream ribbons hung from every pew, secured by small arrangements of light purple roses and baby's breath.

As I continued to walk, my eyes made their way to the altar. I smiled at Jeremy, who looked about as excited as a kid on Christmas morning. Then my gaze found Riley where he stood to the groom's left. Our eyes met and held and suddenly, it didn't feel like I was the maid of honor in my best friend's wedding: it felt like I was the bride in my *own* wedding. It felt like Riley was looking right into my soul, and for the second time in my life I could see who was in the wedding of my dreams. I could see what I couldn't see with Rick or anyone else. With Riley, I saw it.

I reached the end of the aisle a moment-that-seemed-like-eternity later—there goes the trick of time again. I broke eye contact with Riley as I took my place to the left of the altar and tried to shake the vision I'd had. I wanted to return to the occasion at hand, but what I'd been able to see once more—with the same man as the first time all those years before—left my heart beating wildly. And this time, I acknowledged, I didn't feel afraid.

I took a couple of deep breaths as the music transitioned and the bride began her walk up the aisle. I was certain I heard a collective gasp of admiration ring out as everyone caught sight of Meredith; her eyes were sparkling and her cheeks glowing as she walked toward her soon-to-be husband on the arm of her father. A quick glance at Jeremy showed his expression had changed from excitement to a mixture of awe and disbelief at the woman who was about to be his wife.

When Meredith and her dad reached the altar, he leaned over and kissed her on the cheek, blinking hard to keep his tears at bay. He took her hand, placed it in Jeremy's, and after an assuring pat on the groom's shoulder, took a seat beside his wife.

Meredith and Jeremy seemed lost in each other's eyes. Reverend Thomas hadn't yet spoken, the vows hadn't been uttered, and no rings had yet been exchanged, but I knew by the looks on their faces and the way they smiled at each other as though there were no one else in the universe, that I was about to witness the start of an enduring marriage.

After a ceremony that resulted in nearly everyone shedding a tear or two despite our best efforts not to, I walked back down the aisle on Riley's arm behind the newlyweds, nearly tripping when Riley leaned over and whispered in my ear to tell me how amazing I looked. I was afraid to speak, so I simply smiled at him as we made our way to the carriage.

It took us a little longer to get to the Miller Place via horse than it did everyone else in their cars, but it gave Meredith and Jeremy a nice respite before the craziness of the reception. When we arrived, we entered the barn to a chorus of cheers and raised champagne glasses, and even though I had helped set everything up, I was momentarily amazed—as Meredith seemed to be—with how beautiful everything looked. Long tables covered in white linen lined the edges of the barn, which was essentially a giant, open room with stalls at one end (they hadn't housed animals in quite some time, but Meredith had plans to change that soon after settling in).

The tables were topped with mason jars of spray roses, bluebells, and baby's breath surrounded with candles. The door had been opened wide, and from the newlyweds' position at the head table, they had a perfect view of their new house; lights had been turned on in nearly every room, so when the sun set during the festivities, they'd see their home lit up from within for the very first time. It was all very romantic.

Meredith and Jeremy were all smiles as they took their seats, flanked on either side by Riley and me. The warmth and ease that came with the wedding of two well-loved individuals in a small town like Riverdale could instantly be felt. There were no formalities, which would have completely gone against the personalities of both the bride and groom, and before long the barn was alive with celebration.

Riley and I gave our speeches before everyone got too wrapped up in drinking, and eating the food that had been prepared by my mom and aunt as well as both Meredith and Jeremy's moms. We'd been told not to, but there was no way we could go without saying a few words each. So we did. After we finished and tears were wiped away, things really got into swing. The same band that had played on the Fourth of July was in charge of the music, and I'd been pleasantly surprised to learn they knew quite a bit more than just '50s hits. Their sounds were accompanied by the singing of Samantha Gibson, a local girl who everyone was convinced would one day be the town's claim to fame—her voice was that good.

The newlyweds were, of course, the first to step onto the dance floor. Samantha summoned them after it was apparent most everyone had had their fair share of food. As soon as she sang the first line to Etta James'

"At Last," Jeremy pulled Meredith close, and they began moving about the room. I watched with a small smile as they spun around beneath the twinkling lights we'd wrapped around the beams overhead. The two of them were framed by the open door, and the scene behind them—a dusky sky with a few stars beginning to blink sleepily and the farmhouse glowing warmly—made it all the more picturesque.

"Can I get you another drink?"

I turned to Riley and nodded. He got up before I could tell him what I wanted, but then I realized he probably knew, as he always seemed to. I smiled, then focused once again on my best friend being twirled around like a true princess.

"And here we are in heaven," sang Samantha. "For you are mine at last."

As the song came to an end, she invited other couples to step onto the dance floor, and automatically my eyes scanned the room in search of Riley. I caught sight of him for a moment, heading back toward me with a glass in each hand, but my view was suddenly blocked.

"Annebelle Roth, you look gorgeous."

I smiled up at Mark Nichols, who was looking rather fine himself. "Thank you, Mark."

He held out his hand toward me. "Dance with me?"

While I'd had it in mind to dance with Riley, I wasn't about to turn down a nice guy like Mark, so I placed my hand in his. He pulled me up and we walked onto the dance floor together. As soon as he placed his hand on my waist, I focused on the feeling. Nope. No tingles.

"What a great wedding. You must be really happy."

"Wasn't it? And I am. I couldn't have imagined anyone more perfect for Meredith."

"Jeremy's a great guy," he agreed.

Silence followed the brief exchange, as we continued to move along to the song. I smiled to myself, remembering when I'd momentarily thought I should pursue a relationship with Mark after seeing him at the parade.

"It's real nice to see you back in town," he finally said.

"It's nice to be back," I admitted.

"I thought I heard somewhere you were only planning on staying a week or so."

I shrugged. "I was, but things happen."

"Ah, you mean Clara and the bakery."

I nodded. "That was definitely some incentive to stick around, along with my family and friends of course."

"Well, I'm glad you're here. I dunno how long you plan on staying now, but before you decide to run off—if that's your plan—I was wondering if you'd like to..." He looked over my shoulder and trailed off, then relinquished his hold on me a moment later. "Well, never mind that now. Thanks for the dance, Annebelle. I'll see you soon."

I stared at him confused as he walked off, considering there was still half a song left.

"May I?"

I turned around and came face to face with Riley. I looked at him in disbelief. "Did you really just do that?"

He slipped his hand around my waist, and I felt it instantly: tingles. "I sure did." He grinned. "What? Don't look so shocked—people have been cutting in for centuries."

"Actually, that wasn't really 'cutting in.' If it had been, you would have politely tapped Mark on the shoulder, not scared him off." I felt light as air as he spun me around, and I was sure I'd float right up to the ceiling if he released his hold on me. "You didn't even say anything to him!"

His grin widened. "Technicalities. And sure I spoke to him—I just didn't use words." He let go of my hand, then made a slicing motion across his throat followed by an outward gesture of his thumb. "That means get lost, or else..."

I laughed. "You didn't!"

"I did what I had to. I'm supposed to have the first dance with you."

My heart started playing hopscotch in my chest. "Oh really? And why's that?"

A frustrated look crossed his face. "Jesus, are you completely blind?"

I was taken aback by his tone and stopped dead. Memories of Rick yelling at me for no apparent reason came flooding back. It was strange, considering thoughts of him had dwindled since sharing everything with Clara. And this was Riley, I reminded myself, not Rick. They were polar opposites.

"Belles, are you okay?"

I shook the thoughts of him away and began dancing again. "Yes. I'm fine. Sorry... What were we talking about?"

"You sure didn't look like you were okay," he seemed to mutter more to himself than to me.

"Oh!" I interjected. "Why the first dance..."

He looked into my eyes. "Because I..." There was that hesitation again. "Have you thought about my idea?"

"What idea? Oh, you mean the business? A little. I wanted to focus on the wedding before really taking the time to think it over and make a decision. But that doesn't answer why you—"

The song ended then, and he looked visibly relieved. "Our drinks are waiting at the table. Shall we?"

I smiled and led the way back. After being hit with a not-so-pleasant memory of Rick followed by Riley's confusing interest-then-hesitation, that drink sounded extra nice. I was getting sick of these mixed signals. I planned on bringing it up with him again after a few sips of liquid courage, but I never got the chance. Soon we were separated and swept up in the celebration. My nieces came to claim my attention for a while, and Riley was beckoned for a cigar break with Jeremy and some of the other men. Before long, dusk had turned to night, the cake had been cut, and the already happy mood was elevated. Music, love, and laughter were heavy in the midsummer's night air. Meredith mingled with each of her guests like the perfect bride, periodically breaking away to rush over to me with a grin spread from ear to ear.

"I feel like I'm on a cloud, I'm so happy!" she'd declare breathlessly, then float off for more mingling.

"I'd say today was a definite success."

I turned to Clara who had appeared beside me, and nodded. "It certainly was. Meredith Larson seems pretty pleased with it herself. Meredith Larson." I tried the name out to see how it sounded, then shook my head.

"Not used to it yet?"

"No, I'm sure it'll take some time. But I'll get it eventually. Meredith Larson! See, it'll still work for yelling at her."

Clara laughed then let out a yawn. "Sorry."

"Don't apologize." I looked from her to Rett, who was sleeping in her arms. "Seeing you yawn lets me know you're still human. Do you ever put him down?"

She looked lovingly at her baby. "I like holding him. Sometimes I'm afraid if I put him down... I don't know, I'm afraid he'll vanish. Like he's only a dream, you know? That's silly, isn't it?"

"No, it's not. But he's not going anywhere, Clara... he's yours forever."

She ran a finger over his soft cheek and then smiled back at me, stifling another yawn. "He looks a lot like Jackson..."

"He must have been really handsome."

"He was. Looking at Rett and seeing Jackson... it makes me only slightly sad. Mostly it makes me happy. *So* happy—to have a piece of him still with me... you know?"

I remained silent.

"Do you think Meredith would mind if I went home and got some sleep? I can barely keep my eyes open."

"I don't think she'd mind at all. You've done so much. You've helped with the wedding, you're a miracle worker at the bakery, you're a wonderful mother... I don't know how you do it. Besides, you need some sleep so you'll be rested for your restful spa day tomorrow."

Meredith had given both Clara and I gifts for being "such exceptionally good friends" throughout the wedding process. Clara's was a spa package at the Tea Rose Inn, and mine was a gift card to my favorite department store and the promise of a day of shopping together after the honeymoon.

A dreamy look came across Clara's face at the reminder of what was in store.

"It seems funny to worry about being rested for a day of rest... but that was so thoughtful of Meredith. I've never been to a spa before..."

"Meredith has been saying for a while that you need a break—a spa day should be just the thing!"

"Are you sure you don't mind watching Rett?"

"Are you kidding me? Knowing him, he'll probably sleep all day, or just sit there and stare at me with those big blue eyes. The question should be are *you* going to make it a day without Rett?"

I was kidding, but her pause before answering told me she was going to have a hard time of it. I placed a hand on her shoulder. "You'll be fine, Clara. It's just a few hours—not even a full day—and I'll take good care of him."

"You're right, of course you will. It's just... you're sure it won't be keeping you from anything?"

"I've got absolutely nothing planned for tomorrow apart from looking after the little guy and maybe whipping up a pie or two. The bakery will be closed, Mr. Carter will be at church... Rett and I are going to have some one-on-one time. It'll be nice and relaxing. Now go on home and get some sleep. I bet Mr. Carter is about ready, too. Why don't you see if he's set to leave and head home together?"

"That's a good idea." She wrapped her free arm around me for a hug. "Good night, Annebelle, I'll see you tomorrow."

"Night, Clara."

She headed in search of her grandfather and then left with him a few minutes later. After Clara, other guests began to leave as well, mostly the elderly and families with children tired out from good food and dancing, like Jules and Nathan. But despite this, there were still plenty of people left to carry the celebration well into the night. And carry on it did, right up until the champagne had Meredith so excited at finally being able to have her slumber party at the Miller place—we kept reminding her it was now the Larson place to no avail—that Jeremy decided it might be best to get her in to bed.

"Especially considering we've got a plane to catch in the morning," he added, to which Meredith's excitement increased ten-fold.

"Oh my God! I forgot I get a honeymoon! Belles, I'm going on a honeymoon!" She jumped up and down like a kid and grabbed me for a hug. "My life is so freaking amazing."

Jeremy rolled his eyes lovingly from behind his wife.

"A honeymoon *and* a slumber party at the Miller place with my *husband*!" She spun around and flung herself onto Jeremy. I couldn't tell whether she was hugging him or holding on to him to keep from falling after her dizzying display, but a moment later she stepped back and took hold of his hand. "I love you all," she announced to the room. "But it's time for us to go... you know." She winked at no one in particular and started pulling Jeremy toward the door.

We all laughed, and Jeremy shrugged in submission as he followed his wife outside. "Thank you for such a memorable wedding, everyone," he called out to us. "It wouldn't have been the same without you."

We called out our goodbyes and best wishes for their honeymoon as they headed toward their glowing farmhouse, and that was it. Soon the rest of the guests dispersed as well, and I was left in the giant barn with the twinkling lights. The long tables were now covered with plates of unfinished wedding cake and the candles, which were now burnt out. I sighed quietly and contentedly, contemplating cleaning up a bit even though Meredith and Jeremy's moms had told me they'd take care of it. I was about to at least gather up some of the dishes when a sudden wave of exhaustion had me flipping the light switch and pulling the heavy door securely shut instead. I'd come back tomorrow.

I turned at the sound of a starting car and the sudden flash of headlights on me. I shielded my eyes from the light, and realized it was Riley's car. I'd lost track of him some time ago and was certain he'd left.

"What are you doing?" I inquired as I approached the driver's side window.

"What does it look like I'm doing? I'm waiting for you."

"But why?"

"How else were you planning on getting home? Walking?"

I thought for a minute then realized he had a point. I hadn't driven since I'd come in the carriage, and Clara and Mr. Carter were long gone. "I could take Meredith's car."

"Do you really want to go in and disturb them for a set of keys when I'm sitting right here?

I frowned. That probably wasn't the best idea.

"What did I tell you about frowning? Get in, will you?"

I walked around to the passenger's side and did as he said. "You're so bossy."

"Only because you're so stubborn."

I remained silent.

"Did you enjoy yourself?"

"Mmm," was all I could manage as he turned around on the gravel drive and headed out onto the street.

"Tired?"

"Mmhmm."

"Alright, we don't have to talk."

Suddenly I remembered our unfinished conversation earlier and I straightened in my seat. "No, let's talk. I feel like we didn't finish earlier."

"No," he asserted firmly. "We didn't finish, but we're finished for now."

"Why?"

"So now that the wedding's done with, you're going to think about starting up that business, right?"

"I told you I would. Why do you keep dodging my questions?"

"I'm not dodging any questions. I just don't feel like answering them right now."

"That's dodging."

He sped along the dark street, heading toward the bridge. "Technicality."

"Well, then I don't have to answer any of yours."

"Look, I'm just interested in knowing if you've figured out what you want yet—because if you figure out what you want, that means you'll have figured out whether you can get it in Riverdale or not."

I thought back to the vision of my own wedding—of him at the altar. *I think I want you*, I thought to myself. "Why are you so interested in whether I stay or not?"

"I told you I want you to stay in town Belles."

"Yeah, but you didn't say why."

He pulled to a stop, and I blinked, surprised at already being home. "What do you want me to say?"

I turned to look at him. The streetlight lit up the interior of the car just enough to create an outline of his face and cause a glimmer in his eyes as he looked at me through the night.

I remained silent. What did I want him to say?

"Figure it out." He said it sternly, then leaned over and pressed a quick kiss on my lips before reaching for the door handle and pushing it open. The kiss, brief as it was, made me tingle from head to toe. I got out of the car, disoriented, and shut the door behind me. Riley rolled down the window a moment later. "This belongs to you," he said.

I took what he held out to me, and he sped off into the night. I looked down at the yellowed envelope now in my hand. The word "Riley" was scribbled across the front in my own handwriting, and the weight of the contents told me exactly what it was—the necklace. I headed inside, pleading with my mind to stop reeling and my heart to stop fluttering so I could get some sleep.

18

What did I want Riley to say? I contemplated this as I walked over to open the bakery door with Everett in my arms. Although we were closed, it was too nice to keep the door shut, so I pushed it back as far as it would go and secured it with a rock. Instantly, a warm summer breeze burst into the room. I smiled and inhaled. "That's better, isn't it?" I asked the baby, who was looking curiously around.

A part of me, the part of me that had gone against everything I felt—or *thought* I'd felt—about Riverdale and what I wanted, knew the answer. I brought my free hand to my neck and touched the apple charm. As soon as Riley had given it back to me last night, I'd ripped open the envelope. All these years and he'd never taken it out. I'd laid it on my bedside table then slipped it on when I woke up. It rested just below my collarbone, and the light weight of it was comforting. I'd never really been one for necklaces, but this one—it had always felt like it belonged. I should have known.

I settled Rett into his seat on the counter, then headed to the kitchen and acknowledged to myself that my heart had always known. It was my heart that had realized, long before I'd let my stubborn self admit it, that I didn't really hate Riverdale—that I never hated Riverdale. I just never thought I'd be able to find everything I wanted here—but I could. In fact, most of it was already here; my family taught me that. So did my friends, and some people I never expected to learn it from, like Doris, and, perhaps most importantly, Riley. Riley's idea made me realize the other things I wanted could be mine here as well—a successful career, the ability to travel and keep from feeling stuck. His idea wasn't a bad one. In fact, thinking about it made me excited, the same way helping out with the bakery had. It was perfect, really, and would allow me to have everything I'd been searching for. Well, almost everything. There was one thing I wasn't sure I'd be able to have anymore, and that's where the 'but' came in.

I picked up the pan of raspberry-peach filling, then returned out front to where a pie crust waited—the kitchen had no windows, and I couldn't bring myself to stay back there on such a beautiful morning.

What did I want him to say? I wondered again. My brain was telling me not to say it—not to admit it, but the tingles, the flutters, and the games of hopscotch my heart liked to play when he was around outweighed the protests of a stubborn mind. And so, I found myself coming to the conclusion that I wanted Riley to say he still loved me.

I began pouring the filling into the crust, as my heart did a little skip for joy at my admission. Looking back now, I could see how stupid I'd been. How stupid I was for breaking things off like I did, running away like I did, only to realize years later Riley was the only one for me. But now, now I wasn't positive he felt the same. Sure, he'd kissed me— *really* kissed me—at the picnic, but the way he'd pulled back made me wonder. It was almost as though he regretted his decision. And sure, he took me out, but he'd also made it clear he had everything he was looking for. And if he had everything he was looking for, then he didn't need me. Perhaps he was toying with me after all. I couldn't say I'd blame him, not after hurting him like I did...

"Annebelle." All thoughts came to a halt at the voice that uttered my name. I dropped the pan of pie filling on the countertop, splashing the remaining bits of raspberries and peaches around the room. The clatter startled Rett, who began to cry. I looked up, and there, standing in the doorway staring back at me with a thundercloud expression, was Rick. Apart from the look on his face, he appeared as crisp and put-together as he always had. He was still handsome—I'd never deny he was handsome—but he was ugly, too, grotesquely so thanks to the side of his personality he kept well hidden, like a secret just for me.

He didn't look the slightest bit happy at discovering me. Instead, he looked furious. All the memories came flooding back in one ice-cold rush, and it suddenly felt like someone had knocked the wind out of me. Rett's cries seemed distant because of the ringing in my ears.

"What is this!?" He looked from me to Rett as though he'd caught me committing a crime. I realized he probably assumed the baby was mine—he was too angry for any logical thinking about the length of time since I'd left and the length of time it takes to have a baby—but I couldn't bring myself to speak. He had a way of making me feel like a deer in headlights.

He started walking toward me with heavy, angry steps. My shock gave way to panic as I began to fear for the baby. Instinctively, I moved in front of Rett's seat so it was hidden behind me. His cries continued to escalate. I turned back toward Rick just as he stepped behind the counter, and put up my hands to protect myself from whatever he might do. He grabbed me firmly by the arms and began shaking me like a rag doll. The memory of being thrown into the coffee table caused a pain to sear through my right shoulder. While there no glass tables here, I suddenly felt afraid of the display case.

"...and this is how you thank me?" Dazed, I tried to focus on his words. "I've been giving you your space. Waiting. I knew you'd miss me. But I'd given you long enough. So I come here for you..." He paused, his breathing heavy. "I come here..." He continued through gritted teeth. "To find this?" He turned me in the direction of Rett, who was now screaming at the top of his lungs. He spun me back around and grabbed my left hand to search for a ring. "You're not even married, you whore! At least I offered to marry you!" He took me roughly by the chin and placed a wet kiss on my mouth. "Didn't you miss this?" I felt like throwing up. "What does he have that I don't? I've never been insulted like this before. I *refuse* to be insulted like this. Especially by a little bitch like you who doesn't know what's standing right in front of her!" He raised his hand to strike me, and I closed my eyes tightly, waiting for the sting.

But instead he released his grip on my arm, and there was a loud crash. I opened my eyes to find Rick getting up off the ground. A table and a set of chairs were toppled over beside him, and there, standing above him, was Riley. I could only see his profile, but even from that angle I could see an expression more threatening than Rick's—but in a way that made me feel protected, not afraid. His eyes were dark and fierce, and he stared down at Rick as though he could tear him to pieces.

I couldn't take my eyes off them as Riley grabbed the now thoroughly stunned Rick by his pressed shirt collar and tie. I stepped back and picked Everett up from the carrier, holding him against me. In the next instant I flinched involuntarily as Riley drew back his fist, then slammed it into Rick's face. The resulting blood trickling from his nose told me it was broken—or close to it.

"You like beating up women, do you?" Riley said as he drew back his fist again. "In case Annebelle didn't make it clear when she turned you down the first time—" Surprised, I looked at Riley and wondered how he knew, then realized just as fast Clara must have told him. I should have been mad at her for breaking our confidence, but instead, I was infinitely glad. "—she. Doesn't. Want you." Riley continued. He brought his fist to Rick's face again, and his head fell back at the impact. "Get out of here," Riley said as he grabbed another fistful of shirt, and shoved Rick in the direction of the door. "Get out of this town. Now. The sheriff already knows you're here, but if I see you again we won't need him. I'll take care of you myself."

Rick didn't say a word. He turned to look at me, wiping blood from his mouth with the sleeve of his shirt.

"Go." It wasn't said with a raised voice, but there was so much rage behind that single word it sent Rick out the door without further hesitation. As soon as he was out of sight, Riley turned to me. "Are you all right?"

At his inquiry I felt my eyes start to water and my lips begin to quiver. He was beside me in two giant steps, wrapping his arms around both me and Rett, whose cries had calmed to a quiet whimper.

"Yes," I mumbled against his shirt, despite the fact that tears were streaming steadily down my cheeks. He pulled back to look at me, and, cupping my face with his hands, he used his thumbs to wipe the tears away.

"Don't you lie to me, Annebelle."

I looked in his eyes and suddenly felt more love for a human being than I ever thought possible. My heart ached with it, and my mind finally stopped protesting.

"I'm not." My shaky reply did nothing to reassure him. He frowned, pulling me against him once more. "Don't frown. You'll get lines," I said, and he let out a rough laugh at my copycat jest, then stepped back and placed a gentle kiss on my lips. Tingles, not nausea, ensued. "How did you know?"

"Know what?" He asked as he steered me over to one of the chairs along the counter.

"About Rick. And that he was here."

Everett had gone back to silently looking around as though nothing had happened, so Riley brought his seat over and I placed him back down.

"I knew about Rick because Clara told me weeks ago." He glanced at me. "And don't be mad—she was worried about you."

I shook my head. "I'm not."

Riley disappeared into the kitchen then returned with glasses and some ice in one hand, and a bottle of brandy in the other.

"Brandy?" I asked with a raised eyebrow.

"It's all I could find. But it'll do the trick. And I knew he was here because I saw him at Amy's. He came inside to ask where to find you." A distressed look came across his face. "I should have come right away. But his look... I don't know. For a minute I wondered if all Clara said had been true. He looked so pulled together, so gentlemanly." He opened the brandy decanter and poured out the liquid.

"He's a great pretender. And you got here just in time. You rescued us." I said as he handed me the brandy.

"Drink," he ordered, and lifted his own glass.

I took a sip, swallowing the potent liquid. I felt it glide, hot, down my throat, and a calm began to settle over me.

"Better?"

I nodded.

He rested his arms on the counter and looked at me with a mixture of concern, uncertainty, and thoughtfulness on his face as I continued to sip. Then his gaze lowered as the necklace caught his attention. His eyes seemed to brighten at the sight of it, but a questioning look crossed his face shortly after. He broke the silence. "Have you figured it out?"

"Figured what out?"

He hesitated. "What you wanted me to say, and how you feel about the idea of staying in town. Because, honestly Belles, I'm tired of waiting."

I was caught off guard by the sudden change of topic, and I looked down into my glass, swirling the liquid around as I thought. My heart, which had ached only minutes earlier with the love I suddenly, unmistakably, and undeniably felt for him, now ached for a different reason.

"I can't stay here." I looked up at him and nearly cried out at the expression on his face. He looked like I'd given him back his class ring all over again. It made me want to take back my words, but the reaction they'd caused also left me confused.

A moment later, Riley's face changed as though he'd put up a wall. He cleared his throat. "Why not?"

I took another drink of brandy. "Do you want me to be honest with you?"

He raked a hand through his hair. "Christ Belles, of course I do. That's all I've been trying to get you to be!" I bit my lip at his raised voice, and he noticed my frightened look. "I'm sorry, Belles."

"It's okay. I'm just a little spooked." I wondered how long he'd known about Rick, how long he'd been concerned. "Look... I thought maybe I could stay," I began. "I think your idea is brilliant, and I was gonna give it a try. But then I realized I can't."

"Why?"

"Because..." I bit my lip again, but for a different reason this time. Was I really about to say this? I wouldn't be able to take it back. I paused and waited for my mind to spout all the reasons I shouldn't—to tell me all the reasons I should keep what I had to say hidden and go on like the feelings weren't there. But for once, it remained silent. The only sound I heard was the steady beating of my heart. I took that as my cue. "Because you made it clear you have everything you're looking for, and I don't. I have to go because now, I know what I'm looking for, too. I figured it out, and now that I've figured it out, staying here would hurt me more than ever."

"You mean you still don't feel that what you're looking for is here? In Riverdale?"

"No, that's the thing—it is."

A look of confusion crossed his face. "That doesn't make any sense."

"It's you. And now that I know that... knowing you already have everything you want means I could never have everything *I* want. So even though I'm not as adamant about staying away from Riverdale for the reasons I had when I first came back, now I need to stay away for this one."

"Belle..." He stepped closer to me. Fueled by the brandy and a need to get everything out now that I'd started, I placed down the now empty glass and held up my hand.

"Wait. I have to say this to you even though I know it can't change things. I'm sorry. I'm so, so sorry for what I did to you. I was so stupid. I thought there was no way the feelings we had for each other could be real. Only now, years later, when it's too late, I realize that they were. They were *so* real, in fact, that I still feel them. And I can't deny them no matter how hard I try, no matter how much I work to convince myself I want to deny them, which, I don't think I ever really did. Before Rick made me stay away, I stayed away from Riverdale because I was certain I couldn't find everything I wanted in this small, old town... but I was trying to find something that was right in front of me the whole time. Well, now I have to stay away from Riverdale because I know that to be true. And I ruined it years ago."

"Belle." It was said as a whisper, like the word hitched a ride on an exhale of breath—a repeat of our reunion at my graduation party, when I looked deep into his honey brown eyes and was so completely happy, yet nervous at the same time. I could have looked in his eyes forever that day, just like I could today. He came and knelt in front of me, then took hold of my hand and looked up at me with the most serious, sincere expression I'd ever seen.

"Don't apologize, Belle. Don't. I blame myself for how things happened. I don't blame you. I was young, stupid, and selfish. All I could think of was how much I loved you. I didn't want us to be apart even if that meant you didn't follow your dreams but followed me as I pursued mine instead."

I opened my mouth to speak, astonished at his words and the fact that he didn't blame me, but he shook his head and continued.

"When you broke up with me, it hurt like hell. But I think it was the best move for the both of us. You were smart and levelheaded when I wasn't—and now look at us. We did what we said we'd do. We went to the places we said we would go. And now we're back, with good experiences—and bad. But all of it brought us right back here." He raised my hand and pressed it to his lips, sending shivers throughout my body. "What you did wasn't stupid. It was smart. The only stupid thing about you, and I say this in the most endearing way possible, is that you haven't been able to let yourself see that it's you."

"What's me?"

"I knew what I was looking for a long time ago, so I knew when I had it *a long time ago*. It was you, Annebelle. I had everything when I had you. I lost it, and I've been waiting for a long while to get it back—to make sure I'd never lose it again."

My heart thundered in my chest. Was this really happening? Was he really right in front of me, saying all this? "But if you... if I... why come close to me, then back away? Why kiss me, then pull back and regret it?"

"I've never regretted a single one of our kisses, Belle. There's nothing to regret about you, about us, but there's plenty to hope for." He paused. "I pulled back—I backed away because I didn't want to scare you off. At first I was cautious because of our past; If I came on too strong, I was afraid you'd run in the other direction. I dealt with it once, but I couldn't handle it again. So in a way, I was protecting myself. I didn't want to give in before I was sure you wouldn't leave again. That's why I've been pestering you about the business idea. But then, when I learned about Rick, of course I was cautious because I didn't want to do *anything* that would remind you of him."

The fierce look returned to his eyes, and I touched my hand to his cheek, willing it away. "I know that. I could never think that. You and him are as different as night and day."

He sighed visibly in relief. "It means so much to hear you say that."

I began to see just how colossal my errors had been in regard to practically everything related to Riley, Riverdale, what I wanted and thought, what I didn't want and more—it made me feel like such a fool. "You know, like you said, I always thought of myself as logical and levelheaded and pretty smart... but apparently, when it comes to you—when it comes to this town—I'm none of those things. Breaking up with you, assuming you were with Alexis, misreading everything you said and did, blaming my uncertainties on Riverdale... you have to admit, that *does* make me a bit stupid."

He shook his head adamantly. "No, that's not true at all. I just realized a long time ago what it took you years to find out. And like I said, everything that happened brought us here."

I looked around the bakery, at the countertop soiled with raspberry-peach pie filling and the overturned table and chairs. "Yeah. It's led us to a fiasco in the bakery and the fact that Clara is never going to let me watch Rett again." I looked over to find he'd fallen asleep.

"Sure she will. He looks content as can be." He smiled at the baby, then stood, keeping his hold on my hand and pulling me up with him. "Annebelle Roth, have you figured it out yet?"

"Figured what out?"

He wrapped his arm around my waist and began dancing with me. "What it is you wanted me to say—while we were dancing."

I looked into those honey brown eyes again and said it without hesitation. "That you loved me. I wanted you to say that you loved me."

He grinned down at me, and his expression was similar to the one I'd seen on Jeremy's face when he looked at Meredith just the day before.

"I love you." He said it with such certainty there could be no question as to the sincerity. "I've loved you since you bruised me with an apple. I've loved you since we sat in your backyard peeling fruit together. And when we kissed in the tree that first time. I've loved you since you broke my heart, and all the years from then 'til now. I loved you while you were gone, I loved you while I was waiting for you, and I love you now that you're back. I've always loved you."

Now I was absolutely sure my heart would burst right there, dancing in the bakery to music no one could hear but the two of us. "I love you, too," I responded, hoping even a small portion of what I was feeling would be conveyed in those words—for if it was, he would know without a doubt it was true.

He bent his head down and kissed me, and in that kiss—in that moment that spread tingles from my lips down to my toes and sent my heart into a frantic, fluttering state of euphoria—I knew I had found everything I was looking for. And somehow, it all managed to be within the small parameters of Riverdale.

I guess now I knew why some people never leave.

Keep reading for an excerpt from

Finding Forever

Geeta's next adventure with the residents of Riverdale.

coming soon...

Prologue

Drops of condensation slid slowly down the sides of his glass, and he watched as they raced each other to the bottom. Until he'd stepped into Clancy's dark, air-conditioned rooms, sweat had beaded down his face in the same manner; hours of physical labor in the hot summer sun did that to a man. Now on his lunch break, the only "meal" he intended to ingest was a handful of nuts from the never-ending bowl on the bar, to go along with as many glasses of bourbon as he could down in 30 minutes—or before the bartender cut him off.

"Hey man, join us for lunch—there's a place just up the road with some killer seafood" was the invitation he'd received before heading off on his own. It was a new job. A new location with a new crew—they didn't know any better. Eventually, after he turned them down enough, they'd stop asking. When that day came he always felt relief, but it was a feeling soon followed by disappointment—it was so easy to make people give up on you.

He picked up the glass and stared at the amber liquid it held. As he did so his mind decided, as it had so many times before, that the surface was the perfect screen on which to replay images from his past. Some of those images were beautiful—what once was—and he felt the already shattered pieces of his heart crack just a little bit more each time they appeared. Most of them, though, came straight from his nightmares, but the fucked-up part was they weren't nightmares at all. No, they were things that had actually happened. There was blood. There were screams. There was loss. *So much loss.* And an emptiness impossible to fill. Worse still, that emptiness seeped into his present, and he wasn't fool enough to think it would—or could—ever change.

He muttered a curse under his breath and tossed back the drink, signaling for another as he brought the empty glass back down.

1

With a shudder and a shake, the plane touched ground and I let out a sigh of relief. Why wasn't teleportation a thing yet? My love of travel was seriously inconvenienced by the necessity of flying. Uncomfortable seats, bad food, and over six and a half MILES between my feet and solid ground? Not exactly my idea of a good time. Then again, the alternatives weren't exactly stellar either. Car? Bus? Train? Ship? No thanks. Sure, a picturesque train ride or a scenic road trip was fun every now and again, but when it came to journeys that'd take more than a few hours by car, planes were really the only logical way. So basically, the options equated to the slow peel-back of a bandage or a quick rip; neither were pleasant, but at least the latter was over faster.

As soon as the pilot gave the "ok," I unbuckled my seat belt and took my phone off airplane mode as the plane taxied up to a gate. A moment later, chimes alerted me to messages from my mom, my best friend, and one that made me instantly break into a smile: my long-time boyfriend Riley.

At least... I *think* "long-term" applied to us. I'd loved him since we were kids, and although we dated in high school, we had a teeny, tiny *eight-year* break—my fault. But when I came back to town after finishing graduate school, Riley was there too. And, luckily for my heart and happiness, he never gave up on, nor got over me. And so, Annebelle and Riley, the town's favorite couple, was back together and stronger than ever.

Actually, hard as it was to admit, there was a chance the title was up for grabs by my best friend Meredith and the sickly-sweet love she shared with her husband Jeremy. And I was pretty sure a fragile love was blossoming between our good friend Clara and one of the firefighters in town, but that had yet to be seen...

I looked at the message Riley sent: "Miss you already. Stay away from peach trees!!"

"I miss you too! ...What's wrong with peach trees?" I hit send, then stood up as the passengers who'd been sitting beside me stepped into the aisle, grabbed their bags from the overhead bins and headed toward the exit. I followed suit and felt my body relax as I stepped off the plane to freedom and fresh air—well, air-conditioned airport air anyway. But my breaths of truly fresh air came just a few minutes later, when I left the airport to find North Carolina greeting me with a mid-August day boasting 85 degrees, blue skies and plenty of sunshine.

I settled into one of the taxis that lined the curb and told the driver my destination. As they sped off, I returned my attention to the messages I'd received while flying. I let my mom know I'd arrived, as requested, then shook my head at Meredith's request.

"Can you bring me back some Shrimp and Grits? Researched famous NC food—it made the list."

"Ew! Mere, that sounds gross. And even if I could, I wouldn't torture my fellow passengers with a bowl of shrimp on the plane!"

She responded immediately: "Better than 'Snakes on a Plane!'" Then, a moment later, "Haha, I crack myself up! Literally. LOL'ing."

I groaned inwardly at her horrible pop culture reference. "Don't you have some animals to tend to?" Since moving into a big old farmhouse after getting married, Mere's new favorite hobby was browsing online for animals in need of a home the way some women—myself included—might browse for shoes. This was in addition to being the town veterinarian, so caring her animals was kind of her thing.

"Yes, actually… and look at this baby I'm going to bring home!"

"Baby" seemed like the wrong term, considering what followed was a photo of a large pig lounging in a mud puddle. I shook my head and tapped over to the message that'd just come in from Riley.

"Yes. Absolutely no peach orchards. I can't have you throwing a peach at some unsuspecting Rhett Butler and having him fall in love with you."

A laugh burst out of me that made the driver jump in surprise.

"Sorry about that" I blushed, slumping slightly in my seat from embarrassment. But the grin only Riley could give me—the kind that made my cheeks sore—remained as I responded.

"That's never gonna go away is it?"

"Not a chance."

"Well, don't worry, my fruit throwing days are done. Besides, 'Gone with the Wind' takes place in Georgia."

When I was eleven, Riley and I had a "property dispute" over an apple tree that bordered our yards. Things got a little heated—that is, he ruined my plans to spend the afternoon reading on one of the boughs by lounging up there himself—so I picked up an apple and threw it at him. In hindsight, it wasn't the best reaction, but since we ended up becoming best friends and then falling in love all was forgiven, and Riley loved to refer to the incident as the moment that started it all. Not that I was trying to rush the future or anything, but I could already picture him as an old man telling the story again and again to our grandchildren.

"Did I tell you the tale of your grandma and the apple tree?" The answer would be yes, of course, but he'd nod and continue anyways. *"I was just minding my own business up in a tree in my yard* (our yard), *chewing on a piece of hay* (he wasn't), *when along came the neighbor's daughter. I was surprised to see her (*I found out later it'd been his plan to talk to me all along) *and I was about to invite her up into the branch next to me (*never happened) *but I didn't account for how vexed she'd be that I tossed a hitch in her reading plans, because before I got a word out* (there were, in fact, quite a few words exchanged) *or had a chance to prepare my lightning fast reflexes, your cheeky grandma threw an apple at me and hit me square in the head!"*

I wasn't sure why Riley of the future used words like "vexed' and "cheeky" but there we had it. Of course, such a tale would have to be followed up with a few lessons and explanations like the importance of sharing and, of course, that throwing an object at someone is *not* an appropriate way to express your upset. Looking back, I could pinpoint several instances throughout my life where I acted rashly, made hasty assumptions, or otherwise sorely lacked in the communication department—it was something I'd been working on. So, yes, I was now a retired fruit thrower, and the Vanna Wilder of the School of Communication.

I shook my head. That last thought was something Meredith might say; I guess after being friends most of our lives, it was inevitable her cheese-soaked ways would rub off on me.

"Georgia... NC... technicality. How is The Tar Heel State, anyway?" Riley replied.

I looked up and out the window and was surprised to find we'd already exited the highway we'd been on; the stretch of asphalt surrounded by trees that looked practically the same as home had given way to a downtown area I was instantly drawn to. I'd always been a fan of city life, and it looked like Juniper, North Carolina wasn't going to disappoint on that front. But unlike a city such as New York, with skyscrapers so tall they'd block out the sun, the buildings here were only a few stories high, which meant they were complemented by—not competing with—the sky. The street was lined both ways with sidewalks dotted with benches and evenly spaced trees. The bright green leaves the trees boasted looked lovely in front of the red brick façade most of the

3

buildings featured but they were, of course, there for more than just aesthetic; beneath the branches of some of the larger trees we passed, benches and café tables were shaded from the sun—and both were filled with people enjoying their lunch hour.

The place was bustling, and a thrill of excitement raced through me— it would be nice to spend some time in a place with a quicker pace than Riverdale. I loved my home—it was a quaint little New England town where you knew everybody and their grandma and life was perfectly pastoral—but every now and again I craved a taste of city living. That was a big reason I'd ended up in NYC for college—there were several schools where I could have studied business closer to home, but I was looking to experience life different from how I'd grown up, and that's precisely what I got. But when all was said and done, and despite fighting it for a while, I eventually came to realize Riverdale was where I wanted to be and the only place that had ever truly been "home."

Still, that didn't change my love for cities, so I was ecstatic when the first big contract my fledgling consulting company Branch + Bloom garnered was with a store in Juniper, North Carolina. With a population around 55,000, it wasn't NYC or LA, but it was a big jump from the 4,000 that made up home. I had a feeling it was going to do just fine satiating that craving and, even more importantly, provide my company with a nice bit of exposure. No one who happened upon my website needed to know I got the job on the recommendation of the owner's great aunt (who lived in Riverdale)—all they'd see is a consultant so sought after she was asked to travel over 600 miles to do the job, despite a plethora of consultants already in the area. It was all about the wording.

"1059 Lexington Street."

I jumped at the sudden sound of my driver's voice, which also reminded me I'd been in the middle of texting Riley.

"Oh! Great, thank you!" I said as I handed them some cash, grabbed my bag and got out of the car.

"So far so good—just got to the store. Talk later. Love you!" I hit "send" on Riley's message then looked at the building in front of me and let out a *whoosh* of air. Before me stood a three-story building with a wood frame and brick masonry that had been painted white and was currently faded and peeling. Unfortunately the effect wasn't like the perfectly weathered-on-purpose look that'd been trendy lately: it just looked shoddy. I could tell right away it was a historic building, albeit one in dire need of updating.

A door was centered on the ground level, while the upper floors had two windows each. There was a large tree out front, and it was—or rather, could be—a lovely spot, but I was slightly confused at what I was seeing. Or, that is… *not* seeing.

Considering the store's downtown location I'd expected some serious curb appeal including—at the very least—a large sign advertising the business, but there was none to be found. If it weren't for the numbers displayed in the middle of the building, I'd think I was in the wrong spot. It also looked like the door should be flanked by large windows but instead, there were two benches, and the space behind them was used like a bulletin board. I walked up and glanced at the flyers. Advertising other businesses and events instead of your own? Oh no, that wouldn't do at all.

I tugged on the door but it was locked tight, so I looked closer at the wall. There was a crack between the wood on which the advertising was displayed and the ornate frame that surrounded the door. I leaned in and tried to peek between the two; I had a feeling there *were* in fact, windows behind there. Promising.

"Everything alright ma'am?"

I jumped back and turned to face a couple who had paused on the sidewalk. My cheeks reddened. "Oh, hi—yep. Just um, looking for… the way in?"

"I can tell you there's no secret door," said the man. He nodded toward the edge of the building. "The entrance is around the corner."

"Oh! Right. Thanks." I could only imagine how I looked creeping around the building. I hoisted my bag over my shoulder and hurried around the corner, noticing *then*, of course, the painted black arrow on the wall and the word "entrance" pointing the way I was headed. Even so, that was some poor advertising. It looked like I had my work cut out for me.

The side of the building featured a single door, painted black with shiny brass hardware. There was a mat on the ground with the word "welcome" written across it in black, cursive letters, beside which sat a terracotta pot filled with vibrant petunias. This was a little more promising—it showed the owner actually *did* care about their business, despite the slapdash front.

I pressed the thumb latch on the door and tugged, only to strike out again. As I let go, I caught sight of a small sign reading "closed" that hung from the handle.

"Really??" I looked at my watch. 12:22 on a Tuesday and she's closed?! Oh no, this would not do *at all*. Plus, our first appointment was scheduled for 1. If I were the owner, about to have a meeting with a consultant in the hopes of saving my business from ruin, I'd be in there preparing—not off doing whatever it was she was off doing. I let out an exasperated sigh, turned back onto Lexington Street and started walking. So much for my plan to wow her with my punctuality.

A few buildings up, a black sign with gold lettering that read "Clancy's" caught my attention. I had no idea who Clancy was, but if I was going to judge by a name I'd bet he'd have a cold drink and some fish and chips to offer. My stomach let out a rumble in support of my new plan.

I took a quick glance at my reflection in the darkened window just outside: the teal blazer I wore had thankfully remained relatively unrumpled on the flight, as did the white tee shirt I wore beneath it, tucked into a pair of dark jeans. The look was completed with some tan, peep toe booties with a chunky heel; I knew it wasn't the same for every woman, but a sturdy heel always made me feel extra powerful. I tucked my shoulder-length chestnut hair behind my ears as I pushed my way into Clancy's and stood for a moment, allowing my eyes to adjust to the dimly lit space.

"Welcome to Clancy's! Are you here for lunch?"

A girl at a hostess booth came into view. I gave her a smile. "Hi, yes, but I'll just sit at the bar if that's ok?"

"Of course! Go right ahead."

A quick glance around the room showed it earned checks for all the typical "Irish pub" requirements: lots of dark wood, at least one Irish flag visible, and signs written in English but styled in a way that was supposed to give off a Gaelic vibe. The bar was the main attraction, taking up a large portion of the left side of the establishment, which was bigger front to back than side to side. Behind it, the wall featured four thick wood columns that broke up the space and created five little alcoves—the two closest to me housed stacks of glasses and the register, respectively. The biggest space was in the center, where a full bar was illuminated from beneath, causing the glass alcohol bottles of various hues—mostly shades of amber with emerald mixed in—to glow like a mountain of leprechaun treasure.

The counter was surrounded by wooden stools topped with black leather cushions, almost all of which were full. I headed for the first available spot I saw, which I quickly realized had been left vacant due to the awkward position of a large square column just a foot behind it. When the seats on either side of it were occupied—like they currently were—it made for a tight squeeze to reach it. Ah, the quirks of older buildings.

"Excuse me," I said to the man sitting to the left of the column. He didn't budge. "Excuse me," I said a little louder, aware that other occupants were able to hear me just fine and were beginning to look. But this guy—nothing. Well, third time's the charm! I repeated my request and followed it up with a light tap on his shoulder—a move I instantly regretted when it startled him from the daydream he'd apparently been in, causing him to jump in his seat and splash his drink over the counter.

He whipped his head around to face me, giving me an angry look that seemed a little excessive considering the situation.

"Sorry I uh... just want to get by." I felt my cheeks redden, not for the first time today.

He said nothing but scooched his chair in ever so slightly. I sucked in a breath and squeezed past, trying not to hit him with my bag. I took a seat, tucked my belongings down by my feet, and busied myself by looking at the signs that hung above the bar listing drinks and specials.

"What can I get for you?" the bartender asked.

"A cider and the fish and chips would be great, thanks."

"You got it."

With ordering taken care of, I glanced at the patron on my right to see if they'd be up for some friendly chatter, but he was half turned away from me already talking to someone else. Guess not.

I looked at Mr. Overreaction out of the corner of my eye; he seemed lost in thought again and after our last interaction I had a feeling he wasn't up for chitchatting either. So much for the "everyone's friendlier down south" view. Oh well. I pulled out my phone—which I typically hated to do in social situations—and sent Riley a text.

"Grabbing lunch before the meeting. Sitting next to a total jerk. I startled him and he spilled some of his drink; he looked at me like I'd just called his mama a name. Makes me miss you all the more, Charming."

I cleared out my inbox—mostly junk per usual—while waiting for a reply. I knew he'd get back to me soon unless he was meeting with a client of his own; having your own business meant you got to be a little more relaxed on the cell phone front, and Riley was an attorney at his father's practice—which would eventually be *his* practice once Cliff retired.

A ding followed by a notification at the top of my screen told me his schedule was currently clear. I clicked through.

"Well... what was he drinking? Maybe spilling it was *worse* than calling his mama a name? What if it's the most expensive drink they have and he's saved up for a year for it and you just wasted half?? Get him another one."

I let out a snort and rolled my eyes. "Seriously?! I mean, I doubt it, but what if it IS the most expensive drink at the bar??" I replied. I took a sip of the cider that'd appeared in front of me and waited. He had to be joking.

"Yes—serious" came the reply. "And that's all the more reason to replace it. Don't be mean in return. You don't know what's going on in his life. And we can afford a replacement drink."

The way he said "we" made my stomach do a happy little flip; it didn't matter how much time passed—all things "Riley and Annebelle" had always, and likely *would* always, give me butterflies. And he had a heart of gold, that man.

I turned toward the subject of our discussion: still staring off into nothing. Well, I'd already learned a tap wouldn't do, so I cleared my throat and slid my red painted nails into what I hoped was his line of sight and tapped them on the bar. The result was what I imagined would happen when a hypnotist snaps their fingers to wake you from a trance.

He shook his head, seemed confused for a moment, and then looked at me. This time his expression was a stark contrast to the angry face from before—he looked totally brokenhearted, complete with glassy eyes. Considering the location, I couldn't be sure whether the sheen was due to tears or alcohol but regardless, the change caught me off guard.

I gave him a little wave and a smile. "Hi, me again. Look, I'm uh, sorry about before. I didn't mean to startle you. My boyfriend told me I should buy you a new drink. Especially in the off chance you were celebrating something big and that was the most expensive thing in this place, which, I'm kind of hoping it's not, but I'll get it either way."

The bartender headed over with my lunch. "He's good," he answered for the man as he set the plate in front of me.

I looked from one man to the other. They'd started a stare down, and I swore I could literally see the guy's face darken as I looked at his profile. After what felt like forever he stood, pulled a folded bill from his pocket and tossed it on the bar

"I guess I'm good" he said, then walked out.

The bartender picked up the bill and gave me a smile. "Enjoy your meal."

"Are you kidding me?" I shook my head as, my delicious drink and meal consumed, I returned to the giftshop and noticed the A-Frame sign that had appeared at the corner of Lexington and Halston Street.

It read "Reverie Gifts" in white, flowery font on a black background, framed by dark wood. At least it wasn't plastic. But advertising your business ONLY when it was open? We'd have to work on that. A successful business needed a constant presence—and a front door too, not a side entrance that, pretty as it was, made it look as though you were about to make a purchase off the black market instead of a gift shop.

Having been refueled with my delicious fish and chips and a crisp cider, I was ready to get this show on the road—and put the weird interaction back at Clancy's behind me. I guess I shouldn't have expected *everyone* to be friendly.

I took hold of the handle like I had earlier except this time, it opened with ease when I pushed, and I stepped into the store as a bell tinkled overhead and a light, refreshing scent reached my nostrils. The mental list of suggestions and to-dos I'd started as soon as I saw the exterior began to grow: the inside reminded me of Clancy's, which only matched the atmosphere one of the two places should be aiming for. It was dark and awfully cluttered. There were so many different wares on display cases and tables I hardly knew where to look, and considering I wasn't there to shop and was beginning to feel anxious, I could only imagine how an actual customer would feel.

"Welcome to Reverie!" said a cheery voice. I looked in the direction the greeting had come from, just as a woman popped into view from behind one of the tall display cases—this one filled with stuffed animals.

"Are you Nora?"

"I am!" she wove her way over to me—"wove" being necessary because of the number of fixtures; there was no walking in a straight line here. I took in her appearance as she approached: charcoal cigarette pants paired with strappy black flats and a white, cap-sleeved blouse covered in tiny grey flowers; hair piled on her head in a tidy bun; a pretty face made extra so due to the giant, Julia Roberts-esque smile she wore. "Who are you thinking of today?"

At her inquiry, the name "Riley" sprung out of my mouth so fast it felt almost involuntary. I mentally shook my head. Considering it was 1 p.m. on the nose, I figured she'd assume who I was. I held out my hand. "I'm Annebelle Roth of Branch + Bloom."

"Oh?" she looked at my hand with a raised eyebrow but clasped it for a shake. "Well hello, Annebelle… and who's Riley?"

"My boyfriend" I said with a smile, and then I shook my head—for real this time—to bring myself back to focus. Why did I just tell her that? "But I'm not here for him," I added. "I'm here for you!"

"Excuse me?"

"Our appointment… it was scheduled for 1 o'clock right? Did you have to change it? I'm sorry, I didn't get any message."

9

She started to move through the store and I followed behind her. She walked behind a big wooden counter where the register was held and began rummaging through a pile of papers stacked beside it—office papers on the sales floor? That'd have to go as well.

"I'm sorry, I don't recollect scheduling an appointment for today. …now where is that calendar?? When did we speak?"

"Oh, we haven't, actually—your Aunt Doris set it up?"

Nora stopped searching and straightened up. "Aunt Doris! As in, Yankee convert Doris?"

I let out a laugh. "Er… yes?"

She began tapping her plum painted fingernails on the countertop, pursed her lips and glanced up like she was searching her mind for something. A minute later—one that felt much longer considering I was just standing there—she held up a finger. "Just a moment."

Nora pushed some more papers aside and picked up the phone—complete with cord and all—that was buried beneath them. She punched in some numbers then pressed the receiver to her ear and stood with one hand on her hip.

"Bonnie Lorraine Martin did you and Aunt Doris make an appointment with one Miss—" she looked at me. What was your name again?"

"Annebelle Roth. From Branch + Bloom."

"Roth? From some florist!?"

"No, no, I'm not a florist" I corrected, but she didn't seem to hear.

She stood silent for a moment listening.

"…What! Mom, seriously??" She turned away from me, leaned against the counter and lowered her voice. I could, of course, still hear her. "First off, how could you? And second, how COULD you??" More silence. "Right, but— I know, but— I don't think— fine. But don't think we've finished discussing this momma. And I— yes. I'll be there Sunday. Of course I'll remember the casserole. Love you too."

Nora let out a sigh, then turned to face me. Her peach-tinted lips curled up into a bright smile as she hung up the phone with a bit more force than necessary—a satisfying feeling you just couldn't replicate by pushing a button on a cell phone.

"Miss Roth, I sincerely apologize for my earlier reception. Might we start again? I'm Nora Martin, owner of Reverie Gifts."

I nodded, reaching for her extended hand for a second shake. "Annebelle Roth of Branch + Bloom—business consultant, not florist."

We shared a smile.

"How about some tea?

About the author

Geeta Schrayter decided she was going to be a writer when she was eleven and never faltered in that decision. Over the years she has been a blogger, magazine intern, freelance writer, reporter, and assistant newspaper editor. When she isn't writing, Geeta loves to travel, read, cook, run, and savor the magic in the everyday. She currently resides in New England with her family.

@geetawrites

CPSIA information can be obtained
at www.ICGtesting.com
Printed in the USA
FSHW011127161020
74794FS